I0674121

STIRRED

a love story

TRACY EWENS

STIRRED

a love story

Stirred: A Love Story
Copyright © 2016 by Tracy Ewens

All rights reserved. No part of this book may be used or reproduced in any manner whatsoever including Internet usage, without written permission of the author.

This is a work of fiction. The names, characters, places, or events used in this book are the product of the author's imagination or used fictitiously. Any resemblance to actual people, alive or deceased, events or locales is completely coincidental.

ISBN: 978-0-9908571-9-8 (print)
ISBN: 978-0-9908571-8-1 (e-book)

Book design by Maureen Cutajar
www.gopublished.com

For my Jack.
He knows why.

Chapter One

Sage Jeffries never backed down from a challenge. "There's nothing you can't do if you set your mind to it" was practically a family motto growing up. She and her three sisters spent their childhood outsmarting, outrunning, and out-achieving one another. Hollis graduated high school in three and a half years; Sage did it in three. Annabelle rode in her first competitive horse show when she was seven, so their youngest sister Meg made sure to win her first blue ribbon by the same age. To say the Jeffries girls were competitive was an understatement. So, it took the family by surprise when Sage bowed out of corporate life to become a bartender in Los Angeles. "Not simply a bartender, a mixologist," she had said, but her sisters mocked what they called her foolishness while her parents offered up some extra cash. She'd been in LA almost three years now, and mixing drinks wasn't all that different from building robots. She'd always loved pieces and parts—figuring out what worked together and fixing things that were broken. Shortly before turning thirty, she'd announced during a family dinner her desire to experience more than what she'd learned in a classroom or the boardroom. She wanted stories and adventure. Since renting her little 1960s-style, one-bedroom bungalow, Sage had become an experience junkie. She went to festivals, had jumped out of a plane, traveled, hiked, and competed in cocktail competitions. She loved her job and after reading a book on giving back, she'd become involved in her local community center. In a few months, she would be teaching bridge, which would have made her grandmother so proud. Sage was up for anything that brought her closer to life—real life.

Of course, even with her recent "renaissance" as her father liked to call it, there was still one area of "experience" that had eluded her. In school, Sage was shy, and now that she'd grown up a bit, she was sort of clumsy or awkward, she wasn't sure. All she knew was the opposite sex was a weakness, an area in which she'd never managed to excel. That was exactly why her sister Hollis had downloaded the book onto Sage's Kindle in the first place and stuck a note on the screen while she was packing. After settling into her seat on the plane, she read the note.

> *Good seeing you. You've been in LA long enough now. Stop being so damn nice. It's time. You're a bartender, little sis. Happy Reading! XO Hol.*

She'd finished with one of those stupid winky faces. Damn her and her winky face, Sage thought, peeling the note off and stuffing it into the seat pocket in front of her. The moment she touched the little book icon, she was happy she had a Kindle. Not that she was embarrassed to be reading a book titled *Nice to Naughty in Ten Easy Steps*, but it wasn't something she wanted to advertise either. The plane began to taxi and Sage held the blue quartz stone hanging from her necklace as if it could somehow aid in delivering her safely back to Los Angeles. She knew better; she knew how planes were made but still brought something with her every time she flew—a piece of good energy, in case there was more to life than moving parts.

Sage read the "How To Use This Book" section and began questioning her sister's suggestion the minute the author compared women to fruit salad. As the plane lifted off, she took hold of the armrest and prepared for that moment in flight when everything drops a little from the turbulence. Once she made it past that point, Sage had learned through countless trips out of San Francisco, she could relax.

Settling back into the virtually nonexistent cushion of 14C, she noticed the man sitting by the window. Seat 14B, between them, was empty, so Sage had a little room to observe. Casually glancing up from his dark leather loafers, Cole Haan if she had to guess, she saw he was reading *Maxim* magazine. Once he flipped the page, the cover folded out of sight, but not before she caught a glimpse of a gorgeous woman in next to nothing, her hands over her impressive breasts. Sage looked around the cabin as if some alarm was about to go off and found herself shocked that he was reading what should be a guilty pleasure right out in the open. And what was he so intent on reading? Was there anything to actually read in *Maxim*? She'd seen the magazine on the stand but never opened it, so she supposed she shouldn't judge, but she did anyway. Crossing her legs to the other side and attempting to focus back on her own book, Sage learned that apparently naughty women were the grapes of the fruit salad.

She shook her head as her eyes drifted again, this time to the man's hands and quickly to his face. No wedding ring, nice suit, and he was good-looking. At least from what her side-glance could gather. She noticed the soft leather briefcase at his feet and deduced that he was traveling for business. Did businessmen read smutty magazines on the plane? Out in the open?

As if she'd said it out loud, he looked up, brushed past her eyes, and asked the flight attendant for a ginger ale. His voice was deep, nice. Sage turned, realizing she'd been caught staring at a complete stranger, and told the short woman with blond hair and a huge turquoise ring on her middle finger that she was fine with her bottle of water. Smiling, the attendant moved away for a second and returned with a fizzing plastic cup, square napkin, and a bag of peanuts. She reached past Sage to hand them to the man and, with effort, pushed the cart on to the next row. Wondering for a minute

3

how heavy those carts actually were, Sage again returned to her book and vowed to try to act normal.

"Business or pleasure?" the man next to her asked, folding his magazine and putting it between the seat cushions.

Sage reacted with a bit of a jump, as if she'd suddenly noticed another human being was sitting next to her. So much for normal. His eyes were brown and he had a cute little birthmark right below his ear, on his neck. Now that he'd spoken to her, she turned and noticed he was definitely good-looking—good-looking and smiling. Big, super-white teeth.

Answer him, you creeper, her mind yelled.

"Yes, sorry. I'm. . . pleasure. I was home for Christmas." She smiled back. "You?"

He let out a breath and opened his peanuts. "Business, unfortunately."

"Hopefully you had a little time for the holiday? Or maybe you don't celebrate Christmas. Oh wow, I'm sorry. You're Jewish."

Here we go, crazy lady.

The cute guy laughed. "No, I'm not Jewish. I'm the only one of three associates who is still single, and our Japanese client couldn't care less if it was Christmas, so they sent me."

Giving him a look she hoped conveyed commiseration and made up for her odd outburst, she returned to the safety of her book.

"I'd much rather be spending time in San Francisco with a beautiful woman," he said as easily as he took a sip of his ginger ale.

Sage felt her heart jump, like it did any time she wasn't behind her bar and had to make conversation with a charismatic man.

Don't assume he's referring to you, she told herself as she was suspended in uncomfortable silence.

"I'm sure you get that all the time, huh?"

Okay, so he is talking about you. Be gracious.

"Oh, not exactly. Thank you."

Finishing his handful of peanuts and twisting the bag into a tiny bowtie, he moved on, asking her what she did for a living and commenting that he liked her necklace. Sage closed the black cover of her Kindle, took a sip of water, and talked with Chris, who introduced himself with a great handshake. He explained he was a lawyer traveling home from San Francisco after several long days of depositions.

"Do you live in LA?" he asked with the confidence Sage recognized in men she served drinks to at The Yard. Success brought with it an ease Sage usually found interesting when she had three feet of mahogany in front of her. Without it, packed into an airplane, she found it unnerving.

"Yes," she managed, bracing herself for the next inevitable question.

"Me too. Let me get your number and maybe we can get a coffee or I can take you to dinner."

Sage looked down at the cover of her Kindle, her head now swirling with the fruit salad analogy. She had no idea how to be a grape in the female fruit salad yet, but she'd observed enough grapes to know it often involved exchanging numbers. So, even though she barely knew this man, even though she wasn't sure she was attracted to him, and even though he had a subscription to *Maxim*—she'd seen the mailing label—she let out a shallow breath and gave him her number. As Chris typed her name into his phone, she noticed his hands again. They were tan and well-groomed. Peeking out from his starched cuff was a woven bracelet. As they were departing, he explained he'd brought it back when he hiked Machu Picchu last year.

They exchanged pleasant smiles, and he looked back again as he wheeled his bag out to the curb after they said good-bye. Sage realized her hand was sweating as she clutched her own bag, but she also felt flushed with something else—pride. She'd actually sat on a plane with a handsome guy, been social, flirted a little, and with the exception of a brief blip into Judaism, she hadn't once made an ass of herself. It wasn't quite naughty, she thought as she scanned the curb for a shuttle that would take her to long-term parking, but Hollis had a point. She had been in LA for a while now and other than her infatuation with her best friend's older brother, which was going nowhere, Sage hadn't made much of an effort in the male department. A new year was right around the corner and she had tried so many things since moving to LA, so perhaps it was time to give "naughty" the old Jeffries try. She was only on chapter one of the book and would probably never make it to a grape, but she'd settle for a banana, maybe even a strawberry.

❧☙

Garrett Rye was up before the sun and happy the holidays were over. He loved the tradition of it all, but there wasn't much down-time on the farm, and juggling schedules throughout November and December was always a hassle. With only four more days until he could flip the office calendar to the new year, he welcomed a return to routine. After breakfast and feeding Jack, Garrett hopped into his truck, Jack riding shotgun as usual. It was Monday morning, and he had a meeting in the office with a new company that wanted to provide recycled bands for the farm's lettuce and kale. Their bands contained "no wire" which meant "less of a footprint," or so they'd said on the phone last week. When Garrett had asked if they actually worked, he was told they held together better than the ones he was currently using. He would believe it when he saw it. He'd spent his entire life farming, striking a balance between need and rejuvenation. Lately, it felt like a dear friend had suddenly become a celebrity. The environment was big business now. Garrett still found it difficult to catch up with the latest do and don't list. Only last week, his niece informed him that recycling his paper bags from the market wasn't enough. He needed to buy cloth bags. Garrett had bought the damn things but never remembered to take them out of his truck when he went shopping. Paige had told him he was a "work in progress." Garrett laughed, thinking about his niece, or as he liked to call her, "your highness."

The thought of an hour-long meeting talking about bands made his head hurt. Someone had to take care of this shit, but he often wished it didn't have to be him. "Eh, quit your whining and focus on all the things going right," he could hear his father's voice in his head as he pulled over to check the newly installed drip system on the south field. Jack jumped across his lap as soon as the truck door opened and was off between the rows of newly planted radishes and carrots.

The sun was starting to make its way up the horizon. Garrett crouched down and grabbed some soil, rubbing it between his fingers. It was moist, perfect actually. He looked toward the horizon and found that most things were going right. Despite the fact that he had to wear a starched button-down shirt today instead of his preferred long-sleeve T-shirt, despite his list of "have tos" waiting for him on his calendar today, most of which had nothing to do with this sunrise or this soil, Garrett was right where he wanted to be. The good outweighed the bad when he put his hands to earth or when he thought about his family or looked out and saw Jack running around, ears cocked and stub of a tail wagging. This was his center, and even though he was now responsible for so many other things, it was all part of the effort to keep things as they were.

He grabbed another handful of soil and brought it to his nose before returning it to the neatly laid-out row. Whistling for Jack, he glanced over at the south barn as the guys were opening the doors, starting up the motors. He missed it, that work, he missed it every day, but his father needed him where he was, and Garrett was never one to complain.

He pulled his truck into its usual spot in front of the old assembly building, which was now the administrative offices of Ryeland Farms, and waved to George, who was unlocking the door, a thermos of coffee dangling from one finger.

"Did you bring any more of those tamales for lunch?" Garrett asked, grabbing a folder off his dash and closing the door behind Jack.

George shook his head and flicked on the lights, holding the glass door open. "Nah, they were gone yesterday morning. Next year, man." He patted Garrett on the back and followed him into his office.

"I saw the guys getting started out there. Checked the latest section of the drip system. Everything looks good. Anything I'm not seeing?" Garrett asked as Jack curled up on his bed under the window.

"No, things are pretty much what you saw. They lay the rest of the drip lines today and the guys will be finished planting right behind them. That part went off without a hitch." He leaned forward and knocked on the wood of Garrett's desk.

George shared his coffee with Garrett, as he did most mornings, while they talked about the day ahead and things that might come up. When Garrett had worked the land himself, he'd used his instincts—smells, texture, or a feeling—but since taking over, things had changed. The risk had grown from simply losing a crop to losing everything, so he had learned to use schedules and calendars; his plans had backup plans, but he still had instinct. He needed it for the unexpected, and there was always something unexpected.

He and George were wrapping things up before Garrett's meeting when George pulled out his phone. They flipped through pictures of their Christmas Eve dinner and as they laughed, Garrett remembered why he spent Christmas Eve with George and his family.

As lead farm manager, George and the rest of the Gomez family hosted a dinner for anyone who wanted the world's best tamales or, more importantly, couldn't get home for the holiday. George and his wife Angela knew how to have a good time, and Garrett went every year. Christmas Eve potluck was a tradition that dated several generations back in the Rye family. Herbert, Garrett's father, usually attended, but once his granddaughter was born, Herb had "no intention of missing a holiday with my princess," so he abdicated the responsibility to his oldest son. Garrett didn't mind. In fact, he looked forward to it every year. Logan, his brother the chef, gave him pickled carrots and jalapenos from his garden to bring, while Kenna, his sister, bought and wrapped all the presents. Garrett was the chosen ambassador, but it was a family effort.

The people who ran Ryeland Farms, the folks who woke up early and put in the work, were important. They worked as hard as Garrett did, sometimes harder, and it was part of his job to make sure they always knew they were valued. When he'd taken over most of the operational responsibilities, his father had told him, "People need to feel they are a part of something more than a paycheck."

George and Angela lived with their teenage daughter on the farm. Their house used to be Garrett's grandparents', before the main house, where his father lived now, was built. Ryeland Farms was barely shy of fifty-five acres complete with three barns, the newly converted offices, a four-bay garage, an orchard, beehives, and a large pond with ducks. The main house was where they were all raised and where Garrett had lived until he was about twenty-five. That was when he moved out to the house he'd designed and helped build toward the edge of the property, near the apple trees. His house was small, but it was uniquely suited to him, and it felt like home. Growing up, Logan and Kenna had left for lives of their own, still connected, but away from the farm. Garrett had always known he would work with his dad and eventually take over. He loved what he did, but there was a sense of blending into the background that he'd only recently started to notice. He'd become a fixture, like Gracie the goat. He coexisted with the image of their childhood, Ryeland Farms, as a whole. He didn't cook like his brother or have a child like his sister. Both of them ran something separate from their shared past, and Garrett had stayed behind.

As they thumbed through the last of the pictures, Garrett wondered if his life would always be this way. Would he spend every Christmas Eve with George or his family and their spouses and children? If that's how it was all meant to play out, he was happy with that. It was all he needed. Garrett would always take "same old, same old" over disruption and uncertainty. The last

9

time he'd been uncertain, he was nine. He'd gone to school one morning and returned to a very different life. Since that day, after the initial "what now?" moment, Garrett had created a solid foundation for his family, steeped in hard work, chores, and keeping things steady. They counted on it, or at least they did growing up.

Walking George to his office and then greeting the sales guys waiting for him by the front door, Garrett knew his family wasn't going anywhere. Both his brother and sister were getting married, but that didn't mean anything needed to change. He and his father ran the farm, and that would always be. By the time he closed the conference room door, he'd answered his own wonderings—yes, his life *would* always be exactly as it was.

Chapter Two

"Wait, is that the actual name of the book?" Kenna asked that morning while she and Sage were rolling silverware and sharing holiday stories.

Sage nodded, and Kenna took the Kindle out of Sage's purse. After flipping through a few pages, she snorted a laugh. "Wow. Well, according to this, I need to work on my naughty too."

"It is pretty. . . comprehensive. Hollis always loves to challenge."

"Huh, well, this isn't you. I'm sure you'll have a good laugh with your sister and then you can delete that thing right—"

"I've read the first three chapters, so I think I'll try out step one and maybe two at the New Year's Eve party on Friday."

Kenna looked like she might laugh again but instead furrowed her brow and continued flipping pages. "Step one, let's see here. Are you referring to the Dress Like You Were Just—" Now came the laughter. "Holy hell, Sage. Do you even know what that looks like? I mean, I'm not saying you're a prude, because you're not. Except when you wear that one corduroy skirt and those Catholic schoolgirl-looking shoes, because no one will ever get laid in that outfit. But other than that, you're middle of the road, right? Not exactly—"

"Just fucked?" Sage leaned over and said quietly, realizing that the need to whisper those words in a closed bar, speaking only with her best friend, meant she had a long way to go toward naughty. "I know, but there are pictures in the book. It's all about heels and showing skin and pouty lips. Oh, and messy hair. Which I've actually mastered already." She ran her fingers through her short brown hair.

Kenna found the pictures on the Kindle. "I. . . Wow. Okay, well this is. . ."

"A challenge. I haven't had one in a while, and my sister's right. I am a bartender in a big city."

"Will you stop saying that? You hiked Mount Whitney a few months back. That was a challenge. You're the queen of pushing yourself. But this? I think you should pass on this one."

"Why?"

"Because being naughty isn't like cutting your hair short or learning to play the cello."

"Hey, don't bring up the cello. I'm still upset about that. Who knew I was tone deaf, right? Sorry, go ahead."

"My point is we all have certain character things we're born with. Like, I'm. . ."

"Pig-headed, crass?"

"Blunt, I was going to say blunt. I am not pig-headed. I'm not even sure what that means. Shouldn't that term stay on the farm?"

"Maybe I'm a closet farm girl."

Kenna laughed. "You wish. Anyway, being blunt is part of who I am and unless I want to change everything else, I can't change something that big. You know?"

Sage thought she understood, but she'd done so many things, learned so much in the last few years, that she wasn't sure why this was any different. There were steps, a guide to naughty, and she would master them.

"You're not naughty, Sage. You're kind and completely unaware of how smart and beautiful you are."

"Aww."

"I'm serious. What if you change that part of yourself in the name of some challenge and you lose all the rest?"

"Have you been watching Oprah with your dad again?"

Kenna shook her head.

"I think you're making a big deal out of this. I have a book, a blueprint. This is going to be fun, and maybe I'll learn some things about myself."

"Like what?"

"Like. . . I. . . like being naughty."

"Don't you think you would have figured that out when what's-his-face, your last boyfriend before you moved here, wanted to break out the blindfold?"

"That was a long time ago and different."

"Yeah, how so?"

"It was. I'm doing this and you are my friend, so you have to be supportive." Sage snatched the Kindle from Kenna's hand and slipped it back into her purse. "I have some naughty clothes, and New Year's Eve is the perfect time to throw caution to the wind and see what happens. Besides, I'll be here, around people I know, so it's like a baby step. Not like I'm heading to Vegas without panties on or anything."

They both laughed, and Sage stood to get more coffee.

"Garrett is babysitting Paige," Kenna said, wincing as if she was almost afraid to say her brother's name.

"You see?" Sage whipped around as the coffee sloshed in the cups. "Another reason why this is important. You assume the only reason I want to be naughty is to get his attention."

Kenna tilted her head and remained quiet.

"Fine. I clearly have it bad for him, but that's why this is a good idea. I'm giving myself a reboot. None of my efforts will be directed at Mr. Dear-Lord-You're-Perfect-And-So-Hot-In-Those—"

"Sage."

"Right, sorry. None of my usual sad, pathetic pining. This could be so empowering. Remember when you wanted to date after the Travis dream?"

Kenna nodded.

"Well, there was a reason I wanted to date too. Garrett and I are not going to have the same happy ending as you two do, but I'd like one, so I need to change things up. There are other men out there, and this book is going to help me learn to have fun. I've never been good with, you know—" Sage set the coffee down, pushed her boobs together, and made an exaggerated pouty face.

Kenna shook her head, laughing.

"What? Too much?"

"Nothing. You're pretty cute, you know. I'm glad you're my friend."

Sage exhaled. "Thanks. Me too."

"Hey, what about hot-guy-from-the-plane? Maybe you could try out some of your moves on him."

"He hasn't called. I may have blown that one with my weirdness. See, if I'd had the steps down I could have tried out Chapter Five—'Tease Me, Please Me' or Chapter Six—'Talk Dirty to Me' on him while we were stuck on the plane."

Both of them laughed.

"Those titles are. . . something else." Kenna said, stacking the rolled silverware into the three empty baskets.

"I know." Sage shook her head and went behind the bar to turn on some music.

"Well, if you need me to cinch anything in for you or troll the aisles of Walgreens for condoms, let me know." Kenna took out her laptop.

Sage was confused. "I don't think I'll be needing condoms."

"Honey, I've known you for almost three years and unless you've been holding out on me, you haven't had any in all that time."

"What about that guy with the huge fish tank that I went out with a couple of times before we ended our online dating nightmare? That got pretty intense."

"Uh huh, until you found out he had a wife and three kids. Besides, close may count in a lot of things, Sage, but sex is one of those where you either have it or you don't."

"Said the woman clearly having it."

Kenna blushed, which made Sage tease her more. Kenna and Travis were engaged and although it took them a while to figure things out, Sage had never seen two people more right. Kenna was a fantastic, sassy woman all by herself, but she was better with Travis. And Travis looked almost lit from within now that he had Kenna and her daughter Paige. Sage wanted that someday, but it appeared her prince charming was on a turtle instead of a horse. Which was fine. She didn't need a prince. What she needed were experiences and to keep growing. Naughty might be a fun part of that process. And even if it wasn't, no way was she letting Hollis gloat that her nice sister was simply a fake goody-goody bartender. *Challenge accepted, big sister.*

❧

By the end of the day, Garrett knew more than he ever wanted to know about produce bands, he'd had to fire a guy who kept showing up to work in flip-flops insisting they couldn't make him wear closed shoes, and he was starving. Logan wanted more Japanese eggplants, so Garrett agreed to hand deliver them if his brother made him dinner. When Garrett pulled into The Yard's parking lot, it was packed. He parked in the back lot by the onsite garden and walked around through the front door. Summer, the receptionist, waved and led a large party back to the private dining room. Garrett made his way to the only empty table in the bar. Servers were buzzing by in a controlled frenzy as he spotted Sage pouring some frilly drink into a very tall glass with what looked like a piece of pineapple.

Garrett liked his brother's place. Even with the noise and the craziness, the energy at The Yard was special. He'd often tried to figure it out: Was it the food or the location? Were the servers' personalities or the music that was playing important? Looking at the menu, he was pretty sure it had a lot to do with the food, but the other stuff was vital, too. His stomach growled, and not wanting to be another demanding diner, he waved off the tall blonde server who gestured she'd be with him in a minute and approached the bar to put in his order.

"The thing is, I've never understood why *Taxi Driver* was such a big hit," some guy in a shirt that looked too tight said to Sage as she finished making his drink and carefully moved it across the bar to him.

"Seriously, Brett? It's a classic. 'Are you lookin' at me, cause if you're lookin' at me,'" Sage said out of the side of her mouth in a spot-on De Niro, complete with the narrow, intense eyes, all while pouring two glasses of white wine and wiping up the spill from a server who nearly lost a beer on his way back to the floor. The Brett guy laughed and said something about her being "fun" and how he "wondered what else you're hiding behind that bar."

Sage's face almost fluttered in a gesture Garrett found odd and said, "Wouldn't you like to know?"

As she batted her eyes and turned to the register, Garrett looked over his shoulder, checking to see if he'd slipped into some alternate world. Apart from the drinks and fun conversation, the whole scene wasn't Sage at all. Not that he knew her, but it sure looked like she was flirting with this tool who had "I want in your pants" all over his face. She had to see that, right? They both laughed again, and Sage moved down the bar. She kept talking, her hands in constant motion. Garrett had no idea how she did it, but he decided watching Sage tend bar had to be another piece of The Yard's success. Finally noticing him standing at the end of the bar, her eyes shifted in that way they often did when she looked at him. Her flirty banter was gone. Garrett never thought of himself as an intimidating guy, but he clearly made her uncomfortable. Maybe it was that he was her boss's brother or that he wasn't usually all that talkative. His sister Kenna was forever telling him to "lighten up" or "smile for Christ's sake." Garrett lifted a hand in greeting to Sage, who dropped a few olives and eventually made her way over to him.

"Hey, you're not normally here for the dinner madness," she said, taking a credit card from an older woman in a green sweater.

"I brought eggplants for Logan. He promised to feed me."

Blowing her bangs out of her face, Sage handed the card and a pen back to the woman. "Oh, great. So what are you having? Or did you want me to see if Logan can come out?" She looked toward the kitchen.

"No, leave him. What's good?"

Sage met his eyes and then quickly focused on his chin. "I think I'm supposed to say it's all good."

Garrett smiled, wondering if she was going to get all flirty in-nuendo with him, and she dropped her pen.

"The meatballs are incredible"—she bent and picked up the pen—"that's what I had, and the pork. If you're hungry, go with the pork because it comes with these amazing potatoes and squash that look like flowers."

"Summer squash."

"I'm sure you grew those, right?" Her eyes were now on his forehead. Had she always been this reluctant to look at him?

Garrett nodded. "I'm sold. I'll have the pork."

Sage entered it into her computer, which printed out tickets in the kitchen, and turned back to him. "Beer?"

"Please."

She reached down and opened the bottle of Duck Duck Gooze from somewhere under the bar. She always picked his beer. There were too many new ones to choose from, so one day Garrett had asked her to pick one and she'd been doing it ever since. It was a talent, Garrett thought, because she somehow managed to give him the beer he wanted, needed, every time. There were some that hit harder on the days he was in a shit mood, lighter beers in the summer, warm heavier ones toward the holidays. She knew his beer, but she probably did that for everyone.

Handing him the cold bottle, Sage's eyes finally held his and for a split second it looked like she was going to say something else, but she must have changed her mind. She released the beer into his hand and was gone, working her bar like no one's business.

Garrett took a seat right as Logan came out of the kitchen, wiping his hands on a towel.

"Big brother in the house," Logan said with a casual tone that told Garrett his brother was not fazed by the crowds or Summer's long wait list at the hostess station.

Garrett pushed the box of eggplants across the small round table and Logan put it under his arm. "It's a shame no one wants to eat here," he said, taking a pull of his beer.

Logan laughed. "Did you order?"

"Yeah, pork."

"Good choice. You look tired." Logan glanced over his shoulder, and Garrett recognized the need to get back to work.

"You too. Do you need to get back?"

Logan quickly told him a story about Kara's shop and that some lady wanted her to make stained-glass sconces, and on his next breath, he was back in the kitchen. The blonde brought out Garrett's dinner and after the first bite, he knew he would travel infinite miles and sit on a damn cardboard box for this food. His brother and Travis were good at what they did, which made Garrett proud. Logan was only a couple of years younger than him, but Garrett had always felt much older. Maybe it was because he'd grown up a little faster working with their dad, or that he'd driven, dropped off, and made sure his brother and sister were able to participate in activities and be kids. Whatever it was, Garrett was protective of them both, and he genuinely liked the people they'd grown into.

Finishing up his last few bites and washing it down with the rest of his beer, he sat in the dimly lit bar and witnessed "pride and purpose," as their dad had often said. Those two things were the keys to a good life. He'd told them that before they were even old enough to understand. Logan's place had both, and maybe the magic of The Yard defied explanation. It worked, and that was all that mattered.

Chapter Three

S age had managed to try several exercises from Chapter Two—"Get Comfortable with You," while working her shift on Wednesday night. She'd "talked about things other than work" with Brett and practiced her "sexy laugh." Even though the whole being naughty business still felt a bit like when she tried to eat a caramel apple with braces at Tim Strough's Halloween party, she kept trying. Brett wasn't exactly her type, and his shirt was a little tight, but she didn't have to marry him. According to the book, Brett could be a "practice man," which sounded ridiculous when Sage read the chapter, but she'd secured a date for New Year's Eve and an opportunity to try out Chapter One—"Dress Like You Were Just. . ." She still had a hard time saying that title but had received confirmation from Brett that her look was spot-on when she'd arrived at The Yard a few hours ago. Now, however, in an effort to "work" her naughty outfit, she'd had too much to drink. She'd been tired of everyone looking at her boobs or her legs, barely noticing that anything was coming out of her mouth, so she nervously kept accepting drinks.

Although technically she could pass for tipsy, Sage was drunk. As she sidestepped through the crowd of pending New Year's Eve revelers on her way to the bathroom, she wanted to tell Brett, who'd been swiping free samples of her ass all night, that he was an idiot and the shirt stuffed under his ugly blazer was still too tight. And, she wanted to add that she wouldn't "ring in the New Year back at his place" if he were the last person on the planet. But that wasn't a nice thing to say, nor was it naughty, so drunk she must be.

Sitting on the toilet in the cramped bathroom stall, Sage watched the tips of her favorite tall black boots with a fascination only tequila could incite. They came up a little past her knees; she always wore them with shorter skirts because she never liked her legs in short anything. Her calves were thick, or as her mother would say, she "thought herself into insecurity." Although she didn't wear them all the time, the boots were favorites because they made her feel different. A few years ago, she'd decided to make a statement with her clothing, and she hadn't looked back since. Flair always had a place when she dressed herself in the morning, but these boots were sexy and Sage had never been too sure how to do sexy. She blew her bangs out of her face with a puff and knocked her knees together as she scrolled through her phone for Kenna's number. Pursing her lips in that my-face-is-numb way she'd seen so often as a bartender, she tried to concentrate.

A few women in sparkly festive heels—she could tell the black ones were Jimmy Choos from below the stall door—came and went as Sage attempted the normally simple task of texting. The music in the bar switched to something pulsing. She couldn't make out the song, but the beat was alluring. It reminded her of the music she'd put on when she was getting ready to go out that evening: club music. She'd been excited for The Yard's New Year's party, happy she wasn't working, and ready to try out her. . . new skills. But as with most things in her world, what she'd envisioned had not been based in reality. Getting dressed proved the easy part and about an hour into the party, Sage found it was hard not being herself. By Brett's second ass grab, she started feeling the weight of the fifth coat of mascara she'd applied before leaving the house. In fact, all of her makeup started to bug her, and her blouse, although cut super naughty low in the front, was itchy. Still searching for Kenna's number, Sage decided she felt sexier right after an hour of yoga.

She pulled out a few squares of toilet paper, cleaned the screen of her phone, and remembered the photo of the *Nice to Naughty* author when she'd googled her a few days ago. She was in a jean shirt and black leggings. She hadn't looked all that naughty, and Sage wondered if she ever actually wore a tiny skirt. If she had, she would have put a few paragraphs in there about what a pain in the ass it was to shimmy into the seat of a high-top bar table or get out of a car without flashing the valet. She could hear Hollis, who by the way, her tipsy mind told her, wasn't all that naughty either, saying, "What's the matter, sis? In over your head?"

The problem still remained that even in her completely "fuckable" clothes and having become well versed in the proposed steps all the way up through chapter seven, which was more than she ever imagined possible on the subject of role-playing, Sage was beginning to think Kenna was right. She wasn't wired for naughty. She was more of a talker, a snuggler. Simply wearing sexy boots did not a naughty girl make, and the desire to mask her discomfort with her outfit was how she ended up having that last shot of tequila. Looking for liquid courage, she of all people knew, only led to sloppy.

Damn it, she didn't like to fail. Maybe she should stay; there were hot guys out there, and Brett had joined some of his friends anyway. She was free to throw caution to the wind and "hook up," as Travis used to say before he fell in love with Kenna. Even in a tequila haze, with great music and the New Year only hours away, Sage couldn't find her naughty. She didn't want to hook up, she wanted. . . *Don't do it, don't go there*. She closed her eyes and felt the tiny stall spin.

He was "emotionally unavailable" as Kenna and many of Sage's relationship books had preached, but Sage, despite vowing to be free and open to new experiences, had tied herself in a knot over him. A knot she wasn't sure the *Nice to Naughty* book, or any book for that matter, could help her untie. The only answer was to leave it alone—leave him alone.

"Maybe you need a tattoo," tequila interrupted, warm and caressing as she heard two women at the sink talking about some guy at the bar who invited both of them back to his place. "See, you should be out there getting propositioned by hot strangers," tequila continued. Sage took in a slow breath and set her phone down on the little shelf provided. Her head was dizzy, even with her eyes now open, and looking down at the phone was making her sick. She wanted to go home.

"This is why you have no sexy stories, or no stories at all for that matter," tequila added, with a cruel bite that turned her stomach. She had to admit it was right. That was exactly why, despite her great wardrobe and super cute hair, she would always be Sensible Sage, middle child of the Jeffries sisters. It was a cliché but often true—sisters, based on birth order or life experience, were rarely alike, and that was certainly the case in her family. She'd designed a bi-cell assembly machine for her final project at Berkeley but never went anywhere other than home for spring break.

Letting out another slow breath, Sage sensed the approaching brand new three-hundred and sixty-five days stretched out in front of her. This would be the year of her hot air balloon ride. She'd signed up to teach bridge at the community center and. . . damn it, she would get through this book. And, although the dirty talk chapter only made her giggle, she would push through. She was a Jeffries after all. Looking down at her feet, she decided the boots should guide her. Daring, seductive, like that show Hollis, her oldest sister, used to watch that had all the great shoes. *Sex in the City*, yes. Even though she'd told her sister when they were in high school that the show was ridiculous, she needed it now.

Sage recognized the next song pounding overhead, so she hummed along as she returned to her phone and finally found *Greatest Friend Ever*. Kenna had made that her nickname when Sage had bought her new phone. After a couple of weeks of looking for her friend under K, she now knew instinctively, even after tequila, that Kenna was always in the Gs. With her thumb hovering, Sage made a decision.

She would still finish the book and keep trying, but not to-night. She'd had enough and wanted the green tea ice cream in her freezer more than she wanted hot sex. Because sex never worked out for her and green tea ice cream was. . . well, things were never awkward with ice cream. Resolved that tomorrow was a new day for naughty, she finally managed to open a text.

> *Hi! I know you guy left early and UR buzy, but I'm a little tippppsy, which I know is crazy ironic for a bartttender, but could you please come and pick up. I've had en fun. I guess I could take a cab, but that's awwkward since most of the cab companies know me because I call them for other drunk people and I. . . Ugh, could you come get meee?*
>
> *Sure. Be there in 15.*
>
> *Thank you. Kiss, kiss, kss. Oh, and my sort of date is here. He's at the bar in a plad blazer, can't miss HiM. He keeps grabbing my ass, which shold be a good naughty time, but no. Rude.*
>
> *Got it. Sit tight.*
>
> *I'm in the bathroom. Come get me when U here. I'm in the Stuart boots so I might need help not falling on my ass.*
>
> *OK*
>
> *Are you sure you don't mind? R you pissed?*
>
> *No.*
>
> *Okay. Thank you. I live you. XXXXXX*

Sage set her phone back on the tiny shelf, rested her head against the cool concrete wall, and sank back into her fuzzy state. She had good friends.

Garrett carefully lifted his sleeping niece off his shoulder and handed her over to Travis a few minutes after he'd received the text.

"You outta here?" Travis whispered, shifting Paige farther up his shoulder.

"Yeah, I need to get back. Early morning."

"Sure, thanks for babysitting."

"Anytime." Garrett leaned in and kissed a slumbering Paige. "Sleep tight, your highness," he whispered, and was rewarded with a tiny arm that wrapped around his head and squeezed. Heart full, he returned her hand to Travis's neck.

"See ya tomorrow morning for deliveries," Travis said, lowering his voice as he turned down the hall toward Paige's room.

Watching after them, Garrett was amazed how comfortable the role of dad looked on Travis. He and Kenna had been engaged less than two months, and they'd somehow already fallen into a rhythm as if they were always meant to be together. As if everything his sister had been through was leading her to this, to Travis. He wasn't sure he believed in any of that crap, but when he was around them, it sure felt destined. Putting on his cap, Garrett woke Jack, who was asleep in the entryway with a belly full of pepperoni and popcorn, compliments of Paige.

"Leaving?" Makenna asked, coming into the small living room.

"Early morning." He clipped the leash on Jack, who yawned in appreciation as Garrett rubbed his curly ears. "Oh, did you still want me to help you put up that bookcase? I noticed it on my calendar this morning. Has it arrived at the restaurant yet?"

"Yes, it came in yesterday. It's still in the box and crazy heavy. If you don't mind."

"Not a problem. I'll see you tomorrow for delivery and then I'll plan on being there for a couple of hours on Tuesday. We'll put it together then."

She leaned up and kissed him and then knelt to kiss Jack. "You two drive safe. Thanks for watching Paige tonight."

"Will you stop thanking me? She's the best, no trouble at all. Did you have a good time at the party?"

"Yeah, I think it went well. Logan is still there if you want to stop by on your way home."

"Sage." Garrett needed to get more sleep because that was supposed to be a thought.

His sister's forehead scrunched in the center, almost exactly like his, and Garrett scrambled for an explanation. He'd randomly blurted out her best friend's name for no reason. *Shit!*

"What about her?"

Hand on the door. "Oh, I was thinking of who's working. I'm sure she's there too?"

"She's not working tonight," Kenna answered, suspicion still in her eyes. "She was at the party, but I'm sure she's gone by now. Sage isn't exactly the partying type, although tonight was her. . . never mind."

"Her what?"

She shook her head. "I'm so tired, I have no idea what I was going to say."

Garrett nodded, eyes on Jack. "Right, well maybe I'll stop and see Logan. Night." He opened the door and if he knew his sister, she'd have one parting comment.

"I love you," she said, standing in the open doorway as he walked toward his truck.

He'd expected more questions, not something so simple. Kenna was rarely simple.

"I love you too." He glanced back at his little sister. A mom and soon-to-be bride, she was so happy, it sort of spilled off her. After her first husband died in a car accident when Paige was only five weeks old, Garrett watched his sister go through more pain than he cared to think about. He'd carried her to her bed in the main house many nights wishing there was something he could do to stop the hurt, something more than pushing Paige in her little swing so Kenna could take a shower. Her healing had been out of his control, which was worse than pretty much anything else. Garrett would have preferred to beat the shit out of someone or work himself to the bone over sitting around and waiting for time to return his sister to him. She was happy now, he thought as he waved and drove away, and Travis had proven himself to be a good guy. Not that Garrett would ever tell him that.

❦

A few minutes later, Garrett pulled into the parking lot of The Yard. He cracked the windows and told Jack, who didn't even bother to get up, to stay. Walking toward the glow of lights and the sounds of partying, Garrett nodded to the valet and told him he'd only be a minute. He was hoping he could get in and out with Sage without being noticed. He was guessing she wanted to sneak away too. That was why she had texted her best friend. Although he wasn't quite sure how she'd mixed up Kenna's number with his, he found that he wanted to be her covert escort anyway. Sage always came across busy, in need of no one, and even if they weren't exactly close, he wanted to help. *How did she even have my number? Was it that time she asked me for extra lemons? Hey, who gives a shit, get in there.*

Garrett walked through the bar unnoticed and made a quick detour to have a few words with Plaid Blazer, then stood at the door to the ladies' room. Running a hand across his face, he wasn't quite sure how to proceed. What the hell had he agreed to? Eh, what's done is done, he told himself and knocked.

"Sage?"

Nothing.

A tall woman, made even taller by heels that reminded Garrett of the fringe on a cowboy vest he wore as a kid, walked out of the bathroom. She glanced at him in confusion but then smiled.

"Hey, is anyone else in there?" he asked, trying not to sound like a pervert.

She started to shake her head of long black hair but paused. "Actually, someone is in one of the stalls. I think I heard her singing."

"Thanks." Garrett slowly pushed open the door with the cut metal sign that read—Ladies. "Sage, are you in there?"

A bang that sounded like someone kicked the stall was followed by a flush and then laughter.

"Sage, I'm coming in."

"Garrett! Why are you in the girls' bathroom? Was the little boys' room broken? Wait, you're not at this party." Her voice echoed in the empty bathroom, which was dimly lit by an old industrial sign.

Garrett locked the front door. There was no sense in scaring the crap out of some unsuspecting guest; he'd never hear the end of it from Logan.

"Sage. Let's get going. I'm your ride."

"What?" One more bang and then the stall door swung open.

Sage stood, holding onto the edge of the door. She wasn't hugging the porcelain bowl, so that was a plus, Garrett thought. She wobbled a little as she walked toward him, but she was balancing on some pretty substantial black leather boots that held his attention.

"You all right?" he asked as she made her way to the sink and he tried not to notice her incredibly tiny skirt.

Sage nodded and blinked her eyes a few times, as if that would somehow sober her up as she washed her hands.

"Was Makenna busy? Why would she send you?" She glanced at him and although she looked like hot sex in that little silver skirt and a dangerously low-cut blouse—*Eyes up, man, eyes up*—the look on her face betrayed her. He'd expected to find a stumbling, drunk party girl he could laugh at before delivering her safely home. Instead, he was face-to-face with a beautiful woman who was genuinely surprised to find herself in this situation. Her eyes were dark and glossy as she waited for an answer. One benefit of the alcohol, Garrett thought, was she didn't seem as nervous as she normally did around him.

"No. She doesn't know I'm here. You texted me," he said.

"I . . . no." She pulled her phone out of some mystery pocket in the tiny skirt. "Oh shit, shit! I'm. . ." She put a hand to her face. "Like you have nothing better to do other than pick up my silly drunk ass? I mean, I didn't have that many. I probably could have waited it out. God, I'm sorry. Why didn't you text me back and tell me that—"

"Sage"—he touched her arm, surprised at the scratch of the fabric—"we're standing in a women's bathroom and I'd like to get out of here. You texted that you needed a ride. I was right at Kenna's babysitting Paige, so it's not a big deal. Let's go."

She appeared to pull herself together, but then Garrett took her hand and she paused, eyes closed and smiling. It was only a moment, but long enough for him to notice how small her hand felt in his, and then her eyes opened. He unlocked the door to two women waiting.

"Sorry about that, ladies," he said quickly, and Sage laughed.

"What?" he asked as they made their way through the bar.

"Nothing. This is a little funny."

"I suppose it is." He glanced over his shoulder, still moving them toward the door but stopping at the end of the bar. "Before we leave," he tapped Plaid Blazer on the shoulder and could feel Sage's hand tense in his. "We're leaving. Did you have something you wanted to say?" he asked the guy whose ego was now a little deflated. Garrett always liked it when slimeballs knew enough to be uncomfortable.

"My apologies for putting my hands on you, Sage. No hard feelings?" He looked at Garrett as if waiting to be prompted for his next line. "And. . . I'm a tool?"

Sage laughed, hand to her mouth, as Garrett patted him on the back and turned them toward the exit.

"Do you have a coat?" he asked as they pushed through the front door.

"What kind of coat did you want me to pair this with?" She ran her hands up the sides of her body, completely unaware he was a male and they were standing under the stars.

Hello, eyes up, asshole!

He shook his head, took off his coat, and wrapped it around her shoulders.

❧❧❧

"My God, that was classic. How did you get him to apologize *and* call himself a tool?" Sage asked, still laughing and reluctant to let go of Garrett's hand as she slid into the warmth of his truck. "Oh, hi there, sweet baby Jack." She kissed the dog sharing the bench seat with her and leaned against him, all soft and wonderful, kind of like his owner but far less dangerous. Jack was a Britney, brown and white with what Paige called "freckles," and the most well-loved eyes Sage had ever seen. He was always with Garrett whether he was at the office or out in the fields. As if the man needed any help being her ultimate hot-and-damn, he had a great dog too.

"I asked him to say he was sorry," he said, starting the truck.

"Uh huh."

The corner of Garrett's mouth turned up as they pulled into traffic. The truck, a 1957 Ford, smelled like rich oil and potted plants. It had been restored for as long as Sage had known the Rye family. The story, according to Makenna, was that Garrett had worked on the engine and the bodywork all during high school and then their father surprised him at graduation with all-new upholstery.

She'd only been in his truck one other time when he'd picked her and Kenna up from the movies because Kenna's Jeep wouldn't start. That had been over a year ago, and not much had changed. Running her hand along the leather of the seat, Sage told herself, through the haze of tequila, to sober up and not make an ass out of herself. Her cheeks were warm, and she wanted to switch places with Jack and climb right into Garrett's lap.

"Let's do it," tequila, its voice a little fainter now, said.

Stop it.

Sage closed her eyes, petting Jack and knowing that the body of knowledge she'd gathered on Garrett Rye, through his family and eavesdropping from the bar, was a touch pathetic. Her interest in him was a little "consuming" according to pretty much all of her books, but Sage wasn't sure how to stop. There was an energy she felt every time he was around that was hard to ignore. He wasn't flashy and she knew she wasn't his type, but that didn't matter to her heart. She wanted him. And until she could move on and get a grip on herself, maybe learn to be nasty, no other date, or man for that matter, stood a chance. That was her problem. He was hers. He simply didn't know it yet.

She let out a slow breath, listening to the low, rhythmic lilt of a country song she didn't recognize. Jack made himself comfortable and rested his head on her lap. Sage peeked at Garrett, driving silently beside her, his face lit by the dash, and her heart settled into her chest, content to stay right where it was. Her eyes were heavy and as she drifted off to sleep, she heard tequila, in a voice that sounded a lot like her own, say, "I love you, Garrett Rye."

Oh, me too, tequila, me too.

Chapter Four

S age woke up the next morning with yuck mouth, but only a slight headache. At least she'd been aware enough not to mix alcohol during the party; there were some benefits to being a professional. Sticking with tequila but forgetting that she hardly ever drank anymore had landed her in the bathroom last night. *So, she told herself as she pulled on her yoga pants and prepared to detox the final night of the old year right out of her system, you're allowed to have fun.* After wrestling into her sports bra, she lay back down on the bed. The headache throbbed a little more now that she was moving around. The evening had not gone as she'd expected. It turned out dressing naughty brought out all sorts of other problems, namely Brett's hands. She'd followed Chapters One and Two to the letter and still ended up texting. . . who? Suddenly, Sage remembered her ride home.

Garrett. She closed her eyes, inhaled, and exhaled. "Focus on the breath, be in the now," she told herself as she began to drift back to sleep. Maybe one more hour. Rolling over to her pillow, pieces of her brief drive home with Garrett floated to the surface. Holding his hand, being wrapped in his coat, Jack, even the weight of his body as he leaned over her to help find the seatbelt. How had she been that close to him and fallen asleep? He'd looked over at her when she'd said. . . when she'd said. . . Her eyes flew open.

"I think I told your brother that I love him," she blurted out to Kenna minutes after scrambling to grab her phone off the nightstand.

"Hold on," she mumbled. "What now?"

Sage closed her eyes, not quite sure she could say it again. "I told Garrett I loved him, at least, I think I did. I was in his truck and he gave me his coat and Jack was there. It was so warm and the tequila and I sort of fell asleep, but before, I think I told him. Oh crap, I can't remember if I was thinking it or if the words actually came out of my mouth. Oh, oh my God. Say something, Kenna. Why did you leave me alone with him?"

"Okay, we need to back way up here. When did you even see Garrett?"

"Last night. I was in the bathroom and then I texted you, but it wasn't you. Oh holy shit, I need to sit down." Sage sank to her couch, folded her legs into her chest, and told Kenna about the mix-up, Garrett showing up, and even Plaid Blazer. Kenna listened and laughed at some points. Despite being pretty sure she needed to leave town, she had to admit parts of the story were funny.

"So you told him you loved him and then fell asleep. That's not a big deal. For all he knows, you were saying that as a way of thanking him for picking you up. You know, like, 'Hey, thanks for getting me. I love you for this.' It's not like you went into detail. You fell asleep."

Sage was silent. Hand rubbing her temple, she tried to remember what was real and what was imagined. She'd had so many fantasies about Garrett without the help of alcohol that it was hard to pinpoint reality.

"Right?" Kenna asked. "You fell asleep on the way home?"

"I think so."

"Well, did he walk you to your door? I'm sure he did. Do you remember him walking you in?"

"Yes, I remember getting my keys and thanking him. I remember shutting off my alarm and turning and then. . . oh, oh, shit, Kenna. I think I said other things. I'm pretty sure I said stuff about his eyes, and I touched him."

Even through the phone, she could tell Kenna was holding back a laugh.

"This is not even close to funny. Are you laughing at me?"

"No, no, sorry. Well, was he in your bed when you woke up this morning?"

"No! My God. Like I'd be calling you if he was in my bed."

This time, Kenna did laugh. "Okay, so whatever you said, it's not a big deal. Honey, you had too much to drink. Most of us are stupid when we drink. I'm sure whatever you said has been forgotten. Garrett probably shrugged it off and went home."

"Could you call him?" Sage knew it sounded high school, but she didn't care.

"Me?"

"Yeah, get a feel for what happened. I mean pieces are coming back to me, but if you call him, he'll tell you how bad it was."

Kenna let out a sigh. "Okay. I'm sure it's nothing, but let me get Paige to her friend's house. Her mom's taking them to a movie, so we can't be late. I'll call him on my way to work."

"Great, okay. Yeah, let me know."

Sage hung up and sat on the couch trying to find the missing pieces of her memory. There had been something about summer camp. She remembered mentioning the name of her camp. Something about making a fire, maybe? Right, yes, because she had a faint memory of describing Tim Strough, her first crush. They must have been talking about crushes. . . and maybe the one she had on him? Oh no, this was not good. How had this happened? She dealt with silly drunk women all the time and after three measly shots of tequila, she'd become one.

This wasn't even a good story for her bottom drawer. It was a sad little unable-to-hold-her-liquor story. Now, if she'd been dancing on the bar or had some gorgeous guy take her up against the wall in the bathroom, that would have been a story, something to feel a little naughty about before she tucked it into her life experiences. This was more like a cautionary tale of a lightweight naughty girl wannabe who probably blabbered herself silly to a guy she'd been in love with for far too long.

Sage felt like she was going to be sick from the stupidity of it all. Why couldn't she be comfortable in her own skin? Why had she dressed that way and found herself drunk in a bathroom? She put her face in her hands. *Shit, shit, shit.*

Finishing up her pity party and what was left in her water bottle, she grabbed her phone and read her positive affirmation of the day: "You are not your yesterdays," the words of her app informed her above a picture of a road.

"Wanna bet?" she said out loud to her empty house, snorting a laugh.

Her horoscope wasn't much better: "Brace yourself for a period of uneasy, but know you'll get through it." Damn it. Only a few days ago it said she was going to have the best month of the year. Had the stars moved around that quickly?

Finding her yoga playlist, Sage plugged her iPod into the cool speaker thing she'd bought off an infomercial late one night while she was trying to unwind after a shift. Soft flutes and steel drums filled her living room. No words, Sage thought thankfully as she stepped out onto her patio and took in a breath of cool morning air. Things would be fine, she told herself as she rolled out her thick black yoga mat. Feet mushing into the foam, she took a seat, closed her eyes, and tried to quiet her mind, which was easier said than done. Her brain still desperately wanted to know exactly how stupid her heart had been.

Breathe in, breathe out. Sage stretched out on her mat and remembered why she practiced yoga.

❦❦❦

A little over an hour later, sweaty and much closer to normal, Sage grabbed her ringing phone. Pulling on a sweatshirt, she hoped as

Kenna began with, "Okay, I have good news and bad news," that her chi wasn't about to start screaming again.

"Which do you want first?" her friend asked as Sage grabbed another bottle of water.

"Bad."

"All right. It's not exactly bad, but you did quite a bit of talking."

Sage moaned, collapsing back onto the couch, the hand not holding the phone now covering her face.

"You mentioned that you loved him in general terms, which he did dismiss as you being tipsy and grateful for the drive home."

"Okay."

"But then you sort of. . . described in detail the things you loved about him. His eyes, the way his forehead wrinkles and makes that crease, his hands, the way he loves his family."

"Oh my dear Lord, please stop."

"Look, I know you're dying right now, but maybe this is a good thing. You let it all out. Finally saying it has to feel good."

"Yeah? How the hell am I supposed to move on from this? I sounded like some pathetic love puppy. I'm surprised I didn't launch into how great he smells all the time or that I love his dog too."

"You did."

Sage closed her eyes. "Great. Okay, well, I'm going to start packing now. It was nice being friends with you."

Kenna laughed. "Stop. He was a little confused, but come on, everything you said was flattering and. . . nice."

And there it was, the word Sage should probably have tattooed on her forehead: nice.

"Right."

"I'm sorry, honey, but I don't think it's such a bad thing that he knows. And who cares? So you're hot for him. You said some great things about him. There's nothing to be embarrassed about here."

"Okay, let's stop talking about it. Maybe I'll drink again tonight and finish myself off by trying to jump his bones. Make myself a complete laughingstock."

"Well, you sort of. . ."

"Shut the hell up. I would have remembered that. Wouldn't I?"

Kenna's laughter grew louder. "I'm kidding. Take a shower, do your bendy exercises, and make one of those plant shakes you drink. You'll be fine."

"Will do," Sage said with more resolve than she felt. "I'm off today, so that's something."

"Yes, you are. Now go be kind to yourself."

"Sure, see you tomorrow. Oh wait, what was the good news?"

"There wasn't any, but I thought that sounded better than 'Oh my God, it's as bad as you thought.'"

"Great. Very considerate, thank you." Sage tried to laugh and hung up the phone.

She'd made a fool of herself in front of the one man who mattered. Adding more spinach to the blender, she stopped and gripped the edge of the counter. Chapter Three in the naughty book was "Life is a Stage." It was completely absurd but talked about setting the scene for things, sort of a precursor to role-playing, which had its own chapter toward the end of the book. Staging. Sage was pretty sure what happened with Garrett was not what they had in mind. Had the author been in charge of last night, Sage would have certainly woken up with Garrett in her bed.

Damn it, building semiconductors was easier than this crap. Stupid book, Sage thought as she took a glass from the cabinet and pushed the pulse button on the blender.

❧

Community Supported Agriculture, or CSA as it was called now, was something Ryeland Farms had been doing for years, but now that it was a trend, business had picked up considerably. The program was a way of bringing local produce to restaurants. Garrett remembered being a kid and delivering boxes to two local restaurants once a week. Now they had a truck route and delivered to various locations around Los Angeles six days a week. Their distribution had tripled in the last two years alone.

Garrett had two core supervisors. George, who, as he liked to put it, "handled all things earth," and Richard, who handled distribution. George was one of Garrett's favorite people; he'd been a teenager working the farm back when Garrett was a kid. Now he was in his forties, with the last of his three daughters entering high school. He'd been a grower his whole life and Garrett not only loved working with him, he loved him as a friend. As of right now, Garrett, with the help of Kenna, handled everything else and the employees. They probably needed more help, but he never liked to throw bodies at things. Once he had a handle on all the tasks he needed to delegate, he'd get someone, but the thought of moving further and further away from the parts he loved made him uneasy.

Garrett and Logan worked farmers markets and had thought for a while about having a farm store, but that was put on the back burner once the CSA program blew up their business. Kenna continued to push for a farm store, but Garrett always managed to squash the idea by telling her if she wanted a store, she could run it.

Garrett delivered The Yard's order every morning, and sometimes in the afternoon if they needed more. He didn't need to. He could put them on the route with the rest of the stops, but he brought Logan's order himself. It was a chance to see his brother and sister, to check how things were going, and to find out if they needed anything before their family meetings on Wednesdays. He didn't mind the little extra effort of driving an hour each way. It was on his schedule, and it kept them connected. Besides, Jack loved riding in the truck almost as much as he liked the tractor.

While the guys loaded the flats into his truck, Garrett noticed the lemons. They were for her. Picking one up, he tossed it in the air and put it back in the flat. He wondered if she was working today.

"You heading out?" George asked, pulling up next to him on a tractor.

"Si."

"Can you pick up a tray of lasagna from Logan before you come back? Angela could have any Mexican feast she wants for her birthday and she chose your brother's lasagna instead. That's almost embarrassing, right?"

Garrett laughed. "You should cut her a break—it's pretty powerful lasagna. And yes, I'll bring it back with me. Everything good this morning?"

"Things are good. Kind of slow now that everything's planted. We're pruning the trees today, getting ready because you know we'll be up to our *culos* in a few months."

"That we will. I'll be back soon. By the way, did that guy show up to finish the electric in the barn?"

George nodded. "First thing this morning."

Great, Garrett thought, one thing off his list already.

"All right, I'll let you know if anything new comes up with these dinners they're planning."

"It's going to be great having fancy events out here with us farmhands." George laughed.

"Yeah, apparently we're trendy now," Garrett said, using finger quotes.

"I know. Marisa told me some celebrity recently had a farm-to-table wedding. I asked her if she wanted to help her papa get that food from the farm to the table and she looked at me like I was nuts. I was cool for about a minute."

Both men laughed, and Garrett still couldn't believe George's daughter was old enough to care about what was trendy and what wasn't. Seemed like yesterday she had braids and braces.

"It's good though, people paying attention to what we're doing out here. Even if it's only while we're trendy."

"True." Garrett kicked the tire of the huge machine. "See you in a few."

"Take your time. I've got this, amigo."

"Yeah? I should take my time? You want to handle the paperwork on my desk?"

"I will if you want me to."

Garrett shook his head. "Get back to work."

George laughed, tipped his hat, and left in a cloud of dust.

Garrett whistled for Jack and they were on the road by nine. As he drove past their old school, he thought about Jenny Kapoot. He was nine when she wrote him a love note on a napkin during lunch. The bell rang and while they were all going back to class, she'd handed it to him and smiled. Jenny had strawberry blonde hair and freckles on her ears. He remembered because he'd sat behind her in class the year before. She was pretty and wore incredibly shiny lip gloss that he knew smelled like bubble gum even a few desks back; a lot of the boys liked Jenny. The letter said she wanted to be his girlfriend and he should ask her so they could hold hands. Pretty forward for a nine-year-old, he thought now, putting on his sunglasses.

On that day, as he'd walked to class, his heart had drummed in his chest at the thought of holding her hand. He'd never thought about a girlfriend until the moment she'd put that napkin into his hand. Class started and he'd shoved the note into his pocket.

Later, after school, two older kids were messing with Logan, who was seven at the time. Some shit about him not wanting to help them with their worksheets. By the time Garrett had arrived, it had escalated to pushing and his little brother hitting the dirt. Garrett punched the biggest of them and knocked his short, chubby sidekick into the trashcans.

He and Logan had picked up Kenna and walked home. Logan's lip was bleeding, so Garrett handed him the napkin from his pocket. The next morning at the breakfast table, their dad told them their mom had left and she wasn't coming back. Makenna ran to her room, Logan cleared the breakfast dishes, and Garrett helped his dad with the harvest until dark. Jenny's love note had ended up in the trash; it wasn't until she sat glaring at him a couple of weeks later that he even remembered her handing it to him.

In the space of a few days, the thought of walking down the hall with a girl became silly, and the thumping of his heart and his sweaty hands were all but forgotten. Things had changed and Garrett, even nine-year-old Garrett, no longer had time for silly. Jenny Kapoot moved on to Cory McCoy. She probably sent him a note too. Just as well.

Sharing his bag of granola with Jack, Garrett considered if he'd ever received another love note. He supposed what happened with Sage was similar, although more adult. The unfiltered declaration that she wanted him came out of nowhere and was probably nothing, but his heart had thumped a little.

She had too much to drink, and the woman barely speaks to you.

The texting episode and how small and shiny and relaxed she'd looked in his truck had been unexpected. The vision Garrett now had, as he changed lanes to let some guy in a Lexus race past him, was of Sage rubbing Jack's ears while crossing and uncrossing long, shapely legs Garrett wouldn't soon forget. She was a beautiful woman—that wasn't up for debate—but he'd always thought of her as more than that. She was funny and flashy with her crazy clothes and her ever-changing nail color. Her hair was long and then it was short; she looked great either way. He didn't know much about her or where she came from, but beautiful was too simple a word for her.

"Your eyes are like. . . they're green, but like a watercolor. Different and swirling," she'd said when he had walked her to the door.

Who said things like that? She immediately had him thinking the ordinary eyes he saw in the mirror every morning were somehow art museum worthy. She'd put her hand on his chest before reaching up to kiss him on the cheek as thanks for picking her up. There had been no sign of her usual nerves, only a warm, grateful woman. And despite knowing this was a one-time thing and reminding himself she was drunk and this was a favor, his heart thumped again. He'd barely noticed the damn thing for the last few years and there it was, thumping away.

As he'd moved away from her front door, Sage had handed him back his jacket. He smelled her sweet but spicy-like-rosewood scent all the way home. Even her perfume was confusing.

Being with her like that, with her defenses down even for a few minutes, had felt like something he didn't want to explore. At the same time, it was nice to be noticed, nice to put that look in someone's eyes. Pulling up to The Yard, Garrett decided he'd leave it at that. Sage Jeffries was nice and even though he didn't have time to be her boyfriend or hold her hand in the hall, grown-up Garrett would try not to shove her feelings into his pocket, either.

Chapter Five

*S*age had been a little relieved when Garrett delivered the vegetables through the back door without incident. She'd returned from dry storage to find the lemons she'd ordered on the bar. Before she could delude herself into thinking this was some kind of gesture instead of the simple fact that it was on the order, Garrett walked, well rather, heaved his way through the front door of The Yard carrying what looked like a tree trunk on his shoulder. Sage tried to hit slow motion in her brain because she didn't want the image to end. Kenna had mentioned some new bookcase that looked like a tree for the corner of the restaurant, but she failed to mention Garrett would be delivering it. Sweet Mother Mary, his blue flannel flapped open, exposing a white T-shirt that hugged a broad chest and woke up her already-active imagination. *Who the hell carries in a tree?* How was she supposed to be normal around this crap?

Kenna came through the door next and ran to guide her brother through the maze of tables to the corner she'd cleared for her latest find. As Sage finished putting the pieces of the blender she'd fixed back together, she heard grunts, the sound of a drill, and clapping. Makenna flew by her saying something about a meeting and that she'd be back. Garrett was right behind her, brushing dust and dirt off the front of his shirt. She wasn't sure how he did it, but the man managed to make everything seem second nature. She was sure if she put him at a ballet or an art show, maybe he would look out of place, but watching him saunter past her, she doubted it. The ease and comfort, the pureness of him were things a person simply couldn't fake.

"Sage." He nodded and continued into the kitchen.

Oh perfect. Now I'm relegated to a head nod. Well done, Jeffries. Rush right in there with your stupid heart and scare the guy into head gestures. Right as she was about to bow her own head in embarrassment, she remembered Chapter Four—"Balls Out." "Naughty women never back down from conflict, and they simply don't get embarrassed," it read.

"Wait."

Garrett stopped, hand on the door.

"I . . . don't want to do this. I had too much to drink and I called—"

"Texted," he interrupted and moved away from the door.

"Right, well, whatever. It's not important."

"It sort of is, because if you'd called, you would have heard my voice and probably would have hung up. We'd be in a different situation."

Wow, someone was awfully technical this morning. "Okay, sure, good point. Irrelevant, but I'm glad you got that out. Anyway, my point is it's one of those things, and I'd like to move past it and go back to being civil, friendly." *Confident, moving on, good, this is good.*

"Were we ever friendly?"

"Sure, I think we were."

Garrett grinned and sat at the bar, leaning in on his forearms as if he were watching a game or trying to figure out a puzzle.

"Are you saying we weren't?" Sage finally broke the silence. "Coffee?"

"Please." He took his knit cap off, and his deep brown hair danced with static.

Sage slid the cup across the bar to him and brought up the sugar from the shelf below. She turned to get the cream out of the small fridge, because of course she knew he used cream.

"Yeah, I guess we were friendly."

"Were?" She turned, still holding the pitcher of cream.

Garrett appeared to be choosing his words carefully. "I, yeah, things were said and I'm not sure how you want me to respond. If I'm completely honest here, it's a little weird now."

She couldn't remember a damn thing in the book when he looked at her. If he was going to be honest, she'd try that too. "I. . . meant what I said, but it was still. . ." *Completely humiliating*, she wanted to scream, but didn't.

"Embarrassing," he finished her sentence.

Yup, he was a mind reader too. Sage laughed because laughing was easier than dying.

"I was being honest. Sometimes that's embarrassing I guess."

"You had too much to drink. It's not a big deal."

"True, but you still have great eyes," she said, accepting the space she was in and enjoying the bit of freedom honesty allowed.

His mouth curved into a slow smile, and she wondered if he even knew the way he looked, the effect he had. "Thank you," he finally said. "It was all very flattering."

"I'm glad. See, there's nothing wrong with being told you're hot."

"You didn't actually say I was hot."

"Didn't I?"

He shook his head.

She laughed. "Oh, well, hot is sort of a general term. You can throw that in there, too."

"Thanks again, it was nice."

"Nice?"

"Yeah, you're right. There are worse things. So, we're good?"

Nice. It was nice and I was nice. Damn it.

"I'd rather be naughty," she heard herself say.

Garrett choked on his coffee. "Excuse me?"

Sage, shocked at her own words and certain that was not what the book meant by "assertive flirting," shook her head. "Nothing," she said quietly. "I have some things, I mean I need to"—*Good God*—"bye, Garrett." She all but crawled to the dishwasher station to pick up her shakers.

Sage took a psychology class her sophomore year in college. The instructor had been crazy, which was ironic considering the subject. He'd started off the semester breaking them into groups and asking them to "interact as if you are the produce section of a grocery store." Sage had never quit a class in her life. It simply wasn't an option in her world. But when he gave her a C on their first exam with the comment "not enough heart," she'd reached her limit. Not enough heart? The test was multiple choice. That day she went straight to the registrar and dropped psychology. She'd cut her losses and moved on.

Garrett was like psychology class, Sage thought as she continued making chitchat with the dishwashers until she was sure he'd left. She needed to cut her losses while she still had a tiny bit of dignity left. She would continue practicing her naughty skills, but not on Garrett. She returned to the bar and wondered if she should take it as a warning that her psych teacher wanted his class to play produce section and her naughty book author had a fruit salad analogy. She should probably throw the damn book out because they were both nuts. "Are you looking for excuses to quit again, little sis?" Sage heard her sister's voice in her head.

"Oh, screw you," she said to no one as she selected Green Day on the audio system and cleared Garrett's cup.

❧

"What do you know about Sage?" Garrett asked Logan as they grabbed a booth at the Chicago Hamburger Company. It was early; they'd beaten the lunch crowd.

"She's great, why?"

"Does she date often?"

"I. . . know she did the whole online thing with Kenna months ago, but other than that, I'm not sure. Oh, she did date the Twisted Tree Winery rep. I think they've gone out a couple of times."

"Huh."

"Are you going to tell me why you're asking?"

"No reason. I don't know much about her, and I'm sure you've heard about the New Year's Eve pickup thing."

Logan nodded.

"She said a bunch of things and I guess that got me thinking, but shit, I don't know. Forget it." Garrett shoved a straw into his Coke and wondered why this kept popping into his head.

"I heard she told you she loves you." Logan wiggled his eyebrows and it was official, Garrett felt like they were seventeen.

"She was drunk."

Logan sat back in the booth with a stupid grin on his face. "I don't think that matters. She's been looking at you for a while."

Garrett's brow creased. "Looking at me? What the hell does that mean?"

"Exactly what I said. She has a thing for you. Always has as far as I can tell. It doesn't surprise me she told you. I'm glad she did. Sage is great."

Garrett shook his head as the guy with the white paper hat put two red plastic baskets in front of them. "Very funny. She does not have a thing for me. She doesn't even know me."

"You don't need to know someone inside and out to have a thing for them. Shit, have you been out of the game that long?"

"I'm not out of the game." Garrett grouped some fries together and looked to Logan, who laughed and went to get ketchup for his brother.

"Last date?" he asked, setting the plastic cups of ketchup and extra napkins on the table.

"None of your damn business. I date." Garrett dipped and ate.

Logan took a sip of his soda and waited.

"Like, last month, maybe a couple of months now. It was forgettable. That woman you set me up with who knows Kara—the florist. I can't remember her name."

Logan shook his head and bit into his burger. "Sandy? Yes, you're right, she is a florist, but that date was before Halloween."

"Was it? Shit, where does the time go?" Garrett wiped his mouth. "Anyway, I date. Actually, I saw her a couple of times after that too."

"No, you had sex with her a couple of times after that date be-cause she told Kara you were an asshole and dropped her, stopped returning her phone calls."

Garrett shook his head. "A perfect example of why I... limit my dating."

Logan laughed.

"Don't you ever think about it?"

"Sex? Yes, it's one of my favorite topics after the perfect pH-balanced soil."

Logan finished chewing. "Dating, meeting someone. Starting a family?"

Garrett wasn't sure why the question made him feel stupid and a little naïve. His first thought was—What the hell are you talking about? I have a family. But Logan's definition of family had expanded. When Kenna got married years ago, Garrett barely felt the shift because they were all young and Adam kind of came into the fold. The two of them added Paige, who loved the farm, so not much changed. Then Adam was killed in a car accident and Kenna came home to heal. That was when Garrett realized what the farm meant, how important it was to keep their family intact. But this time, with Logan close to getting married and Kenna newly engaged again, Garrett could feel the shift. Even if he didn't want to talk about it, he knew it was there. Logan continued looking at him for an answer, and Garrett suddenly felt like he did in precalculus during senior year. He had no idea what the hell was going on.

"No," he finally said.

"No, that's it? You're thirty-four. Do you want to have children?"

Garrett shrugged. "What the hell? We sound like women. Are you going to ask me about my cycle next?"

Logan laughed and thankfully dropped it. "So when Sage told you she loved you, did you make your move?"

"She was drunk."

"Right, well, are you going to make your move?"

Garrett kept eating his fries and tried to ignore the images of what that move would look like, feel like. "Probably not a good idea. Work is the priority right now. We're making all these changes and planting. It's not a good time. And I don't think I'm her type when she's sober."

"What's her type?"

He shook his head. "No idea. From the looks of her, probably some artsy guy. You know, the ones who hang out in that coffee shop she and Kenna go to. But, the other day I told her all the stuff she said that night was nice, and I swear she said something about wishing she was naughty."

Logan almost choked. "Sage? She actually said that? Naughty?"

Garrett nodded.

"Well, that is new. I can't say I've ever thought of Sage as. . . naughty." Logan laughed. "Sounds like something's up. You should talk to Kenna. She knows her best. I highly doubt Sage is going to tie you up."

Garrett shrugged, not allowing that particular image in, and finished off his fries. "I'm not asking Kenna. It's been a crazy few days, that's all. One minute we're passing each other in the mornings and maybe I see her a few times socially, and now I'm the love of her life and she wants to be naughty?"

Logan smiled big and sarcastic so Garrett threw a balled-up napkin at his face.

"Yeah, enough of this shit. Let's get down to why we're here."

Logan gave in. "Okay. I was up at the farm last night. The new barn looks amazing."

"Coming together. They're sealing the floor today."

"Great. So we're all set for the dinner there? It's going to be small and intimate. We're sold out. Travis and I will cook. Sage is doing drinks. It's our first one, so there'll be kinks, but I think it's going to be great."

"Should be. Do these people need to see us actually pulling the stuff out of the ground to get the full farm-to-table experience? Is this like a field trip?" Garrett laughed.

Logan explained that the food only needed to come from the farm, that it wasn't interactive. Garrett wasn't big on "a day on the farm" events, but he couldn't dismiss the notion that having people see where their food came from would benefit the greater good. If that meant he had to answer a few questions like, "So, do you guys still drive tractors?" then so be it.

"This will be our only one in January, and then the one in early February is going to be pretty special," Logan said, as if he had a secret he wasn't ready to share.

Garrett nodded, finishing his burger and washing it down with the last of his Coke. God, there was nothing like a good burger, he thought as his brother smiled at him.

"What? What's that look?" Garrett asked, wiping his mouth.

"Nothing. I'm looking forward to this year."

"Okay. . . me too?"

"Yeah, you should be, naughty boy."

Garrett raised his brow and was about to raise his middle finger, but Logan continued with his "love smile," as their father had taken to calling it, and Garrett wondered if he had some kind of surprise in February or if he simply enjoyed looking goofy.

"How's Dad?" Logan asked.

"He's good. Why?"

"I haven't been out there that much lately."

"Well, you guys are busy. We're fine. Ramping back up after the holidays. You see him every week. He looks fine, doesn't he?"

"Sure. I wasn't saying something was wrong, but it's different."

"What's different?"

"Garre, I'm getting married. Kenna got engaged. New people in our lives. I mean it's all good change, but it still takes some getting used to."

"I guess," Garrett said, pulling out some bills and paying the check. There it was again, a twist in his chest and the feeling he was missing something. Maybe he was oversimplifying, as every woman he'd ever dated liked to point out. He supposed they were in uncharted waters here. It had always been the four of them. Garrett figured he would stay focused on keeping the farm running smoothly; it was all he could control. The rest would work itself out.

"Okay, so we'll bring everything up Saturday night and then we'll try to be cleaned up and out of your hair Sunday night."

"Sounds good." Garrett stood and threw their trash out.

"So, Sage," Logan said, holding the door as they walked to the parking lot.

"Bye." Garrett closed the door to his truck, leaving Logan standing in the parking lot laughing as he pulled away.

Once on the highway, Garrett replayed the part about starting a family. It was honestly such an odd thing to think about—the first time he'd thought of the word outside the family he had. He was sure some therapist would have a field day with that one. All right, he thought, things were changing. If he'd adjusted to taking his shirts to the damn dry cleaner, he could work a few extra people into his family.

Shit. Naughty didn't sound like such a bad idea either.

Chapter Six

*S*age spent the morning doing laundry and working her way through the Friday *New York Times* crossword puzzle. The *LA Times* had a crossword too, but her father and her sister Annabelle did that one. Sage subscribed to the *New York Times* because it was more challenging and. . . well, she was probably a head case. She'd been doing some kind of crossword for as long as she could remember; her father always had one at the kitchen table and encouraged his girls to "challenge your brains." Some- times, he'd tie money to the first daughter to finish.

Last year, after reading an article about its history, Sage challenged herself to the *New York Times* crossword every day. She started with Monday, the easiest, every week. Each puzzle got progressively more difficult as the week went on, all in preparation for the mother lode: the Sunday crossword puzzle. She had yet to finish a Sunday. It was a goal, something she looked forward to e-mailing her entire family once it was achieved. At the moment, she wasn't feeling too confident about her less-than-half-finished Friday puzzle and stuck it in her backpack before leaving for work.

Pulling out of her one-car driveway, Sage watched her neighbor, Ms. Beachwood, dragging in her recycle can. She didn't know much about Ms. Beachwood other than she brought Sage fresh-baked cookies a few times a year, and she had a tiny dog named Smurf with eyes that were too big for its face. As she waved and pulled away, Sage wondered if her neighbor had lived alone her whole life. That certainly wouldn't be the worst thing in the world. Sage was only thirty-two, but time zipped by faster these days. It's not that she didn't want to share her life with someone, but her parents encouraged school before anything else for her and her sisters. Her mother and father were both architects, well read, and "drinkers of life," as her mother liked to say. By all accounts, they were happily married and had their children early on. Married young, right out of college, they had Hollis a year later. Her mother had three children by the time she was thirty, Sage realized as she took a sip of her morning shake. It was a new one, called The Green Goddess, and she was grateful for the pineapple she'd added to take the edge off the kale.

Sage rarely thought about children aside from Paige, and honestly, what were the chances of another little girl like that? She was fine on her own—made a point to be—and didn't *need* a relationship. But, what her parents had was special, and she'd be lying to herself if she didn't acknowledge there were times she wanted to hold someone's hand or put her feet in his lap. Sage enjoyed the daily rituals of life, the surprises around every corner, and if she ever found the right person, maybe he would make her journey even better. Maybe. Before she jumped right into playing house, she should probably start with something smaller, like having a boyfriend for more than a month or a goldfish even, Sage thought, laughing in the silence of her car.

She'd dated a couple of guys in college and prior to the man moratorium brought on by her Garrett Rye obsession, she'd been on a few dates in Los Angeles, but nothing ever stuck. Her mother said that her generation was too picky with the scrutiny allowed by social media, but Sage didn't filter much. She went with her gut, waiting for that click. The click was important; if she was going to share half her closet with someone and make the type of compromises her parents had over the years, she needed the click. Her mind filled with Garrett carrying that damn tree. She reminded herself the click had to work both ways, and she willed her thoughts back to Chapter Eight—"Double Entendre and Other Naughty Doubles," which she'd read last night before bed. Kenna was right. The titles were pretty funny, but there was nothing funny about Chapter Eight. Sage had a hard time flirting without wordplay, so by the time she'd closed the book and clicked off her light, her head was spinning with where and when she was ever going to practice something so out of her comfort zone.

❧❦❧

Garrett was sprawled across the floor as Sage came around the bar to set her stuff down.

"Whoa, sorry. I didn't see you there," she said, taking in all six-foot whatever of him propped on his side on a couple of towels. The hem of his navy long-sleeve T-shirt rode up, teasing her with a tiny glimpse of tanned skin. Sage clasped her hands, as if that would somehow curb her urge to rip the damn shirt right off him. *Wow, that was naughty. Well done, you!*

Garrett didn't look up, head crooked with a wrench in his hand. "I'm almost done. I'll be out of your way in a few minutes."

"You're fine." Sage forced herself to stop looking, to stop being stupid. Prior to moving to Los Angeles, she had rarely been silly, let alone stupid. In fact, before she ditched the professional world for shakers and olives, she was the smart one among her group of friends. She was the go-to person for advice or when things fell apart but rarely considered for a good time. So it struck her as ironic that Garrett made her stupid. Maybe it was a sign?

Yeah, a sign of stupid. Get a grip.

"Sage," Garrett said, because, like a magnet, she'd somehow moved closer to him and was now standing on his towel.

"Oh, sorry." She stepped back. "Are you fixing the ice machine again?"

He grunted.

"It's the compressor. I looked at it last night. Something's drawing on the compressor and the breaker's not tripping, so it blows." Sage knew she was rambling, but it was a tight space and he was stretched out on the floor for Pete's sake.

"What'd you say?" Garrett stood slowly, pulling down his shirt and refastening the tool belt around his waist.

Sage didn't want to be an idiot in his presence, but it was a damn tool belt. Slung loose around his narrow hips, and as much as she absolutely was not one of those silly women, tool belts were a weakness. She left him standing there, question unanswered, and pushed through the door to the back kitchen.

Kenna was unloading their morning order and cursing at her laptop again. Sage grabbed her and pulled her into the office.

"You told him about the tool belt?" she asked, turning on her once she'd closed the door.

"I'm sorry, one more time?" Kenna sat.

"The tool belt—he's wearing one and being all cool like he knows that 'let me help you fix something' routine drives me insane. You told him?"

Kenna laughed and leaned forward to steal a doughnut out of the box on Logan's desk. "What would that conversation even look like? 'Hey, Garrett, Sage thinks tool belts are hot, so the next time you save our ass at The Yard by fixing the damn ice machine for the hundredth time because our handyman service keeps bankers' hours, could you be all sexy for her?'"

Sage stared ahead and then sank down in the chair next to her.

"I'm losing my mind," she said, resting her head on Kenna's shoulder.

"Probably. Here"—Kenna shoved the rest of the doughnut into Sage's mouth—"eat and you'll feel better. Let me see if I have a gross Garrett story I can share to help balance things out."

Sage chewed, but she couldn't taste. Which kind of sucked since she rarely indulged in a doughnut.

"Oh yeah, I have one. When we were little, Garrett was always getting banged up."

Sage's eyes must have shifted as she sat up to look at her friend.

"Jesus, cut it out. You're picturing him all sweaty and bruised, aren't you?"

She was but remained silent.

"He was a kid. I'm discussing kid Garrett here. Try to focus." Kenna waved a hand in front of Sage's face. "Anyway, he had lots of scabs and anytime we were sitting around watching TV or whatever, he'd pick them." Kenna looked at her with a scrunched, disgusted face.

"And?" Sage asked.

"And nothing. He picked his scabs. Gross, right?"

"That's all you've got? The man is standing in my bar, a little sweaty, a lot woke-up-delicious-this-way, wearing a tool belt, and that's all you have for me? That he picked his scabs when he was a kid?"

Kenna shook her head as Sage opened the door to the office.

"Jeez, why do I hang out with you?" Sage asked on a huff.

Kenna laughed.

"Fail, Conroy. Complete fail." Sage mocked exasperation and pushed through the kitchen doors back to her bar.

She *was* losing her mind. She had some kind of obsessive lust disorder, and she'd lost all ability to be normal. She was certified in scuba, instructor level, damn it. Women certified in anything, except maybe the *Naughty to Nice* book, didn't pant at the sight of a tool belt. Okay, so maybe she'd finished reading that particular book last night. Sage put her hands over her warm face. She needed Alanis Morissette and she needed her right now.

Walking behind her bar, avoiding Garrett, who was now sitting and putting his stuff away, she grabbed the remote for the stereo. She selected *Jagged Little Pill* and knocked the volume up three notches. The mere sound of Alanis's angsty voice brought her back to her senses. If Alanis could survive being all pent up, so could she.

Kenna entered the bar, looked up at the speakers, and did nothing but laugh as she passed by with her laptop. Garrett stood, wiping his hands on what she should have registered as his faded old jeans, but the man wore them so well they might as well have been a tuxedo. If there were some sort of farmer magazine—there had to be, right?—Garrett would definitely be on the front cover. *What are you even talking about? A farmer magazine? Stop!*

Sage leaned against the counter and picked up her Friday crossword. If she could get four across, that would open up a whole section. Wondering if the sound a baby bird made actually had a name, she felt Garrett slide behind her to leave.

"Baler," he said into her ear as he passed. She almost dropped her pencil as she became acutely aware of every detail, even with her eyes still on the puzzle. The warmth of his breath on her neck, the nearness of his body, even the vibration of his voice as it moved in the small space between them. Sage leaned on the counter to keep herself steady.

"What?" she asked, face still in the paper.

"Sixteen across. Machine that makes bundles. Five letters. B-A-L-E-R. . . baler."

Sweet Lord.

"You do crosswords?"

"No, but I have a baler."

"Of course you do," she said, rolling her eyes, trying to mask the image of Garrett, shirtless, loading. . . bales of hay or something equally manly. She sighed again at her inability to keep her shit together.

Garrett laughed. "What's that supposed to mean?"

"Nothing"—she shook her head—"thank you."

Garrett moved to one of the tables and was checking his phone when Jeremy from Twisted Tree walked in carrying their wine order and looking like he'd recently returned from some tropical vacation. The man was tall and blond and always looked good in a salesman kind of way. Similar to Chris from the plane, he was neat and put together, complete with a great watch and nice shoes.

"Hey, beautiful," Jeremy said, setting the box on her bar.

Sage looked at Garrett, his attention still on his phone, and saw the difference clearly. Jeremy, and men like him, were open and available. Granted, her palms still felt a little sweaty and she was a bit jumpy around any good-looking man, but none of them made her stupid. She needed to focus on that, focus on them.

The minute Sage was about to draw from the chapter of her book called "Ferocious Flirter," Alanis wailed her famous naughty line about going down on her man in a theater. Sage closed her eyes.

"Interesting music," Jeremy said.

"It's a classic."

"Sounds a little angry."

"You can tell a lot about a person's mood by the music they listen to."

"Is that so?" Jeremy leaned against the bar.

Sage nodded and bit into the soft wood of her pencil, willing both men to leave her bar before she bit the damn thing in half.

"So you're angry?" Jeremy asked, all playful and ready to flirt. Well, that figured.

"Me"—she glanced at Garrett and became distracted—"no. This song is about frustration."

Garrett looked up from his phone as if he'd heard the squealing tires before a car crash while Jeremy's eyes lit with acknowledgment.

She hadn't done that, had she? Sage mentally cringed because she knew what was coming. *You volleyed that one right at him, nice girl.*

Silence. She and Jeremy had gone to dinner a couple of times, so she knew he liked the chase. Peering up from her crossword, she caught his eyes. His smile would probably make most women swoon, but Sage found herself pissed. Garrett was still watching them, probably waiting for her to fall on her face.

Before she could pretend to be busy, Jeremy said, "Something you need to get off your. . . chest? You frustrated, Sage?"

She was sure she turned red, that she was now entertainment for Jeremy and probably Garrett too, although she hadn't heard a word from him. All the same, she vowed to take it like a big girl. Her mind raced for a response, a way to turn the tables. Glancing back at her crossword, Sage's eyes landed on forty-one down: L-U-S-C-I-O-U-S.

"Go for it, girl," Chapter Eight whispered.

Dragging her tongue across her bottom lip and following it with a tiny bite, Sage looked back up at Jeremy through her lashes and slowly dragged her hands over the smooth wood of the bar to push herself up to standing. Her eyes met his and she held.

"Sometimes." That was all she said. It was well played. She let out a slow breath and folded her paper.

Jeremy, who had clearly committed Chapter Eight to memory, didn't even flinch. His smile broadened, and Sage could see a faint outline of where his sunglasses sat across his nose as he slowly leaned over the bar toward her. Faking a little to the left, he took an olive out of her jar and popped it into his mouth, eyes never leaving hers.

"Huh, let me know if you ever need any help with that."

He smiled and Sage couldn't be sure, but she may have let out a squeak. Jeremy made his well-earned cool-guy exit, and when Sage looked over, Garrett was gone.

Crap, crap, crap.

Fail. Jeffries, complete and total fail.

❧❧❧

What the hell is going on? Garrett returned to his office after lunch and wondered when watching a bartender and some wine guy flirt with each other had turned into soft porn. The guy, who looked like he hadn't seen dirt or a shovel in a while, was irrelevant. He'd barely heard that joker, but when Sage stood, her hands sliding across all that polished wood, Garrett felt like he should almost be embarrassed to watch her in broad daylight. The wine guy was clearly into her with his stupid question about her frustration. It was kind of a cheap shot when Sage was obviously talking about her music, and Garrett fully expected her to go all pink in the face and pull the nervous act she did with him. That was not what happened, oh no.

She looked up at the guy with those take-me-right-here-on-this-bar eyes, and Garrett had almost dropped his phone. Where the hell did that look even come from? He'd picked her up when she was drunk, driven her home. Shit, she'd said she loved him, but he had never gotten that look, had never seen her bat her lashes and pout like that.

Garrett wasn't sure which pissed him off more: that he'd been deprived of the look in all the years he'd known Sage, or that she was flashing it at the wine guy. He stopped reading and rereading the same e-mail and stepped outside for some air. *Let it go. Who cares?*

It was unexpected, he told himself as he walked toward the fields. Garrett stopped at the edge of the first dirt road and rubbed his hands across his face. Until a couple of weeks ago, he could count on one hand how many times he'd noticed Sage Jeffries, let alone thought about her. Now, here he was up to his ass in maintenance reports and pricing structures and his mind kept tripping over shit like—*If she loves you so much, why the hell is she getting naughty with the wine guy?*

That didn't even make any damn sense. They'd talked it out and brushed it off, hadn't they? She'd had too much to drink, plain and simple. Sure, she said that he still had great eyes and she'd meant what she'd said, but who knew with women? Clearly it was good he hadn't listened to her because only a couple of weeks later, there she was burning up the bar with her. . . frustration.

He'd wanted to punch the guy when he leaned toward her. Garrett hadn't wanted to punch someone since. . . shit, he couldn't remember. He didn't do that stuff anymore. There were other priorities, decisions to be made requiring his full attention so he didn't fuck something up. Punching a guy, or even the urge to punch him, was so far out of his wheelhouse Garrett wasn't sure he'd even remember how.

"Um. . . hell yeah, we would," his ego cried, beating its chest as Garrett turned to walk back to the office. He didn't need this right now. Things were crazy enough without his newfound awareness of Sage Jeffries. Where the hell had she come from? He thought about calling Kenna but decided that was stupid. There was nothing to say. Nothing had happened between the two of them. She was obviously hot for the wine guy, which was good. Great. Why shouldn't she be happy?

Garrett dropped his face into his hands and for the first time in a very long time, he felt out of control. His mind raced and he couldn't control his thoughts. All over a little naughty music and Sage's pouty lips? Hell no, he thought, picking up the phone. She did have a great mouth, but he needed to clear his head now.

"Hey, is that tractor engine still in pieces in the shop?" Garrett asked George when he picked up the phone.

"Sure is. Does someone need it? I've been meaning to get to it, but I can't figure out the manifold."

Garrett closed down his e-mail, most of them unopened. "I'll be right down."

"You're. . . going to work on an engine? Don't you have—"

"I'll be there in twenty." He hung up, took the cap off his desk, and put it on backward. Whistling to Jack, Garrett jumped into his truck. He'd be working off-site today, as the white collars put it. He needed to clear his head and get his hands on something he understood.

Chapter Seven

She was being tested, Sage decided when she arrived Monday morning to find him sitting at her bar. Or maybe Garrett liked the naughty exchange between her and Jeremy last week. It was entirely possible. She'd seen enough interactions at her bar to know that lots of men responded to the grapes in a fruit salad. Maybe he was one of those guys, because unless it was her always-hopeful imagination, he'd been stopping by the bar alone more often. In the past, he'd sat when Kenna was around or would talk with Logan, but this was different. He was stopping by and sitting alone.

His gloves lay on the edge of the bar, so she knew he'd already delivered the produce for the day. Usually he'd be gone by now. Instead, he sat drinking coffee and scowling at something on his phone. Scowls were supposed to be ugly, scrunched-up looks, but his was more of a smolder that made her soft everywhere.

It figured the minute Sage decided to move on and practice her naughty exercises on men her heart could handle, Garrett would be everywhere.

"Maybe we should try one on him," her stupid heart suggested.

"That's a great idea. Remember how things turned out the last time you got involved?" her mind chimed in, putting her heart firmly back in its place.

He knew her feelings already. Whether or not he believed her, she'd been vulnerable. The naughty book strongly discouraged vulnerability. Sage recalled a few of the more progressive exercises from the book, and looking at Garrett, she was certain she'd pass out before anything happened.

She replaced the sanitized caps on the soda guns and tried, as the book instructed, to think of Garrett as a conquest. He was staring down at his phone, seemingly preoccupied, and she felt like one of those predators on the nature shows Paige watched. Sage smiled at the thought and heard the whispering voice of the host in her head, "As the female lioness surveys the herd of male gazelles. . ." Testing the shots of soda water from the now-clean guns brought her back to reality. Garrett Rye was no gazelle. He'd eat her alive.

Right on cue, he looked up.

"Are you waiting for Kenna?"

Garrett shook his head. "Having coffee. Am I in your way?"

"No, no. It's. . . you're here."

What the hell are you doing? Cut oranges or something.

"I am." Garrett grinned and then grew serious. "When did we meet?"

After a moment's hesitation, she answered. "Summer, three years ago. Logan had given me the job that day and you were helping with the garden out front. My hair was still long back then." Sage touched her now bare neck on instinct and wondered where this was going.

"You had a big flower on your purse."

She didn't reply. Her mouth was open a little.

"What?" he asked.

"You remember my purse?"

"I do. It was some purse."

"It was. Still is. I have it, but I don't use it much anymore. So, that's when we met. We shook hands."

"I remember now." He set his phone aside and gave her his full attention.

"You wiped your hands on your jeans before extending one to me." Sage refilled his coffee without asking. "The entire front of your T-shirt was soaked with sweat. It was white and you were wearing boots and a backward Dodgers cap."

"If it was backward, how'd you know it was Dodgers?"

"I. . . I'm not sure. I must have looked back."

"Okay." He laughed. "If memory serves, I was filthy that day. Almost embarrassed to shake your pretty hand, but not quite."

She basked in the memory, at how simple it felt to be with him now. "I think I interviewed on a Friday," she said, wanting the conversation to continue.

"Good memory."

"Yes, it was Friday, because I bought a couch that weekend. I was so excited."

"About the job?"

"About all of it. I felt so free and ready for anything when I moved here from San Francisco."

Garrett looked down at his coffee and if she didn't know any better, she'd guess he was thinking of something to say. That was ridiculous, considering it was Garrett, but that's how it seemed.

"Is your family still in San Francisco?" he asked.

Sage nodded. "Yes, Marin County."

"Beautiful up there."

"It is."

They went on like that for several minutes: he asked Sage questions she never thought would interest him, and she answered with an honesty that felt organic. She wasn't sure what had changed, why they were suddenly sharing, but she wanted the sun to stop right where it was, for time to stand still while she soaked in a little more. Garrett wasn't exactly forthcoming when it was her turn to ask questions, but he did share that he'd never been out of the country once it was established, with some laughter, that Mexico didn't count and that he'd had one other dog before Jack—an Irish setter.

"Do you like what you do?" he asked.

"I love mixing drinks and I love working here. I'm not sure I'd want to tend any bar, but I love what I do here. You?" she asked, cleaning out the coffee pot and slicing some oranges for the afternoon.

Garrett let out a breath and quickly glanced at his phone. "I love the farm. It's important work. I'm still learning a lot of what I do now, but yeah, I guess."

"You'd rather be in the fields."

Garrett nodded. "It's the best part, but things can't stay the same forever, right?"

Sage agreed.

"I'm working on moving forward, 'embracing change,' as my father likes to preach."

"Oprah?" Sage laughed.

Garrett confirmed and laughed, too. Deep and rich. Sage lost herself in him for a minute and cut her finger.

"Shit." She put her finger to her mouth.

Garrett leaned over the bar, reaching out to help, but Sage stepped back because her finger was bleeding and she wouldn't be able to concentrate if he touched her.

"You all right?"

Sage nodded, still sucking on her finger when their eyes locked. She blinked and when Garrett's eyes dropped to her mouth, the hand not in her mouth hit the corner of the cutting board and her oranges went flying.

Grabbing a Band-Aid near the register, Sage shook her head as she bandaged her finger. Her cheeks were warm and as he came around the bar to help her clean up, they grew warmer.

"You don't have to—" Her words fell when she noticed she had juice all down the front of her skirt. Grabbing a bar towel, she cursed her dry cleaning bill and blotted at the beadwork. The fringe of the towel caught on her skirt, and Sage felt the skin of her bare leg as she tried to untangle the towel. Feeling her stomach flutter, she glanced up, skirt still hiked, to find Garrett with his hands full of oranges, his eyes on her skirt, and his body so close she could see the stubble on his chin.

She cleared her throat and finally pulled the towel loop free, the cotton of her skirt cascading down her leg. Their eyes locked as he stood there with juice dripping through his fingers. Sage wasn't sure where she found the wherewithal, but she put her hands on his waist and turned him toward the sink. Garrett dropped the oranges and turned the water on to wash his hands. Once again, they were standing in that tiny space behind her bar.

He dried his hands and she leaned her back into the bar, not wanting to leave but needing to create space.

"When did you know?" he asked in a voice low and gravelly. The look on his face told her he was asking her how long she'd loved him.

Sage was trying to decide whether to stick with the honesty they'd shared or pretend not to understand when Logan came through the kitchen doors.

"Hey, Sage, can I steal a few of those lemons for a dressing I think would go—" He stopped short at the sight of them behind the bar. "Oh. . . sorry. I didn't realize. . . you were still here. . . bro." Logan's eyes filled with mischief.

Garrett shook his head, visibly finding his place in the order of his life, and returned to his phone on the other side of the bar. "I do need to get going."

"Don't let me chase you off." Logan leaned over the bar and grabbed a few lemons out of her basket on the back bar. "You should stay for lunch. Shouldn't he, Sage?"

She said nothing and stooped to finish cleaning up the oranges, thankful for the dark space and the chance to collect herself.

"No, I need to get back," she heard Garrett say in a hurried voice, followed by the jangling of his keys.

At the sound of Logan's laughter and swinging of the kitchen doors, Sage stood and threw the rest of the oranges in the sink.

"Garrett."

He turned halfway to the front door.

What she was about to say had nothing to do with her book. In fact, the author would not approve because here came the vulnerability again, but she didn't care. She wanted him to know. "About a year, maybe sixteen months."

He laughed and then held her eyes as he realized she was serious. "Am I an idiot?"

She smiled and appreciated the occasional reward for telling the truth.

"I mean here I'm thinking you barely notice me."

"I have great peripheral vision."

They both laughed, and despite her head telling her to focus, to remember the lessons of her book, her heart soared.

"See you at the dinner rehearsal tomorrow?" Garrett asked.

"You will."

He nodded, still smiling, and then he was gone.

⊱⟡⊰

Garrett hated games. Only a few weeks ago he'd had to remind himself he was the adult when Paige had kicked his ass playing Uno. Games were all about luck and chance. Luck was fickle, and chance scared the shit out of him.

But clearly he was on some self-destructive bent because he didn't need to wait for her to come in after he'd made his delivery. He had more shit to do than there were hours in the day. He had no business casually sitting, drinking coffee. It had occurred to him, before she walked in wearing a skirt with what looked like glitter anteaters on it, that she could be screwing with him. Playing a game; most women did in his experience. He'd also thought maybe this was some kind of fantasy thing. Smart proper girl wants to roll around with a sweaty farmer, at least until she needs to clean up and return to her real world. Wasn't that what his mother had done?

Shit, where the hell did that come from?

It didn't matter. He'd convinced himself that this was a game and he wanted his turn. He was ready to bring on the charm, certain he would do better than the wine guy. But then she looked at him, refilled his coffee, and all he wanted was to know more about her. He wanted to know about her family, her world, why she wore animals on her skirt, and why the hell it looked so damn good on her.

By the time he'd finished telling her about his one and only trip to Mexico, he knew he was wrong. She wasn't playing a game at all, or not with him at any rate. Who knew what she was doing with wine guy, but when she looked at him, it was different. Innocent and nervous in a way he couldn't remember ever being. It was like she wasn't hiding anything, anywhere. How was that possible?

Garrett threw Jack the last of his pizza crust and glanced out his office window. It was dark and past time to go home. He grabbed his jacket and followed Jack out into the night air.

He could still feel her hands on him. The woman had great hands. She was so delicate—no, delicate wasn't the right word— she was intricate with lots of moving parts, and he suddenly found himself needing to pay attention to all of them. Most of the women he'd been with were easy to figure out once he identified the game. Sage wasn't like most women, and he wondered if he'd noticed her even before the drunk text. With her short hair, which only managed to accentuate everything else about her, she was hard to ignore. Maybe he'd always known her mouth was full and supple, and maybe he'd internalized the color of her eyes: they were almost silver. He'd noticed her legs in the tiny skirt on New Year's Eve, along with every other breathing male in the restaurant that night. That was nothing compared to practically looking up her skirt behind her bar. After she'd told him she loved him, wanted him, he'd told her it was "nice of her to say, but he didn't see her that way." He'd meant it at the time, but when the towel caught her skirt, when her legs had been right there again, he wanted to touch them, touch her. It was a good thing he could squeeze the damn oranges in his hands or Logan might have walked in on more than free-floating frustration.

Touching her, wanting to run his hand up the length of her, that was new, Garrett thought as he pulled up to his house. Every detail about her was suddenly right in front of him as though he'd turned a light on somewhere. Tipsy Sage, the woman throwing compliments at him and declaring her love, had been nice, manageable. What happened earlier was not nice. He hadn't even touched her, but as he grabbed a beer and threw himself onto his couch, the whole memory felt downright naughty and suddenly he felt things shift once again.

Chapter Eight

Selected staff worked through a mock run at Ryeland Farms on the afternoon before The Yard's premiere farm-to-table dinner. As Sage unloaded her things, the nerves were palpable. The barn was a bustling space of *what if* or *how about we try*. She was happy her bar and the drinks for the evening had already been approved. Now, it was only a matter of working out where she fit into the timeline and if she could help out in other areas. Once she was set up and ready, Sage asked Kenna if she needed anything.

"We have too many damn men involved. Can you do something about that?" she asked before gesturing to two bussers who were leaning against the wall watching something on their phones.

Sage laughed, knowing full well Kenna loved both men who were currently driving her crazy, and slowly walked away from the storm. Turning in a circle to take in the barn, she could tell the entire thing had once been painted red because it was now distressed to allow the natural gray wood to peek through the flecks of red paint. It was beautiful. Sage put her hand on one of the walls and tried to remember if she'd ever been in a barn before. Unless it had happened when she was a child, she didn't think so. Looking up at the beams and light, the angles and seemingly endless space, she had a feeling she would remember if she'd ever been near something like this. She passed through the huge barn door and out into the warm afternoon. The blue sky hung in stunning contrast to the white fluffy clouds that reminded her of the meringues her grandmother put out during Easter.

Fields of green stretched for miles, and Sage was suddenly inspired to create something new. She already had a warm hard cider if the evening turned chilly, but being in the fresh air, with the smell of tilled earth, she wanted to pull it all into a glass. Travis and Logan were huddled together as Kenna chewed something off a small plate and nodded with what Sage recognized as annoyance. She approached and very calmly asked if she could use the main house kitchen for a little while. Logan seemed confused for a minute, but then after looking at Kenna and Travis, he told her she was welcome to it.

"We'll come and get you once we're ready to do a full run-through," he said.

"Unless we kill each other first," Travis added with a smile.

After gathering a few tools, Sage walked past the rose bushes and felt a stir at entering the house by herself. The Rye family home was large by most standards and white with shutters. Placing her hand on the knob, she noticed the dark blue front door looked as if it had been painted at least a dozen times. She wondered if Garrett had painted it growing up. Did he plant the rosebushes with his father during one summer? The privacy of entering alone filled her with wonder.

The door opened into a small entryway that almost forced visitors to engage. A large staircase led from there to a second story. The floors were wood and some rooms, like the living room she peeked in on her way to the kitchen, had large rugs that looked like they'd been there for a hundred years. She'd shared meals in this house and heard stories. Kenna, her best friend, went to prom from this house, and Logan, she'd learned one night, had mirrored his own home, his own small urban farm, off the life he'd lived here. The house was intimate and spoke of a life played out season after season. There were beautiful houses, and then there were homes. This was the latter, and Sage was certain the love she felt for the lives raised in this space made it all the more personal for her.

Mr. Rye was gone for the day, so Sage was comfortable plugging in her iPod and taking over the Rye family kitchen for a bit.

She laid out mixing glasses and checked for ice before realizing she was working on the table Garrett, Logan, and Kenna ate at as children. There was something so omnipresent about the main house. It looked out over acres and acres of farmland framed by a few hills, which, depending on the time of day, looked like a painted backdrop.

Sage wiped her hands on a striped dish towel hanging below the sink and turned on her music. It was only supposed to drop to sixty degrees tomorrow night; it was a Sunday night, so she wanted something with a cleaner finish. Having yet to experiment with her creosote bitters, Sage had an idea.

She could see from the kitchen window that Logan and Kenna were huddled over the long table arguing about something, so she hoped she could squeeze out a little more than an hour. With all her basics prepped, she turned on the playlist titled "Shit Kicker." Kenna had created it for her during her line-dancing phase last summer. Sage rolled her neck, let the twang of the music hit her, and started with a small batch of gin one of the local guys had delivered last week. He'd told her, "It's more lemon peel and orris root than you're used to." Perfect, she thought, adding ice.

The feel of the glass, the clink of the ice cubes, and the smells of the fresh-cut palette swirled around her as she sipped and danced her way to something new. A reporter once asked her if she could only have one sense as a bartender, what would it be? He'd been surprised when she answered smell, assuming the obvious answer for someone making drinks would be taste, but she found her inspiration in smell and without it would probably be stuck serving standard, always understood, drinks.

Sage had worked at a florist when she was in high school, and tending bar often felt the same way: arranging, ordering, and splashing a sprig of a surprise. Making cocktails was like that. Marney, the owner of the florist shop, had said she had a gift, an innate feel for what went together. "Are you sure you're good at math?" she'd asked one afternoon.

"Math figures into flowers. It figures into everything. Math and science get a bad rap for being cold, but they're actually creative," a shy and unassuming Sage had said. She'd found a little of herself working for Marney. The sunlit back room where things were chaotic and clippings could be thrown on the floor had been one of her first creative spaces. It was safe and she was never graded. Sage had often felt like an artist growing up, but her grades said she was an engineer. Her heart and mind were barely getting to know one another at that point in her life.

❧❦❧

"Whatcha watching, big brother?"

Garrett rarely jumped, but his hand did clench into a fist before he realized Travis was standing behind him on the back porch. Relaxing again, he shook his head, as he often did at his future brother-in-law, and said nothing. Garrett had gone his whole life without a nickname, but jackass-soon-to-be-by-marriage had taken to calling him big brother. He would normally laugh Travis off and walk away, but he was glued to the spot on the back porch as music spilled from the screen door of their family home and Sage danced around the kitchen, rolling her body to the beat, hands overhead. It was a sight even Travis wasn't going to pull him from. After glaring over his shoulder, he looked back to find her leaning forward, almost over the counter, to dip her metal straw into a glass and bring it to her lips for a taste. There it was again, that mouth, Garrett thought, forgetting Travis was still behind him.

"She does this all the time when she's working up new drinks. She had some time, so she asked Logan if she could take over the kitchen for a while. If you need her out of there, I was coming to tell her we're ready to get started."

Garrett found that lately he did need Sage, but he still hadn't figured out what for, and none of that needed to be shared with Travis. Instead, Garrett remained quiet, recognizing the song that was now playing. Since when did she listen to country, Zac Brown Band no less? The chorus was building and he didn't want to miss a minute of the show. Sage wore Converse today, green high-tops, tight jeans that made her dancing all the more enjoyable, and a red top with beads or something around the neck. Her hair appeared a little spikier than normal and her earrings looked like playground swings, moving along in time with her hips. Watching her in the kitchen he grew up in, Garrett thought how much his sixteen-year-old self would have loved this. She was a swirling, sipping, smiling vision. The song changed and Garrett held up his hand, stopping Travis from interrupting for one more minute. Sage started to sing and Garrett's head began inadvertently bobbing along to the beat.

"You dance?" Travis laughed.

Garrett flipped him off, eyes still on her.

"She doesn't like to be watched. At least not when she's at the bar."

"What's with the country music?" he asked quietly.

"Huh?"

"I heard her tell someone you can tell a lot about a person's mood by the music they listen to. What does this music say?"

Travis leaned in to get a better listen. "She's inspired by being here and working on something new for the farm dinner. Country music speaks to that, I guess. She needs to come up with things that touch the elements. Sound is one of the senses that heightens all the other creative elements."

Garrett turned, brow furrowed. "Where do you come up with this shit?"

"You asked."

"Yeah, I was looking for happy, sad, pissed. I didn't want to dance around in a field with you."

"But you do with her, don't you?"

Garrett glared at him again. It was his best back-the-fuck-off look, but Travis only nodded.

"Yeah, you do, man. You're watching that like it's the last five of the Stanley Cup."

The song was almost over, so Garrett moved away from the door. "How does someone not watch that? She makes no sense. Right when I think I know where to put her, she changes," he thought, but said out loud.

Travis said nothing and only watched him like a guy who had already been down the path he was barely starting to navigate.

"Anyway, that made my day," he said, and then caught himself a few beats too late.

Travis grinned from ear to ear, like a kid with a secret. *Pain in the ass.*

"Yeah? Did you want me to let her know?"

Garrett shook his head. "It'll wait."

"I always hate window shopping. Seems like shit's always gone when you go back to actually buy, ya know?"

Garrett pulled his eyes off of Sage. "Are you like. . . a poet? That was some kind of metaphor?"

Travis nodded, still with the stupid grin.

"Well, thanks for that. Now get in there and do your job," he said, stomping down the back steps. "Oh"—he turned back—"and remember. . ."

"Yeah, yeah, I know. I'll never be good enough for your sister."

"That's right," Garrett said, trying his best to look like the ba-dass big brother as Travis walked into the house. Steps away from the house, he glanced back and saw her through the kitchen window. She was now talking with Travis, laughing.

When Garrett was a kid, his bedroom was on the east side of the house. He'd always loved being the first to get the early morning light. During the summer months, when sunrise was early, he would lie on his bed for a few extra minutes after his alarm went off and watch the morning slide across his room, lighting up his posters, action figures, and stuffed animals. He'd never been able to put it into words as a kid, but it was as if each morning, the dark was washed away and his room came to life. His childhood hadn't been filled with very many moments of pause. There was always work to do, but those few minutes of twilight were a sweet memory. He wasn't sure why watching her felt like that, but it did.

Garrett bowed his head and went back to work.

Chapter Nine

*S*age had finished the book before bed that night and felt much the same way she did when she left the makeup counter at Nordstrom—scary clown face and a whole lot overwhelmed. She thought, like the makeup counter trip, that many of the steps she'd learned would be tossed in the bathroom drawer because they were either too time-consuming or the wrong color. The "Boss Lady" chapter, for example, was never going to happen, Sage thought before clicking off her light. There was something about tying a man to the bed that went against her nature. "Talk Dirty to Me" probably wasn't going to happen either unless she was drunk again. She couldn't explain it, but after being on the farm for the run-through, the book was even sillier than before. With that much life, that much genuine swirling around, which thong to wear or creative things to do with honey rang absurd.

Sage had read a number of self-improvement books in her life and could usually garner a few kernels here and there to improve either her outlook or the way she conducted her life. That was why she read them. She believed people were works in progress and that if she was going to live her life to the fullest, she needed to work on things. *Nice to Naughty* was mostly about being hot in bed or turning on a man, but there were bits in there about empower-ment and making things happen and feeling sexy. That was all good advice, but most of it, Sage had resolved, would never work in her world. The last chapter had been on fantasy, which she knew a whole lot about, but she wasn't sure how to fantasize about anyone other than Garrett.

❧

The following evening, after deciding to wear the black skirt with the white stripe along the bottom and to also bring three mixing glasses instead of two, Sage arrived at the farm a few minutes early. The path from the parking lot to the barn was now lined with tiny lights threaded through branches. Kenna had been there since the early morning, and it looked like something out of a movie or a magazine. They'd been sold out for months and, as she wheeled her supply cart toward the faded red barn positioned off the rows of rainbow kale, she had to admit she was nervous. Things like this were always a show, a coming together of all the elements that made for an "experience," as their website had touted. She supposed it was similar to her cocktails, mixing things, but on a much larger scale.

A breeze brushed through the silk of her blouse and she was surrounded by the smell of soil, smoked wood, and spices. The barn itself, Sage learned from Kenna a few weeks ago, was old and had been moved from another property up near Temecula. Garrett bought it at auction and had it driven down and reassembled on their property.

There would be twenty-two guests, seated at a massive table that was positioned in the center of the barn. Bunches of local flowers, winter wheat, and candles lit the dining area with a glow that stopped Sage in her tracks on her way to the far end of the barn. It was breathtaking. There were a few overstuffed chairs around the bar, complete with blankets and pillows. Sage looked again at the high, vaulted lofts. It was official, she thought, the barn was nicer than her house.

The sun was setting, their guests hadn't arrived yet, and she already knew the evening was going to be unbelievable. It was in the air, energy so fresh and rooted in simplicity, it was impossible for it to go wrong. Everything looked like a scene in the lifestyle magazines Sage saw at Fisher's bookstore. She liked stopping by Fisher's on her way home after her coffee dates with Kenna and Paige. Sage liked magazines, sometimes thumbing through them for hours, but she often wondered why anyone would pay twelve dollars for a magazine filled with pictures. Now she understood. Twelve dollars was a small price to pay for a frozen glimpse of the magic that was presently all around her.

Taking out her mixing glasses and spoons, Sage opened the cooler that held her fruit and herbs. Jeremy approached, and she decided he was attractive in a clean refrigerator sort of way. She could appreciate it, but she preferred hers packed with food and a little messy.

"Hey, beautiful."

And that greeting, the same one every time, was rehearsed and obnoxious, she thought, but smiled.

He looked over her spread and picked up a bottle of gin before setting it back down. "So what are you shaking up to compete with our wines?"

"Not exactly competing, more like complementing. I've created two drink variations that I think go well with the pork ribs, I'm sure people will love—"

"Sage"—he touched her arm—"I was joking, and I don't need the details."

"Oh, right." No need to clutter things up with the details. Sure. "Sorry, I'm a little wound up." A buzz of energy that had nothing to do with Jeremy coursed through her body. "Maybe it's the night air or this spot. I mean, look at this place, it's gorgeous."

As if he had been cued from some back door, Garrett joined Travis and Logan while they tended to the short ribs smoking at the front food station on the other side of the barn. Another breeze kissed the back of her neck, and she shivered. Sage had brought a sweater but didn't want to put it on.

He wore jeans and a button-down shirt with patches on the elbows. The shirt was out, his hair still wet from a shower Sage refused to allow herself to imagine. Everything about him, about his look, was unstudied, practical, and yet rather extraordinary. Or maybe it wasn't him at all, she thought, looking back to her bar. Maybe it was the environment, sort of like a mirage or a lifestyle magazine.

As Jeremy continued to ramble about Twisted Tree's new fume blanc that Sage had already tasted and thought too heavy on the lemongrass, she peppered in the occasional "oh" or "that is so interesting," all while watching Garrett. Setting out her bitters and laying napkins across one corner of the bar, she recalled a bowl she bought last year from The Fig and Frog, a downtown resale boutique. The bowl was cobalt blue, oversized, and had a red dot of glass in the center. She'd seen it one Saturday and decided she had to have it. It sat front and center in a room the boutique had staged as if it was in the kitschiest house right on the beach. Sage remembered wanting the whole picture. It didn't matter what the bowl cost that day.

When she'd arrived home and set the bowl on her own table, it wasn't quite the same. Still beautiful, but not as enchanting as it had been back at the store, in a space she saw as more exciting than her own. Sage knew she tended to project like that; that was all part of why she'd moved to LA. She wanted to start over, change rooms. She remade herself, but as she took in her fill of Garrett Rye, her mind pleaded with her heart to consider he might be like that bowl. Beautiful in his space, but a fantasy that only existed in twelve-dollar magazines.

"Sage? What did you think?"

"Huh? Oh, sorry. Yes, your selections sound perfect."

Jeremy forced a chuckle as he leaned in and kissed her on the cheek before fading out of view.

Garrett looked over, his clean-shaven jaw and guarded eyes lit by the fire of the grill, and her heart told her mind it didn't care. She would pay the twelve dollars like all those other suckers to stay right there with him. Taking a pull of his beer, Garrett nodded and tilted the bottle in a toast to her. Eyes still on him, she reached for the closest glass on her bar and gestured back at him. He laughed, so she glanced down and realized she'd toasted him with a jar of olives. Sage was happy for the distance because once again, her cheeks warmed as the first guests arrived and made their way over to her. Showtime. She greeted the guests, handed out drink cards, and was happy to be doing something she was pretty sure she wouldn't screw up.

❧

Garrett watched as a crowd began to gather around her bar. Her smile was different. Maybe it was the candles, or the evening breeze that mussed with her hair and she had to keep tucking it out of her face. She was even more beautiful in his barn, stirring and mixing in his world. Sage had never spent much time at the farm. She and Kenna were friends, but he always associated her with being in town, behind the bar. She'd been out to his "neck of the woods," as his father loved to say, two days in a row, and it was messing with his head, or his heart, he wasn't sure which as he finished off his beer.

Sage moved with that same rhythm she did at The Yard, only this bar was smaller and the laughter, the conversation as she stirred and poured, felt more personal. Kind of like the difference between an intimate acoustic set and a huge arena concert. Garrett moved closer and wondered if she brought that same rhythm to the bedroom.

Whoa, let's rein that shit in right now.

She was "in love with every piece of him." That's what she'd said. They had both dismissed it, agreed that she'd had too much to drink and couldn't be held responsible, but the words kept playing through his mind along with her legs and her most recent naughty slide up the bar. Her words were so simple, so honest that now, days later, he couldn't seem to shake them. He remembered vaguely reading Shakespeare in high school, something about the truth being in the wine. She wanted him. *Want* Garrett could deal with, that was what, sex, right? He liked sex. Probably not a good idea to have it with his sister's friend, but if she wanted him, who was he to argue? The *love* aspect of her speech was a little harder to get his head around. No way she loved him. Love took time, not that he'd ever bothered, but watching his brother and sister, it seemed like work. He already had enough work.

Still standing on the sidelines, he scanned the barn—there were a few couples, a family of five, and a group of four women who were a little rowdy. Garrett thought he heard one of them say they were all part of the same book club. The whole thing was pretty cool. Once everyone had one of Sage's concoctions or a glass of wine from the guy who had kissed Sage—yeah, he'd noticed that— they took their seats. Logan and Travis began doing what they did best—feeding people. The intimate setting of the barn, plus everyone sitting at the same table, passing and sharing, was fun to watch. He was filled with pride for his farm, his barn, and most of all, his family.

The way his brother took something simple and made it special was a true talent, and he was honored they chose his new barn as the place for these events. It was great business for The Yard. A reflection of a lifestyle that was trendy now, he supposed, although he always thought those glossy magazines made things look far too easy.

After a welcome, followed by a description of what was on the menu, everyone began eating. Sage leaned against her bar, looking beyond the barn toward the back field—kale and butter lettuce, Garrett's mind couldn't help but note. The lights strung through-out the rafters of the barn brought her face into focus as he took a few steps closer. She wore some wispy top that showed off her neck, or maybe he simply noticed it more now. She always seemed to be in something new, but not exactly new. Most of her clothes looked like they came from a different time. She was a discovery: color, beads, texture, and lace. His mind immediately went to the towel getting caught on the detail of her skirt. It wasn't like he hadn't seen legs before, and there was barely anything showing, but standing there with her, he thought he might actually swallow his tongue.

He'd noticed Sage before her ride in his truck. She was kind of hard to ignore, but lately everything was heightened to distraction, as if his mind was trying to make sense of her, and his body hummed in wait. Garrett walked over to the bar.

"Are you and wine guy a thing?" He caught her off guard; she was still gazing out into the night.

"Huh?" she asked with a sigh.

"Wine guy, you two seem cozy."

Her eyes danced around the barn as if she hadn't even heard the question. "It's incredible here. I'm sure you already know that, but I've been here a couple times now and the air, my God. It's like I think I'm breathing at home, then when I get here, I realize I wasn't even close."

Garrett was stunned by her words—they managed to perfectly describe what it meant to live where he did, do what he did. How could she know that?

"I love everything about this place, the sounds and smells."

He raised his brow. "The smells, huh? I could probably find some smells that would change your mind."

Sage's laugh lit up the space, and he knew he wanted her. Garrett had lived a life that made it clear that *want* and *have* were two very different things with an ocean of work between them, but he didn't care. Standing there, almost desperate to reach out and touch her face, he was willing to work. Hell, he'd add it to the schedule.

"Do you still know how incredible it is, or does it get old being here all the time? I've always wondered that, you know." She twirled a straw. "Like people who live in Paris, do they get sick of driving by the Eiffel Tower, or is it a marvel every time?"

"I'd imagine they get used to it," he said, grateful he'd found some words. Was she comparing his squares of dirt to the Eiffel Tower?

Sage let out another breath. "I suppose so. Is it that way for you? When you look out there, what do you see?"

"Work."

She laughed again.

"No, I get what you're saying. It is special here and yeah, it's pretty much always that way for me. I grew up here and the mornings are still incredible. I swear the night sky up here is larger. And I know what you're saying about breathing—I feel that too."

Their eyes met and then as if she'd seen something new, Sage looked toward the table.

"How do you think it's going?" she asked.

"Well, it has that hum The Yard gets on a busy night. I'm taking that as a good sign. The food is fantastic."

She nodded.

"I'm sure your drinks are great too. I noticed on the menu you made an old-fashioned and a rusty nail? I like the names."

"Thanks. The names aren't original to me. Those are both classic drinks, but I put my own spin on them."

"As expected," he said, finding himself looking into her eyes again. He'd never noticed her right eye had a spot of brown; it was a small dot, but another detail. She was something. "You didn't answer me."

"What was the question?"

"You and the wine guy?"

She looked confused but then remembered. "Oh, um, no. I mean we've gone out to dinner, but no."

"So you have dated? I thought he looked friendly. Not exactly your type, is he?"

Sage laughed. "And you would know that, how?"

He shrugged. "I don't know. Seems unlikely you'd have the hots for me *and* that guy too."

Her face flushed and she looked around as if the whole barn had heard him. "I thought we agreed to drop the drunk truck thing?"

Garrett laughed. "Is that what we're calling it now? Sounds a little naughty."

Sage looked at him, her eyes wide, but remained quiet.

"You're right, we did agree."

"You don't seem to be dropping it. I've been to dinner with Jeremy. He's a nice guy, but there was no click. There, happy? Now stop. And since when do you stand so close to me?"

Garrett said nothing and didn't move.

"Click?"

"Yeah"—she waved her hand in a gesture he now recognized as frustration—"as in we didn't click. Like a bike. You know when you ride a ten-speed, or any bike I guess, and at first, you're pedaling and trying to figure out the gears? Then you hit the right one and. . . click, everything smooths out. Huh"—she smiled—"so weird that I remembered that. There you go, relationships are like riding a bike. I need that click."

Garrett could not have spoken if someone had paid him.

Who the hell was she?

"Besides, why are you so interested? We've established that you were flattered by the. . . drunk truck thing."

She whispered that last part and it was so cute, he almost gave in to everything coursing through him right there in front of everyone.

"But," she continued, "I'm not your type, so if I decide to have dinner or anything else with him, it shouldn't interest you."

"True. When did I say you weren't my type?"

"I. . . I'm not sure. It was probably in there somewhere while you were telling me you didn't think of me that way."

A guy in a red sweater approached the bar and asked Sage for another drink. She was gracious, did her smooth dance, twisted a lemon peel from one of the lemons off his trees, and handed the guy her creation.

"I thought you didn't remember what happened that night?" Garrett asked.

She blushed but still managed to look all hot and bothered.

"I. . . recently remembered that part." She knocked over the straws but caught them before they fell to the ground.

"Is that so?"

Sage nodded, looking everywhere but his face.

"Kenna told you."

"She may have mentioned it during my morning of humiliation."

"Shit," he said under his breath and tried to rub the knot out of his neck. "You came out of nowhere, Sage."

"I know. Why are we talking about this again? I. . . you were honest and that's fine. I don't even think about you, about it, anymore."

Yeah, she did. It was all over her face.

Somehow, feeling like an ass for that honesty, he decided the best thing would be to kiss her, but the right thing was to leave until he figured his shit out. As it often happened, Garrett chose right. "Okay, well, I'll let you get back to work. I need to feed Jack. Have a good night, Sage."

"You too." She looked disappointed.

Garret stayed in his house the rest of the night reading over a proposal from the local high school that would allow their FFA students to work after school hours in the fields. It would be interesting to have teenagers around, and it might give him an excuse to be outside the office a little more. That alone was worth it. He sent off a quick e-mail with questions and stood up to get more coffee. His mind was back on work, the details—how, what, and where?

"Things we understand, right buddy?" He tossed Jack a treat. His dog didn't look all that convinced they were back to normal as he settled beside him on the couch. Scratching Jack's ear, Garrett's mind drifted. How could both of those women be in the same body? How could she be high heels and naughty one minute and clumsy farm lover the next? He should leave it alone. He didn't need more work, but damn if he could turn away lately. It reminded Garrett of the difference between seeing a car at a car show, appreciating it from a distance, and lifting the hood, finding out how it works. The more time he spent with Sage, the more he wanted under that hood. He could hear Kenna's voice asking him if he was honestly comparing a woman to a car. His answer would be no. Cars were easy and Garrett knew, even from his safe distance on the showroom floor, there was nothing easy about Sage.

Chapter Ten

*S*age arrived home a little after one in the morning. They'd all pitched in loading the truck and agreed the evening was a success. Of course, Logan had managed to write down a couple of things on his yellow pad, including that he wanted to add the new drink she'd created at the run-through on the next menu for The Yard. The excitement and pride in her work had kept Sage from falling asleep for another hour last night.

The evening went well, and next month they would do it all again. She loved being on the farm whether she was making drinks or not. Walking to her car last night, she'd looked up at the sky and had seen that Garrett was right: it was bigger. He had not returned for the rest of the night, which was probably a good thing. Sage was finding it more difficult to be around him with all the farm-to-table business. It was one thing for him to visit her in her world, at her bar, but being in his environment added an extra layer to Garrett her heart didn't need. Standing in that barn, he was real, so real she could have reached out and touched him. Talking with him out there under the stars, there was a moment when he looked like he almost wanted to lean in and kiss her. That was crazy, she thought, pulling into work.

Who knew fresh air could be so dangerous?

"The last chapter was about being bold enough to share fantasies," she told Kenna as she made more coffee behind the bar. "It seems that's the final straw to becoming a naughty grape."

Kenna laughed. "So are you going to start sharing your fantasies now?"

"Yeah, that's probably not going to happen. There were some handy tips, but I need to accept defeat and archive the book."

"I can't even believe I'm hearing the word defeat come out of your mouth. Did you practice any of the chapters on Jeremy? You two were awfully. . . friendly last night."

Sage shot her a look that said her friend knew damn well she wasn't wasting naughty on the likes of Jeremy.

"Right, so that's a no. Does this defeatist attitude have anything to do with Garrett or being up at the farm?"

Sage threw a stack of towels on the bar and began folding. "No. Maybe. I don't know. I'm pretty sure my fantasies have nothing to do with being naughty. Spending time up there was. . . I want that, not some made-up crap I read in a book."

"With him?"

Sage let out a sigh and ached with need. She knew it was pathetic, but her heart was oblivious.

"Did something happen last night? I did notice him over at the bar."

"No. But I will say I forgot all about the book. I didn't need it because it was so amazing. I was doing what I love and he was there. It felt for a moment like I had everything I needed."

"Oh, Sage, then go with that. Be you."

She shrugged. "Did you notice Garrett left early and didn't come back out the whole night?"

"I didn't notice, but are you thinking that's because you were yourself?"

"I don't know, but I have been more flirty, not with him, but in general. He's been around more. It's strange."

"That he would respond to you being more flirty?"

"I guess. I don't know. The reality is confusing enough with him. I'm not sure I'd survive the fantasy."

As she turned to put the folded towels away, Sage caught a blur of him out of the corner of her eye. Damn it, the man was everywhere.

"What fantasy?" Garrett asked, standing next to his sister.

Makenna promptly stood, smiled at Sage, and walked to the back kitchen. Garrett's eyes followed his sister and then landed back on Sage. She could feel them, all green fields beautiful, but she didn't look up. She simply started drying glasses in the hope he would follow Makenna into the back and be gone. He walked around the bar, stood behind her, and said nothing.

Sage shifted, distancing herself from his natural warmth, and put the glasses away. He still remained quiet, standing there with the palpable weight of his eyes, pressing her to say something.

"What?" She finally couldn't stand it anymore and turned to face him.

He shrugged.

Sage laughed because he was too close, and why not laugh? The whole situation was ridiculous.

"I have work to do, so if you're going to stand there and stare, that's going to make things hard for me. Do you want a drink?"

Garrett looked to the clock above the bar and furrowed his brow, the wrinkle so deep that it was still indented even after he'd relaxed his face.

"Right, probably not a good idea since it's only nine in the morning. Coffee?"

He shook his head.

"Then what do you want?" she asked, impatient now.

"I'm not sure how much more of this I can take. What fantasy?" he repeated in a voice that was pure tension.

"I. . . pfft, it was nothing. We were talking about—"

"Him, you were talking about him. The wine guy from the other night?"

Sage wondered if it was possible for Garrett to be jealous. She decided it wasn't, but didn't answer.

"What's the fantasy, Sage?"

She couldn't breathe. He was serious. He actually wanted her to tell him not only who they were talking about, but the details? She was going to go up in flames. Turning her back to him, she pretended to wipe down the bar.

"This is silly. We open in an hour and I'm sure you have—"

He took her arm and whipped her around, that same tense look or maybe frustration on his face. She couldn't tell and before she had a chance to figure it out, he was pulling her from behind the bar. He stopped, still holding her by the wrist, and appeared to be looking for something, somewhere. He zeroed in on the door to the wine cellar, nodded as if having a conversation with himself, and pulled her toward the wooden door. Opening the cellar, he all but dragged her into the small room lit only by the dim lights under the wood beams that spread the width of the space. Sage was going to say something, put him in his place, but then he locked the door and she lost all ability to speak. Garrett walked toward her and she backed up until she met the back wall of the cellar. He took her wrist and then the other one as he stood inches away from her, still not saying a word. Gently, he lifted both of her hands above her head and held them there, not letting go. She should have felt trapped, pissed at being "handled," but all she felt was heat. It poured off him and she wanted it, all of it.

He leaned into her ear and his chest touched hers. "What's the fantasy?"

She took in as much air as her hollow chest would allow. "We were talking about some book, and I was not talking about—"

"The wine guy."

"Jesus, why does everyone keep bringing him up? No, not Jeremy."

"Then what's the fantasy? Who?"

Sage shook her head. "Do you honestly have to ask?"

Not a word, he kept holding her there as if he was keeping her at arm's length.

"Fine. I might have mentioned you. There, are you happy now? That's all, nothing new. I don't know why you're getting so crazy."

"You're making me crazy."

"Well, I'm not meaning to. If you'd let go of my hands, I'll leave."

"No. Close your eyes."

"Garrett, this is silly. Stop."

His eyes suddenly warmed, and Sage recognized the look as want.

"Help me out here. If there was a fantasy, what do I do next?"

"What?"

"Tell me." He took the last step into her; his lips were on her ear and she could feel the scrape of his jaw on her cheek. "What do I do?"

Dear God, she was going to pass out. "I. . . I don't know."

"Sure you do. We're all alone in here. What do I do next? Is it this?"

His lips touched her neck and her eyes fell closed. Okay, maybe she could come up with something. He smelled like cotton right out of the dryer or the warm wood of a boat dock when she was a little girl. It was intoxicating, and she began to reconsider the value of the book. A moan slipped past her lips as his mouth trailed along her neck and back up her jaw to her cheek.

"You still with me?"

She nodded.

"Tell me what to do."

"I don't know what you want me to say."

"Tell me what you want."

"I can't."

"Sure you can."

"Kiss me," she said matter-of-factly and stared right into the depths of those eyes—they were way more incredible up close and personal.

His face grew serious. "You need to be sure."

Sage suddenly relaxed into the moment. He was right there holding her, and the reality was more than she had expected. "No, that is definitely not one of your lines in the fantasy."

He smiled, and she decided that smiling was something Garrett needed to do more often.

"Sorry." He was still holding her hands over her head. Leaning in, he brushed his lips across hers.

Sweet Mother of God! Sage had no idea how she was still standing.

"More," she said with a boldness that in a different situation would have put her in the running to be a grape.

Garrett kissed her again and this time, he gave it his all. When his tongue slid across her lips, asking for entry, she opened, and he took her past anything that could possibly be real. Releasing her hands, he ran his fingers through her hair, down her neck. Sage held on for dear life and let him work out all the details of a fantasy she hadn't even imagined yet. His hands moved to her back and suddenly it was as if he'd woken up and realized what he was doing. He pulled away.

Sage grabbed him by the front of his shirt. "My fantasy, we're not done." She ran her hands across his chest. Who knew when this would ever happen again? If this was all part of some game, if it was all she'd ever get from him, she wanted to make sure she had enough to last.

Garrett's pulse was pounding in his neck as she opened the collar of his shirt and kissed down the slope of his shoulder and back up to his lips. When her hands snaked under his arms and around his back, she heard him. The sound low in his chest sounded something like surrender, and the power of that flooded her, threatened to wash her away. Garrett Rye, a mass of solid stoic man, was softening, warming to her touch. Easing back, Sage knew somewhere in the haze of heat that she had to stop. She couldn't have all of this, all of him.

Her freshman year in college, she had gone on this diet that allowed her to have one-half an ounce of chocolate every day, but no more. She lasted three days before busting open the chocolate bar and eating the entire thing. Sage knew even back then that it was next to impossible to have certain things in small doses. Chocolate was one, and after that kiss, Garrett was another.

"Holy shit, how long has that fantasy been in there?" Garrett asked, out of breath but still holding her.

Plunging reluctantly back into reality, she pushed at his chest and he stepped back. "What the hell was that? You can't grab me and bring me in here and talk all, 'oooh, tell me what you want, baby.' People don't do that."

"I didn't call you baby. I hope that's not in the fantasy because I'm not an 'oh baby' kind of guy," he said, leaning up against the wall of the cellar.

Sage shook her head and walked out before she grabbed him and acted out every other fantasy her mind was frantically working through.

⟨⟩

Garrett waited in the cellar for a couple of minutes and, of course, ran smack into his sister on his way out.

"Why were you in the wine cellar?"

He tried to give her the none-of-your-business look, but his eyes betrayed him and fell on Sage, who was filling up something behind the bar, looking so flushed and bothered that he couldn't help but smile. His sister hit him on the shoulder like she'd done hundreds of times in their life.

"Probably had that coming." He walked past her and toward the door, wishing she were like Jack and would stay.

No such luck, Kenna followed him. "What are you doing? Or, what were you doing?"

"Have a good day, Sage," he said, passing the bar.

She glanced up at him like someone caught with a secret and when she turned the overhead music on, his smile grew. It had a fast beat, but he didn't recognize it.

"What kind of music is that?" He pointed to the speakers as Kenna followed him through the front door.

She paused her impending lecture and listened. "That's Ellie Goulding, 'Something in the Way You Move.' Why?"

"Good mood music?"

Kenna nodded. "Yes. Why are you smiling?"

He couldn't help it. Somehow the simple idea of a beautifully flustered woman playing happy music after kissing him senseless made him feel mischievous, young. Garrett couldn't remember the last time he'd felt young.

"What were you doing with Sage?" She grabbed the back of his shirt so he turned to face her.

"You'll have to ask Sage."

"Oh no you didn't, you can't."

He laughed and made a move toward his truck, but Kenna stepped in front of him. He towered over her, but his sister had always been like one of George's little dogs when it came to her brothers—fearless.

"She's working on her naughty and that is not supposed to be. . . seriously, what are you doing?"

"No idea."

"Do you care about her?"

"Of course I do. I care about all of you."

"Don't bullshit me. If you're playing tonsil hockey with her in the wine cellar then your feelings are different than they are for say. . . Travis."

He scrunched his face. "Ah, yeah, I definitely don't want anywhere near his tonsils."

"Garre, I'm serious."

"I know, you're always serious. I'm not discussing what happened with you, little sister. So"—he hit the brim of her cap—"I'll see you tomorrow for delivery if you're here early. If not, I'll see you at Libby's on Wednesday."

"But. . ."

He continued walking. "No buts. I'm a big boy, Kenna."

"Yeah, that's what I'm afraid of."

Garrett laughed and climbed into his truck without another word. It had been a while since he was blindsided, but that's exactly what had happened with Sage. It had started innocently enough, but that night in his truck must have shaken something loose. He'd like to think it wasn't the idea of the wine guy being her fantasy, but maybe it was. All he knew was he wanted a taste and now that he had one, he was thoroughly screwed.

That wasn't a kiss. That shit made him feel like he was something more than. . . well, whatever he'd been before he'd damn near melted right into her. She was so open, it was like she'd handed him her heart and asked him not to stomp on it. *Who did that?* Women were supposed to play hard to get, they didn't come right out and love like that, did they?

Garrett pulled up to the stoplight and searched for Ellie Goulding. He found the song and as he headed back to the office, he was listening to happy music too.

Chapter Eleven

*A*few hours into the lunch rush, Sage saw Kenna take a seat at the end of the bar with her eggplant sandwich. Sage slid a Coke in front of her but had other customers to attend to before she could chat with Kenna. From the look on her friend's face, she'd be waiting as long as it took.

Sage explained to the young businesswoman sitting center bar that the citrus in a gin fizz actually cooked the egg white and turned it to the froth she was now pouring onto the top of a highball glass. The woman stared in amazement, which Sage admittedly loved. Cocktails were art to her and the process of creating, blending, and adding to a person's experience gave her a satisfaction she'd always been lacking in her office job. She was fully aware that to the outside observer, she was nuts for leaving her family and a prestigious job, but once she stepped behind the bar at The Yard, her bar as she liked to call it, everything made sense. She wasn't simply "some bartender" as her sister liked to tease. She was alive, interacting with people, and giving and feeling energy. How she made her living was a gift, and that was something people rarely said about their jobs.

Handing off two Bloody Marys, complete with spicy beans and okra, to one of their servers, Sage cashed out the man who had been reading some book about the Hopi Indians for the past hour. She loved studying people: some were so transparent and others were intricate puzzles.

Makenna was still waiting. She could feel it. They had that best-friend connection, to the point that once her mind cleared from the sheer pleasure of being pressed against a wall with the expanse of Garrett Rye's body against hers, Sage's first thought was of Kenna, of telling her and listening as Kenna explained why Garrett was not a good idea. Sage already knew that, but he sure felt like the very best idea a few hours ago. She could try for casual and brush it off, but the truth was, and Kenna would see it too, Garrett was the chocolate and Sage had been dieting far too long.

"Whatcha doing?" she asked, taking Kenna's plate and wiping down the bar next to her.

"Year-end reports for tomorrow's meeting. It's all incredibly excit-ing." She let out a breath and closed her laptop. Her shiny new engagement ring reflected light as her hand lay on top of her computer.

Kenna was newly engaged to super chef Travis McNulty, which Sage still found so damn romantic.

"The question is, what are *you* doing?" Kenna asked with her know-it-all look.

Sage tried to deflect first. "Cleaning up. Lunch crowd is start-ing to dwindle. Did you see that guy reading that big book on the Indians?"

Kenna nodded with a look that told Sage she had no interest in discussing the reading habits of their customers. It was clear what Kenna wanted to discuss, but Sage wasn't sure she had the words.

"I took a class my freshman year on the Hopis. Did you know that their language is considered the most complex?" Sage wid-ened her glace, hoping to incite interest in something other than Kenna's brother and that kiss.

Her friend held her eyes for a moment, and then Sage saw the sarcasm. "Huh, as fascinating as that is, are you seriously using the Indians to get out of telling me what happened with Garrett? You told me you were retiring naughty, that it wasn't who you are."

She should have known—Kenna was never about bullshit. After checking that the last few people at the bar were happy, Sage wiped her hands on a towel and leaned in toward her friend. "I *was* done with it, but you heard him when he came in. What was I supposed to do, not kiss him when he asked me about my fantasies?" she asked before Kenna had a chance to interrupt and recite more from their previous conversation. "Forget he's your brother for a minute. Any man who looks like that and walks into this bar saying, 'What's the fantasy?' Seriously, like either one of us would have said, 'Oh, I'm sorry Mr. Yes-Please-I'll-Have-Another, I remembered I need to be my authentic self.'"

Kenna laughed, and Sage felt the space between them open up like a breath of fresh air.

"I mean come on. What the hell was that? Christmas is over."

"Okay, forgetting he's my stupid brother, I will agree. It was a fantasy-like scene but, Sage, this is real for you. No book, no practice. And, I would like to point out you were not being naughty. He approached you, no chapters in place."

"That is true, but we were talking about the book."

"Oh, come on, that's a reach, don't you think?"

"Probably. I don't know. None of this was supposed to happen. Things have gotten a little nutty."

"Nutty?"

"Yeah, I remember this one time I went to the emergency room with kidney stones."

"Is this the short version?" Kenna asked on a little laugh.

"Shut up. I was in so much pain they gave me this shot of IV Demerol as soon as I arrived. I will never forget it because it raced up my body like it was filling every pore. That's what it was like in that wine cellar."

"Like a narcotic?"

Sage nodded and went off to tend to three women at the end of the bar. After two rum and Cokes and one iced tea, she returned to Kenna, who'd been watching her.

"Yes, like a drug. He pulls me into the wine cellar and says he wants to know"—she looked down the bar and leaned in again—"what the fantasy is. He wanted me to tell him. Show him. I mean, I was not prepared, it was so. . ."

"Uh huh." Kenna shook her head and stood to put her laptop in her bag. "I need to pick Paige up early, dentist appointment."

"Oh, sure, okay." Sage felt Kenna quickly close the door on their conversation. She'd admit to being let down that the awkwardness of the man who had recently kissed the crap out of her was her best friend's brother, preventing her from discussing her mind-blowing hot guy story, but she understood. "See you later."

"Hey," Kenna said a few steps away, "so it was a good kiss?"

Sage leaned up against the back bar, hands instinctively going to her heart, and as hard as she tried to be naughty bar girl, she had a feeling her best friend saw nice and getting in too deep all over her face.

Kenna rolled her eyes. "I'll call you tonight."

"Okay, but make it early. I have the symphony."

"Date?" she asked, looking confused.

"Nope, on my own. The season starts tonight."

"Okay, so before six?"

Sage nodded with relief, grabbed a few mint leaves, and got back to work.

※ ↯ ※

Garrett met his father in the main house a little before noon. Winter brought with it a lull in work. He knew he was supposed to enjoy it, but he often found himself rushing through on his way to the next task. He always wanted to get on with the next plantings, the next harvest. He was fortunate to farm in California where they grew something all year round, but fall and winter weren't the same as spring and autumn. Those were eighteen-hour days, and he loved them. Well, maybe he didn't love them because his father always said, "Don't love things, love people," but they were familiar and what he knew from the time he was a kid. Long, hard days were comfortable; they'd made him the man he was and held their family together. Grabbing a bottle of water and listening to his father discuss which equipment needed repairs, Garrett's mind drifted.

Sage was a surprise, and being that he was the one in his family to sneak down and peel open the Christmas presents before the big day, it could be said Garrett didn't like surprises. That, or he was hell-bent on ruining them.

The need to kiss her again flooded him. It hadn't even been twenty-four hours and he wanted to see her eyes falling closed that moment before their lips met. She had the longest eyelashes he'd ever seen. Maybe they were fake. He'd seen what looked like fake eyelashes in Walgreens, but Garrett was pretty sure Sage wasn't putting those on her eyes. Maybe she was. It's not like he knew her that well. Her sweater had been a swirl of color, sort of like last summer when Paige left her crayons outside the barn and they all melted. The sweater was like that, except it hugged every curve of her body, and there were plenty of curves. Garrett knew Sage must exercise because everything on her body was in the right place and clearly happy to be there. It was almost impossible to imagine walking past her now without being distracted and not noticing her. He'd given into wanting her and was already racking his brain for the next step.

It was his business to be certain about the process. His life was about planning and then planning again in case the first one didn't work. He didn't rest easy when something wasn't figured out or couldn't fit into a schedule or a diagram. Maybe that's why he'd kissed her. It wasn't his smartest move, but with everyone else changing things up, maybe he wanted a taste of that too. The bonus was that the woman could kiss like nobody's business. Full and genuine, it was like the entire kiss said, "I like you." He knew it sounded juvenile, but there was something incredible about the simplicity of that kind of heat.

"You going to stare out that window forever?" his father asked, bringing Garrett back to what mattered.

"No, sorry. Are we ready to head down?"

"Ready as I'll ever be. Are you sure you want me to inspect the crops with you? You seem like a one-man show these days."

"Of course I do. We do this every year."

"Agreed. But I didn't know if you wanted to do things differently."

Garrett was quiet; he'd already done something differently today. He needed normal.

They walked toward the back ten acres, Jack running up ahead.

"You all right?" his father asked.

"Yeah, why?"

"You seem a little distracted."

"No, I'm good."

"Feeling weird at all about Logan and Kenna?"

His brow furrowed. "Yeah, I always feel weird about those two."

His father laughed, familiar green eyes dancing as he fixed his hat and kept pace with Garrett.

"Well, besides that. I was wondering if all the changes were hitting you. All the love."

Garrett shook his head. "No, Dad, the love isn't bothering me."

"Okay, but I wanted to ask. You know Oprah says change is one of the most stressful things to navigate in life or something like that."

"Does she now?"

"She does. People like what they know—it makes them feel safe. Do you feel safe?"

Garrett stopped. "Maybe I should be asking if *you're* okay. Dad, you need to lay off the daytime television."

"I don't watch daytime television, I watch Oprah. Big difference. I get her magazine now too."

"Oh, fantastic, exactly what we need. I suppose you'll start clipping out important lessons for me now."

"Nah, you seem to know what you're doing. But I like checking on you every now and again. Make sure you're okay. It's what parents do."

They started walking again. "Yeah, Dad, I'm good."

The day passed as they walked up and down the rows of plants inspecting a number of things, including viability assessment, on their checklists. Everything was documented after planting and again before harvest. Once they were done, Garrett would transfer the data to the computer so they had their information for years to come. The data they collected allowed for models and predictions. The more he knew, the less he needed to leave to chance.

Maybe he could ask Sage to fill out a questionnaire, Garrett thought as he drove home.

Chapter Twelve

"*Y*ou kissed her," Kenna said less than two minutes after joining them in their booth for the Rye family meeting. It was Wednesday, not even six-thirty yet. She'd sent Paige to play waitress with Libby, and Kenna was raring to go.

Okay, well, I guess we're off, Garrett thought, sipping his coffee.

"Who kissed who?" Logan asked.

Kenna handed out reports and bent as Paige ran back over to have her apron tightened.

Garrett said nothing and started flipping through a financial report he'd never bothered to look at before.

"Uncle kissed Auntie Sage," Paige whispered, leaning into Logan. The entire table went silent. Garrett smiled at his niece, but Kenna was not smiling.

"Paige, how do you know that?"

"Me and My Travis were spying when you were on the phone last night. You said, 'Okay, it was one kiss,' and then you said, 'Are you sure you're okay?'" Paige continued in a pretty dead-on impression of her mom. "And then I don't know what Auntie said, but you said. 'Oh my God!'" Paige fell into Logan with her hand dramatically placed, palm up, on her forehead.

The whole table, including Garrett, cracked up. He knew the entire weight of his family was about to squeeze him into a bad mood, but at the moment, watching Paige shock everyone was fun. And maybe somewhere, way deep down in a place he didn't want to recognize, it was sort of fun to be the topic of gossip, the one with a bit of scandal. He'd examine that later.

Kenna caught his eyes again as the laughter died down, hands on her hips now.

"What?" he asked, now feeling restless and trapped in the booth.

"Do you have anything to say for yourself?"

"To you?"

"Yes, well, to any of us." Her hands spread to encompass the booth as she took her seat and Paige went back to working with Libby.

"No." He poured more syrup on his pancakes.

"No, that's all you have?" She turned to Logan and her father, hoping for support, but Garrett had the advantage. He knew men, there was no way they discussed this shit, ever. She would corner him later, but she was going lose this time. "Aren't you guys going to say something?"

Logan put his face in the reports and their father sipped his coffee, gazing out the window.

"He kissed Sage. My best friend Sage. He initiated it. How is that okay?"

"Did she kiss him back?" Herb asked, turning to Kenna.

"I. . . well, yes, I guess." She was flustered.

He shrugged. "Well, there you go. Probably between the two of them, don't you think?"

Logan nodded, trying to hold back a smile that said, "you're it, my man."

Kenna huffed and pointed at him. "You know what you did." She cut into her chocolate chip pancakes and shoved a bite into her mouth.

"So where are we at with our order from the seed bank? I'd like to get everything in, cataloged, and over to George and the guys before the end of the month."

Kenna shook her head but pulled up the order, and the meeting was finally underway. Garrett had kissed her, planned on doing it again if she'd let him, but at the moment, he was more concerned about preparing for the next round of plantings. He realized that probably didn't make him a romantic guy, and maybe he wasn't, but romance was like television to him: a time waster with nothing much to show for it.

If he gave it another day or two, maybe one kiss would be enough. It was possible things would go right back to normal, wasn't it? Sipping his coffee, Garrett wondered why he kept reading the same damn line over and over again on the order confirmation Kenna handed him, and probably more important, why in the middle of a diner, surrounded by his family, he could still hear that little moan Sage let out the minute his lips took hers. *Shit.*

After there was nothing left to argue about, Logan and their dad left and Garrett stayed behind while Kenna packed up.

"I'm still working on not having Coke in the morning, so I'm not in the mood for your crap."

As opposed to any other day, Garrett thought, standing from the booth.

"So, you put the moves on her, huh?" she asked bluntly.

Garrett wrinkled his brow, ready to pull from his arsenal of sarcasm, but thought better of it. "It was a kiss, Ken. I wanted to kiss her, she was game, so I did. It's none of your business, you know?" He reached across the table, grabbing her jacket.

Kenna took in a breath. "She's not what you think she is."

"And what do I think she is?"

"Like the other women you've dated or kissed, I mean. . . come on, Garre, it's Sage."

He nodded and leaned against the booth while she finished packing up.

"I'm only saying if this is some kind of sex thing or you're only looking to. . . do whatever you do, please don't do it with Sage."

"Do what I do?"

"Do what I do?" she repeated, mocking his voice. "Yes, ignore her after you get what you want. You know she cares about you. Are you going to give her something in return, be in her life?"

"I *am* giving her something." He grinned and instantly realized his mistake.

She shook her head in what looked a little like disgust and started toward the counter to pick up Paige. Garrett held her arm.

"Okay, stop. This is stupid. She's a grown woman. I kissed her. Why are you getting all—"

"Do you know anything about her?"

"She's pretty damn sexy."

Kenna pulled free of his hold, hands on her hips again.

"She likes crosswords."

"I know."

"Fine. But you should also know that she recently got this book from her sister, but"—she shook her head—"forget it. She is sexy, you're right. I'll mind my own business."

Garrett knew she was letting him off easy and he was a little intrigued that she decided not to share something clearly important about her friend. It was probably something very female he wouldn't understand anyway.

After walking two of his favorite females to Kenna's Jeep and buckling Paige into her booster seat, he kissed them both. He loved his sister for worrying, but he had meant what he said. They'd kissed; they hadn't crossed some line they couldn't come back from. She simply needed one more thing to add to her list of concerns.

❧

Sage was off for the next two days and had found a new mirror at a vintage housewares store in Santa Barbara when her mom called.

"Are you calling to tell me I spent too much money on a mirror? Did you sense I was shopping?" Sage answered playfully, stepping outside the store to take the call and telling her mom where she planned on putting her purchase.

"That sounds perfect, dear." Her mother was distracted. Sage could always tell.

"What's wrong?"

"Oh, well, your sister has had a bit of a breakdown."

Sage was going to laugh, but her mother didn't so she asked questions instead. "Meg? Is she home? I thought she was still in South America."

"No, not Meg."

"Okay, well, then I'm sure Annabelle is overreacting. I doubt it's a breakdown. You know how she is and even if she's upset, it's—"

"Sweetheart, Anna's fine. It's Hollis. She came home last night and I thought she needed to talk, but she's been in bed all day. I'm not sure how to handle this."

"Hollis, are you kidding? Was she hurt?"

"No, something at work. She made a mistake, it has to do with a game called Fat Pigs. Have you heard of that one?"

Although Sage was on the phone, she shook her head along with saying, "No." Hollis was the oldest of the Jeffries sisters. She was thirty-four, a hotshot vice president of Dobbins Venture Capital. If every sibling had a role in the family, Hollis's was being the perfect overachiever. Sage was certain that "breakdown" was not a word allowed in Hollis's vocabulary because to Hollis, it was synonymous with failure. She'd been class president and debate champion. The woman spoke three languages. Hollis didn't break.

But her mother explained that she'd eaten three cartons of Thai food last night and fell asleep on the couch after binge watching *The Big Bang Theory.*

"Do you know that show?" her mom asked, as if knowing the show would provide a clue into fixing Hollis.

"I do, yeah. Did she tell you what happened?"

"Bits of it. I honestly don't understand half of what she said and I want to let her sleep, but something about millions of dollars invested in this game that she vetted and the game doesn't work. The developer was arrested, I guess. Sage, it sounds like a nightmare. The poor thing, I've never seen her like this."

"What'd Dad say?"

"Oh, you know him. He's been in touch with our attorney even though Hollis told him she wasn't in any trouble. He's still prepared. I swear that lawyer should live in the guest room as many times as he calls him."

"Wow. I was planning on visiting in a few weeks. Do you need me to come early? I mean, I'm not sure if I can rearrange my schedule, but I can check."

"Don't worry about it, sweetie. I'm sure she's going to sleep and work things out. I'll call you back if she moves on to anything stronger than wine." Her mother laughed and Sage could tell she was nervous. "So I wanted you to know, but don't panic. She's home and it'll be fine. I'll see you in March."

Sage exchanged I-love-yous and hung up. The clerk in the store signaled that her purchase was wrapped and ready. She went back in and left a few minutes later with her mirror, an old abacus with jade beads for her father, and a big repurposed metal sign that read *LOVELY* for her mother. Sage knew Christmas was over, but she enjoyed buying gifts and now that she lived away from home, it was even more fun. Her parents were both architects: her father worked with nonprofits and community beautification programs while her mother worked on residential remodels and interior design. They both loved what they did and as a result, they were brilliant at it. Both her parents, Stuart and Wendy Jeffries, had home offices, and Sage could never quite see either of them retiring, even if everyone else their age did. "Maybe when one of my four daughters makes me a grandmother," her mother had said once when they were discussing it over lunch. She was the only one among her friends who was not a grandmother, and it had become a perpetual source of guilt for the Jeffries girls. They'd tried to tell her they were "making lives for themselves first," but Hollis was approaching her midthirties and hugely successful. Their reasoning was wearing thin. It struck Sage as funny that her mother assumed they would all have children, as if she'd paid into a pot somewhere and expected a lofty return. Sage was pretty sure one or two of them may disappoint her.

She had never thought about having children, which, based on her friends' standards back home, was fine. She'd gone to school with some smart women who saw marriage and kids as an afterthought compared to a second masters' or professional achievement. Although she did learn through pictures and the occasional e-mail that a few of her friends were engaged and one had a baby on the way. Sage had not managed even a steady boyfriend in college, so she was probably behind the curve. Was there a curve? She didn't even need to get married. Times were different, and she could do whatever she wanted. When Sage thought of Garrett, she thought of a full life, and she guessed that included marriage. Right now though, she'd settle for another trip to the wine cellar.

Chapter Thirteen

The yellow couch was already taken when Sage arrived to get seats for Sunday coffee with Makenna. *Figures.* That couch was the best spot for people watching, and she could have used some of that this morning. After putting down her stuff at the blue corner table with a painting of a typewriter on it, she headed toward the line at the counter.

"Oh damn, you look so thoroughly loved. Is that a new sweater?" Sage asked as Kenna walked in and joined her in line.

Her friend smiled and nodded.

"I put my stuff on the typewriter table because apparently the people on the couch forgot it was our Sunday," Sage said.

"I'm sure we'll be fine."

"Yeah, of course we will. Everything is fine. It's all good," Sage said in a mock dreamy voice.

"What?"

"I'm the one taking yoga. I should be calm and relaxed and you should be. . . Well, technically, I guess you're taking yoga too. Sex yoga," she said a little too loud and then turned to see if the people behind her noticed.

"What's gotten into you this morning, loudmouth?"

"Nothing." The line moved up. "There's a guy, three back, with corduroys on and a kitten on his T-shirt. One more bit of info, in case you're not on your game: looks like he's wearing last night's mascara."

They turned discreetly as if they were looking at the pastries to find the man glancing down at his phone.

Kenna took less than a beat before facing forward. "This one is too easy. Went home with a woman last night. She ripped his shirt off, breaking the buttons, so he had to wear her kitten T-shirt on his walk of shame. But, on the way home he decided to stop for coffee."

Sage laughed. "One problem with that theory, the T-shirt is his size."

"Huh"—they ordered—"right. Well, that's because. . . she normally wears that thing to bed. It's oversized on her so it fits him. Or, he likes big girls." She glanced back at him one more time. "Yeah, I think I like that one. Let me do this over. He's best friends with cat T-shirt lady and last night they made mad passionate love. She took his shirt off with her teeth, and now he's borrowed her T-shirt to go get them both coffee."

"The mascara?" Sage asked.

"They. . . went to a concert last night and he's an. . . accountant, but she brings out his wild side. He has no idea how to take it off."

"Oh, you're good."

"I know. Now, you can buy me coffee."

"For that one, I'll even buy your breakfast."

Kenna laughed as Sage paid and they returned to the table.

"No Paige today?"

"She's with Travis and Garrett. There's a Grossest Bugs exhibit at the Science Center. It's sold out. Travis was barely able to find tickets, so they wanted to get there early."

Sage nodded. "I see, so bugs beat bagels now. Huh."

"Guess so." Kenna took a piece of bacon.

They sat in silence.

"No, Garrett and Travis don't normally hang out, but they both love Paige and apparently they both like bugs. Paige told me that every time she's at the farm, Uncle lets her play with the worms." She made a childish yuck face.

"You don't need to explain. I didn't say anything," Sage replied, realizing she was cranky.

"You didn't have to. I could hear your thoughts as soon as I said his name."

"Wow, that's quite the superpower."

Sage sipped her dirty chai and tried to navigate this new thing between them. She was so used to pining over Kenna's brother that she had never thought of what it would be like if she ever, say, kissed him silly in a wine cellar. She and Kenna had talked about it on the phone, but this was their first Sunday coffee since, and it felt a little off.

Maybe Kenna *could* read minds because she said, "All right, let's get this out of the way. You kissed Garrett. He's *the* guy now, so we still need to be able to discuss, talk trash, or get pissed. I can do that with you. I was able to talk about any other guy, including Travis. You should get to do the same. I will say this, he's my big brother and I love him and. . . he's one of the best people I know."

Sage tried to say something, but Kenna held up her hand.

"But. . . you are my best friend. I love you too and you are the best female I know, aside from Paige, because we all know she's better than all of us."

"Agreed." Sage felt her eyes well up. There was something about Kenna's ability to see and speak things clearly that always got her right in the heart.

"So, I guess that's it. Everything else is fair game. I may suffer a little if and when we get down to the sex stories, but I will soldier on."

Sage closed her eyes.

"Sage?"

"Oh, sorry. I was thinking of which sex story I should tell first."

"What! Seriously, already?"

She laughed and Kenna threw a napkin at her. "No way you'd have sex without me knowing."

Sage shook her head. "We are talking about one kiss here. I haven't seen him for days. I'm pretty sure it's out of his system by now, so you won't have to worry."

"I'm not worried. Is that what you want? Is it out of your system?"

"No, it's probably worse now. I don't know. I honestly wasn't expecting it to go past him laughing at my stupid bathroom pickup."

"Which you seem to be handling pretty well."

Sage sighed. "I suppose."

"What? What was that sigh?"

"Nothing."

"Spill. You are not one to waste a sigh."

"I'm not sure what changed. He said he didn't think of me that way, and I think on some level, I was comfortable with that. He was on a shelf."

"Okay, and now what?"

"Now, I think it's all tied up in this stupid book. Maybe I was working those exercises, even if they weren't directed at him, and now he thinks that's who I am. I told him the fantasy; I kissed him back and played along. I'm starting to regret opening the damn book. Remember when you said I should delete it? You were right."

"Oh boy, can I get that in writing?"

"Sure. I honestly have no idea what I'm doing and now that I've kissed him, I think he sees me as some hot mama, to quote my grandfather."

"You are kind of a hot mama, maybe your own version. Be yourself."

"I don't think that's enough anymore. I need to be more... risqué."

Kenna laughed. "I'm not laughing at you but the fact that you used the word risqué. I mean, Sage, you can't be something you're not. So he latched on to the fantasy thing, who cares?"

"I know, but it's all off balance. The whole drunk New Year thing put me in a weird spot and it seems like the only way we connect right now is physically."

"And that's not what you want."

Sage had no idea what she wanted and after another round of caffeine, she and Kenna decided she didn't have to know. She could play along for now, but at some point, she'd need to admit she wasn't the sex kitten she had built herself up to be.

"You need to let him see you, Sage. The real you who is so much more than what you're showing him now," Kenna said as they walked to their cars.

"I know, I'll work on that. In the meantime, we have not discussed one thing about your wedding."

"Oh God"—she climbed into her car—"I haven't even started thinking about it. I'm going to enjoy being engaged for a while."

"Good idea," Sage said. "Hey, Kenna?"

She closed the door and rolled down her window.

"I love you too."

Kenna blew her a kiss and was gone.

Sage often found it hard to believe she'd met her dearest friend only two weeks after arriving in LA. There was something about their lives at that very moment that made sense and now their lives were changing, moving forward, but the friendship, the nut of what they meant to each other, would always stay the same. She swallowed emotion as she backed out and turned up James Bay. He was her most perfect Sunday music boyfriend.

❧❧❧

Early on Monday morning, Garrett watched George and six of their other guys pull up the summer plants that were no longer producing in rows nine through twenty-two. The new cultivator was working. They'd spend the next couple of weeks cultivating and amending the soil before planting broccoli, cauliflower, and turnips. They'd finished spinach and another three rows of brussels sprouts, but Garrett was worried about the cabbage. The seeds were new and despite a few weeks of ideal environment, they still sat dormant. He also made a mental note that they needed to get the peppers Logan requested in the ground by the end of the weekend. Watching his men on their tractors through a cloud of dirt, he once again wanted to be out there in the fields instead of held up behind the damn computer for half the day. There was something about sweating, real work, that cleared his mind.

As he walked back to his office, Garrett longed for the days when Ryeland Farms was still only twenty-five acres and he could see everything he was responsible for while standing on his back porch. Now there was a whole other growing area a few miles away, and by next week, their new prep-and-assembly facility would be updated. The lands were still sustainable and responsible, but it was getting harder and harder to keep it all together. The drip system they used on their first forty-two acres proved a bitch to install at the second grow area, but it was important. California had been in a drought most of his life, so responsible water was sort of his soapbox issue. Sipping his coffee, he felt the weight of the three generations of farmers before him. Garrett was happy that Logan and Kenna were now getting married and he knew he wasn't responsible for them in the true sense of the word, but the big brother thing never went away, which was fine. It was all he'd ever known how to do—farm and be responsible. When he was younger, he was also pretty good at kicking the ass of anyone who messed with his family, but he tried to find other ways of handling assholes these days.

Herbert Rye, their dad, and though Garrett rarely admitted it, one of his best friends, took a seat in the metal chair, padded with fake leather, across from Garrett. He placed two sandwiches wrapped in white paper on the desk right as Garrett responded to an e-mail from an applicant they hadn't hired. He hit send and looked up at his dad.

"Were we meeting for lunch?"

Nodding, his father opened two Cokes and set one in front of Garrett.

"Did you make these?"

He shook his head, nudging a sandwich closer to Garrett and opening the one in front of him.

"Are. . . you going to speak?"

"I'm working on being a better listener," his father finally said before biting into the French roll.

"Okay. I thought you were a pretty good listener before."

"Yeah"—he paused to sip—"but there's always room for improvement."

Garrett opened his sandwich. "So, what's up?"

"What are you working on?" his father asked after a few bites in silence.

Garrett let out a breath. "Well, we still need two more people trained and ready before harvest, and I got a quote to paint the sign out front because Kenna said it looks. . . haggard. I think that's the word she used." He finished the first half of his sandwich.

"That's not what I meant. I know you're working on things here. I meant your personal life."

Garrett put his sandwich down and rubbed the bridge of his nose, hoping like hell this wasn't another "shared wisdom" from his father's obsession with Oprah. He'd already told Garrett that his "tank was empty" and "if he wanted abundance, he needed to nurture himself." He shuddered at the memory and tried to think of something to tell his father that would end the conversation.

"Oh. . . well, I'm working on. . . being more enjoyable to be around." If that made any sense. Apparently, it did because his father's eyes widened mid-chew.

"That's great. How's it going?"

"Great. Dad, thanks for lunch and it's always nice to have one of these. . . chats with you, but if I don't get some of this paper off my desk, I'm going to have a bonfire that will supremely piss Kenna off."

His father laughed, which was one of Garrett's favorite sounds. "Sure, I'll let you get back to it. I'm glad to hear you're working on your personal foundation. Sometimes I think the things I say go in one ear and out the other."

They do, Garrett thought, throwing their lunch trash away.

He patted his father on the back and walked him halfway back to the house. Returning to his desk, he smiled and wondered if there was a support group for too much Oprah.

Chapter Fourteen

*L*ogan had called a meeting to go over "Lessons Learned" at the farm-to-table event so they could prepare for the next one, which was rapidly approaching. He wanted to run through the meet-and-greet flow and promised a tasting menu if everyone was willing to drive up to the barn for the meeting. Sage didn't need to be bribed with food to visit Ryeland Farms. Aside from the fact that Garrett would be there and the place itself was breathtaking, she also loved the drive. It was cleansing to get out of LA and she enjoyed being on the open road with her music. Today's playlist was The Fray. They were always right on the border of depressing, and their music made her think about something other than sappy love.

Rolling down her windows, Sage allowed her fingers to touch the breeze as she looked out over acres and acres of rows. They were different in the afternoon sun, and she noticed more were covered, with what looked like white plastic, than before. For dirt, everything was so clean, precise. Sage guessed it had to be and wondered about regulations. For the first time in her life, she pondered what it must take to run a farm of this size.

What did his job look like? Was it fun or nerve-racking? Probably a bit of both, like most jobs, she thought. Pulling into a space next to Kenna's Jeep, Sage realized admiring him from afar was no longer enough. She wanted to know him, understand him. That kiss had opened a door and even though she tried coming in late to avoid seeing him, nothing had helped her close the damn thing. If she couldn't have all the pieces, she didn't want his body.

"What the hell is wrong with wanting his body?" her own body screamed.

With the door wide open, her stomach knotted at the thought of seeing him, she realized that steps or no steps, she was never going to be a grape.

Reapplying her lip gloss, Sage tried to think about something else. She exited the car and grabbed her supplies from the trunk. She'd spent the last couple of days working on another drink, using bitters she'd made herself, and she planned on mixing up a batch for the tasting.

Sage went around the back of the main house and lowered her sunglasses over her eyes, partly because of the sun and mostly because Garrett was sitting straight ahead and she wanted some kind of barrier. His shirt was stiff and white as if it had recently come back from the dry cleaner. *Did he drop off his own dry cleaning?* For some reason, the idea of him living alone seemed wrong. It didn't make sense that a man like Garrett Rye would be alone. She knew that sounded silly, but those were her feelings as she stared at him, one arm draped over the back of his chair. There were faint blue and red stripes on his shirt. It was plaid, but not exactly. The starched cotton looked as if it warmed and molded to the muscles of his shoulders. She noticed his wire-framed sunglasses and one boot propped up on the base of the wood table where he and Logan were sitting. Even with his back to her, he looked like no other man she'd ever met. He was a rare combination of easy and hard with a casual loping walk that hinted at cowboy. Every time he sat down, he leaned back as if he were going to be there for a while. Sage caught herself being ridiculous and cleared her throat. He certainly wasn't perfect, but when she shared space with him, it felt like he was perfect for her. As she approached, he was arguing with Logan over melons. Was it even possible to have an argument about melons?

"We did the honeydew hybrid two years ago and they were crap. I'm keeping it simple this time." Garrett took a catalogue back from Logan.

"They weren't crap. We put them with that Spanish ham and it was great. The flavor is mellow, it worked."

"Yeah, well, not everyone is a chef or knows what the hell Spanish ham is for that matter. I'm talking about bringing this thing home from our farmers market and cracking it open. There's no flavor. You'll need to find another friend for your jamón because I'm not growing those melons."

"Hey, Sage," Logan said, standing as if he'd been hanging out and forgetting his yellow pad for a minute. "You brought your equipment? Are we gonna be doing some afternoon drinking?"

She smiled. "Only samples. I have another new drink I think we should feature instead of the rusty nail."

"Okay, good. Well, Kenna and Travis are in the barn already and we brought an extra server to see if that helps with the flow. Garre, do you want to come over and play restaurant for us?"

"Oh sure, I'm not working. I've got a tractor George can't get out of reverse, but let me do this."

"Great, thanks," Logan said as if Garrett's sarcasm was sincere.

As he stood, George approached, asking him something in Spanish.

Garrett nodded. *"Deje' las partes en el escritoire en la oficina de enfrente. Regreso en un minuto."*

George said something back that was equally confusing to Sage's one-language brain and shook his head before heading back to the fields.

"You speak Spanish?" she asked as the three of them walked toward the barn.

"No," Garrett said, gesturing for her to go ahead. Logan shook his head at his brother.

"Very funny." Sage glanced over her shoulder.

"I'm working on being more. . . enjoyable to be around." Garrett's grin was wicked, his eyes hidden behind his shades.

"Seriously?"

"It's not working," Logan said, and ran ahead as a truck pulled up close to the barn.

"What's the drink called?" Garrett asked from behind her.

"When did you learn to speak Spanish?" she asked back.

"Some in high school and then community college."

"Impressive."

"Is it? I thought only fancy degrees were impressive."

"Those are too, but I've always been fascinated with language. Like, what did you say to George back there?"

"He was looking for parts. I told him they were on the desk and I'd be back in a minute. Why?"

"I think it's interesting that you two are privy to something I don't understand, but if I had a key and could learn it, then I could communicate. Language never sticks with me. I've tried Spanish and Italian on those computer classes, you know?" She shook her head. "Nothing works. My sister speaks three languages, which pisses me off."

Garrett laughed. "Why does that piss you off?"

"She's smug. You'd have to meet Hollis to understand. Anyway, I envy that ability to communicate. What did he say back?"

"That I was full of shit and he'd see me in a couple of hours. He also said you were beautiful."

She stopped and turned to him again. "You made that up."

"He did say I was full of shit, but the beautiful part may have been mine. You are."

Sage felt her heart jump. "Is this part of your being more enjoyable practice?"

"Maybe." He stepped up to her, inches from her mouth, and took off his sunglasses as if he knew those eyes were a weapon. "Is it working?"

She nodded, noticing he'd shaved.

"Good. What's the drink called?" he asked softly, eyes on her mouth.

"The Rye." She offered nothing else and continued walking. Sometimes being next to him threatened to wash her away, and she needed to concentrate on this meeting so their event went well.

"Really? I thought my drink was a Manhattan. I'm a classic, remember?"

"Yes, but you are not the only Rye in the family. Maybe the drink is an expression of the whole family."

"Maybe."

Logan was way ahead of them now and already in animated discussion with Travis.

"What's in it?"

Sage stopped and turned to face him. "Logan gave me some plants, so I combined them and made a couple of new bitters."

Garrett looked confused.

"Bitters are... essences, kind of like spices for a bartender. They're part of the creative process for me. I have different kinds, creosote, rhubarb from last summer. They're infused with flavors."

"Huh. So you have new bitters from our farm?"

"Well, it's my interpretation of the farm. You may not agree."

"I'm sure I will."

She laughed. "Yeah?"

"Yeah," he said and pulled her off to the side, out of sight near a large tree. "You don't by any chance have any farm fantasies, do you?"

"I do, they involve—"

He slid his hand behind her neck and kissed her before she could say another word, which was perfect because she had no idea what she was going to say or how she would go about describing a farm fantasy.

She could hear the breeze in the leaves above, smell the wood-tinged scent of him, and feel his lips, which were almost familiar. He'd touched her enough now that the initial shock had been replaced with recognition, as if her body knew it was him and welcomed him.

"Sage," Logan called out from the barn.

She started to pull away, but he held her for one more beat and then without a word, let her go. Sage ran to the barn, not even trying to disguise the feeling washing over her. It was impossible to contain so she didn't bother.

❦

Garrett stood where she left him for a few minutes, running his hand over his face because he couldn't seem to get his fill. Rejoining Logan and Kenna, he sat at the table and ate roasted chicken breast with baby turnips that he had thought too small when George pulled them last week, but they were perfect once Logan and Travis added carrots and some sauce with rosemary. The meal, although small because it was a sample, was delicious. Garrett was by no means a food snob, but when he ate his brother's food, it was like not quite realizing how great the rain was and then being reminded.

Eager to try the drink Sage had boldly called The Rye, Garrett pulled the glass she'd poured toward him. He grinned, but her eyes were on the drink, dead serious as if she were figuring out a puzzle. The first sip slid down his throat, and Garrett immediately recognized the rye from the first drink she'd ever made him and then he tasted a hint of spice, like wood, followed by the grand finale of the sip. His mouth was flooded with moist earth and plants. Grass maybe, because he was immediately thrown into a memory of sitting in the fields as a kid and blowing on blades of grass to make that high-pitched sound. Kenna was always pissed because she could never do it. She'd hum with the blade up to her mouth and try to convince him and Logan she was legit. She couldn't have been more than six or seven, and he'd told her the skills would come with practice. He couldn't remember the last time they'd tried to play music on the grass. He looked at Logan, who had finished his taste of the drink.

"How the hell does she do that?" he asked Logan. It was as if she knew them, what it meant to live on this land. Like she'd dropped a private part of his family right there in the glass.

Logan's smile broadened in acknowledgment. "Incredible, right?"

Garrett took the last sip of the sample, relived it one more time, and glanced at Sage, who was beaming with pride.

"I'm not sure how you know that much about us, let alone how you put that into a glass, but however you do it, that's a talent. I could taste the earth. Shit, I sound like one of those foodie assholes Logan used to watch on television."

They all laughed. He caught her eyes and something in his chest reached for her. It was probably his heart, but he wasn't ready to go there. Behind her blue nail polish and snail earrings, she was kind, genuine, and indescribable—like her drinks. She was the best kind of person—the kind who cared about her job, her customers, her friends, and. . . him. He'd tried to be a decent guy most of his life, but he didn't deserve her.

Helping clear the table, Garrett wondered if that level of caring came from being loved. If it had come from a good family, maybe he was capable of giving her something in return.

Chapter Fifteen

*A*fter everyone had gone, Sage found herself in the barn with Garrett. What had started as a good-bye kiss escalated quickly until they were both grabbing at each other's clothes. Garrett closed the barn door, and when he dropped to his knees in front of her, she was certain her heart stopped right there on the spot. Eyes on her, he was hotter than any fantasy she could conjure up. This wasn't a joke; the man was on his knees. He wasn't holding a ring, but from the looks of him as his fingers played with the hem of her shirt, teasing the skin beneath, Sage realized there were many versions of the man-down-on-one-knee fantasy. She should try to define this before it went any further. Kenna's sensible voice whispered in her ear that if she had sex with Garrett, she would do so with her whole heart. The only sex advice her mother had offered growing up was next. "A man is not going to buy the farm if you give the milk away for free." Sage understood the irony that she was now going to give far more than the milk away on an actual farm.

She tried to clear all the voices of reason and instead remember the book. This was a good idea, a very good idea, she decided right as Garrett slid both of his hands under her shirt. She closed her eyes. He was barely touching her and when the warmth of his breath spread across her stomach, she was gone. Gone, completely somewhere else—no book, no voices. Oh, if she could simply let go and fall into the glory of a moment without needing to know how it worked.

"Sage."

"Uh huh." Her eyes remained closed.

"Are you okay?"

Her eyes peeked opened. "Yes, why?"

"Well, your eyes are squeezed closed, sort of like you're at the doctor's office."

She let out a shuddering breath. "Are they?"

Garrett stood.

"Oh no, don't do that," Sage said, trying to save a moment she felt certain she wanted. *Didn't she?*

His face eased from lust to tender, and he ran the back of his hand along the curve of her neck. It was so gentle it felt like a good-bye.

"I'm fine, I mean that was"—she blew her bangs out of her face—"definitely fantasy material. You on your knees and you were surely going to, what like, take my panties off with your teeth and then—"

Stop talking. In the name of all things holy, shut up!

"I. . . okay, is that something you want?" Garrett asked with a curling grin that proved he had no idea she was about to collapse.

"Why are we talking? Let's. . ." She'd never felt more lost in her life, including the first time she'd had sex. Was it possible to regress back to that level of awkward?

"Sage?"

"What?"

"Do you want me to take your clothes off with my teeth?"

"I, sure. How does that work? You know, in a practical sense. I've always wondered how that is even possible."

You're babbling again, Sage. The man was on his knees for Christ's sake, and you blew it.

Garrett laughed and Sage put her hands to her face. He gently pulled them back down.

"I have no idea what I'm doing. I guess I've fantasized about you but more like. . . the essence of you. I'm still at holding your hand, kissing you stupid. This might kill me. I'm a sham, right?"

He smiled but said nothing so she continued, unable to stop.

"This was fun and that day in the wine cellar, you were so. . . and I was. . . and I thought if that's what this is then I'm going to go with it."

"So that day you said you wanted to be naughty?"

"Oh yeah, you heard that? It was barely a whisper."

He nodded. "You said naughty. That word usually rings pretty clear for me at any volume."

Sage laughed. "Well, no, I'm not naughty by nature and I don't have fantasies mapped out. I mean there are images when it comes to you, but they're not all. . . I guess what I'm trying to say is they don't all involve. . . Oh, please, let's forget this."

"Sex."

"Pardon?"

"When you think of us together, you're not always holding the headboard and screaming my name."

Sage allowed that particular image to race through her mind for a moment, or two or—

"Sage?"

"Oh, sorry. Although that one's not bad. Maybe you should be in charge of the fantasies. You're very good at it. I don't actually have a headboard, so we'll need to be at your house for that one."

He laughed again. "So if we're not naked, what are we doing?"

"Oh, come on, not this again. I don't know what we're doing, and you're not some actor in a play. You're you. I find that incredibly attractive and that's that. You don't need to continue playing this game. It was fun making out with you, and please know that I will store away that image of your headboard for a very long time, but this isn't me. I'm so tired of trying to be hot and smoldering. It's exhausting. I'm a fake. You're free to go now." She walked toward the door, hoping she had the strength to pull it open before she died of embarrassment. This crap never happened on television or even in the lives of her friends. Why the hell was she always the strange one? It was that damn bottom drawer. If she had more life experience, she wouldn't be fumbling and acting so stupid.

"Do you want to get a pizza?"

She turned. "What?"

His eyebrows went up and he repeated the question again slowly. "Do you want to get a pizza?"

"Now?"

Garrett looked at his watch. "Well, it is time for dinner. I'm done here and you don't work tonight, so yeah, now. Or we can get Chinese. There's a good place about ten minutes from here."

For a guy that appeared to like routine, he certainly knew how to change gears on her as if it was the most natural thing in the world and expect her to catch up. She still wasn't sure if this made him the most self-centered man on the planet or a damn Zen master. On the surface, he didn't appear to have the same apprehension most human beings possessed. It was sexy, confident, and somewhere in the corners of his water-colored eyes, it was calm. She did want to grab on to his headboard, but this—standing outside a barn with the sun setting behind them—she wanted this more.

"I'm surrounded by pizza most of the time, so Chinese."

Garrett took off his jacket, draping it over her shoulders. "Chinese it is. Let's do it. Please tell me you like egg rolls."

Sage put her arms through the offered coat and walked past him toward his truck. "Um, egg rolls are the only reason to have Chinese food, the rest is filler."

Garrett laughed and opened the passenger door for her. "Do you have a cocktail for Chinese food?"

Sage shook her head. "Even I can't top the Chinese tea. It's all about the egg rolls and the tea."

He closed the door and in the time it took him to walk around to the other side, she felt it. It was simple and overwhelming all at the same time: the click.

❧❧❧

"So, how did all of this start?"

"How did what start?" She picked at the edge of her egg roll.

"Naughty Sage."

She shook her head. "You'll laugh."

"I'll try not to."

"But you will. It's kind of funny, so I guess I don't mind."

He didn't say a thing and simply watched her; it had become one of his favorite things to do lately.

"Well, it all starts with my bottom drawer."

"Okay."

"I don't have one."

Now he was confused.

"Everyone has life experiences, things they did when they were young and stupid. I... well, I guess I woke up one morning, or maybe after a few mornings, and realized that I don't have anything tucked away. I don't have any cool stories or experiences. I wanted those. I still do."

"The bottom drawer is a metaphor for your twenties packed full of stupid and crazy experiences?"

Sage nodded and bit into her egg roll.

"But you're thirty-two, so isn't that time gone?"

"Yeah, but I still have some stories to get in before I settle down. I want stories."

"You're a bartender—I would think you'd have lots of those."

"I do, about other people. I'm a great listener, but those are other people's lives."

Garrett ate and thought about the conversation he'd had with his father a few days earlier. She was sort of quirky and unexpected like his dad, he decided, and then hoped like hell she didn't watch Oprah.

"Moving here and becoming a bartender was my first big step toward changing things. Before that, my life was safe and nice."

"Safe and nice are things lots of people strive for."

"I know, but not me."

"Okay, so you want stuff for the bottom drawer, like ticket stubs and champagne corks?"

"Could be, but mainly experiences. A person is defined by her stories, her journey. Don't you think?"

"I. . . guess, but you have experiences. From what Kenna says, you're always going and doing things. No way you made it into your thirties without things happening to you."

"Not much happened before I moved here. That's why my sister bought me the book."

He dipped another egg roll and noticed she became more and more relaxed. The more she spoke, the more Garrett was starting to understand the puzzle pieces that made up Sage. Almost afraid, he asked, "The book?"

Sage set down her teacup and appeared to brace herself. "Here's where you'll laugh. *Nice to Naughty in Ten Easy Steps.*" She closed her eyes as if saying it was almost painful.

He tried not to laugh, but that was some title, and it explained why things had been so strange lately. He wasn't sure if he should tell her the book was absurd or that she was adorable for reading it. *Would that be condescending?* Damn, women were more complicated than cars. Not knowing what to do, Garrett went with not reacting at all. He took a bite and hoped his face was neutral.

"Go ahead," Sage said, eyes now open.

"What?"

"It's stupid I was even reading the book, but Hollis challenged me and. . . so stupid, right?"

She was smiling a little now so he went with honesty, hoping it wouldn't bite him in the ass.

"I'm not sure naughty can be taught from a book, but good for you for giving it a shot. I'm happy you read the book." He grinned. "Which step was I, exactly?"

"Very funny. You weren't a step. That's the thing, I had no intention of trying it out on you. You were already. . . I mean, I was already. . ." Sage shook her head. "I know this will come as an enormous shock, but I've never been great with guys. I'm not what they're looking for."

"I disagree with that."

"Sure, because you're being kind, but I don't exactly exude a frivolous fun. Hard as I try, I tend to come across as. . ."

"Interesting?"

She smiled. "Yeah, I guess that's a polite way to put it. My brain is usually on, and it's hard for me to let things go and have fun."

"I think I'm understanding. Once you told me you 'wanted me'"—he used the air quotes and was rewarded when her cheeks turned a gorgeous rose pink—"you felt liberated and decided to jump my bones."

She shook her head. "You're having a good time with this."

"I am. But I'm kidding. I think it's great that you looked at your life and decided you wanted more." Garrett sipped his tea. "The book's a little silly, I'll give you that, but since you can't turn your mind off to be what my dad would call a floozy, maybe you could fill your drawer with other stuff."

"Maybe."

"You probably have a bigger bottom drawer than you realize, Sage."

"Said the man who probably has a huge one."

"You'd be surprised. It's not that big."

"Well, someday we'll have to compare."

Garrett smirked at the inherent naughtiness of comparing drawers and sizes and the fact that the whole thing didn't even occur to her. Sage Jeffries was so much more than naughty and sitting with her, he became aware of his heart as it pulsed in his chest. He'd grown very fond of her lips lately, but the woman in front of him woke up a part of him he wasn't sure how to control.

"So, should we talk about this?" He gestured between the two of them.

"Honestly, have I not embarrassed myself enough? You were on your knees, Garrett."

"I was, and I'm happy to get back down there." He grinned,

intending to make her blush, but instead found his pulse picking up at the memory of her.

"Thank you"—she gave him a smile laced with frustration—"but I'm not sure I'd be able to handle that. Ever."

Ever? Now he was definitely confused.

"Wait, so you don't see this leading to. . . ever?"

"I don't think it's a good idea. I've felt this"—her hands flailed back and forth between them—"for a while. And even though you're excellent at kissing me back, you haven't felt anything. I'll always be here, and you'll be. . . wherever you are. If we had sex, I wouldn't recover."

"You're not making sense, Sage."

"I don't care. I didn't think this was ever going to. . ." She closed her eyes and let out a breath.

"Now that's a shame." He tried to keep things light because his heart was back to thumping.

"This isn't funny."

"It is a little bit. We were figuring out the logistics of me taking off your panties with my teeth a few minutes ago, and now you're all worked up and I'm not sure what's going on. It's funny."

She was five shades of scarlet, and Garrett decided to change direction.

"Where is your family?" he asked as their plates were cleared. If she didn't want to have sex with him, that was fine. They'd discuss the "never" part later, but at the moment he needed to spend more time with her. He had to be up at four-thirty, but for the first time in recent memory, he didn't care.

"Up north, Marin County."

"Get along with your family?"

"I do. Three sisters and Mom and Dad."

"Where do you fall?"

"I'm number three of the four."

His mind filled with an image of Sage as a little girl within the context of a family he'd never met. Because she was such good friends with his sister and worked with Logan, she knew so much more about his life than he knew of hers. He'd never bothered to know about her, but as she ordered green tea ice cream for dessert, he felt the need pull at him. She wasn't pretending or trying to flirt anymore, and he found himself more attracted to her than he already was.

"What about you?"

"What about me? You know all about me."

"That's not true. I know what's on the surface and what your family says about you, but it's not like we've ever been on a. . . I mean, sat and had dinner. . . alone."

"True."

"So, do you get along with the rest of the Ryes?"

He grinned and instantly felt uneasy, not at the question, but at the realization that no one had ever asked it. Was that possible? He'd been on dates before—not many—but there'd been women. None of them quite like this.

"Yeah, I do. I mean, there's the usual stuff, but I like both of them, so that helps."

Her eyes sparkled. She was breathtaking when she forgot to critique herself.

"And your dad?"

Taken aback at being front and center, Garrett stuck with short and sweet answers. "Well, you've met him."

"I have. He's pretty incredible."

"He is. I. . . Wow, I'm not sure why this is so weird for me. I guess I'm not used to talking about myself, or no one has ever asked."

"Seriously? When you go on dates, don't women want to know about you?"

"Sage, I'm sure you have this image of who you think I am, but I don't normally date. I've gone out now and then, but all I've done since about nine is work."

"Oh."

"Yeah, I have Jack and my family and the crew that works the farm. I have George. You've met him."

She nodded.

"And so, if we're being all honest over the ice cream here, I'm probably not Sexy Garrett either."

She shook her head, slowly. "Sorry, that last part is simply not true. Sexy Garrett stays," she said with a little bit of naughty.

Yeah, they'd need to discuss the "never" part soon.

Garrett dropped her off at her car back at the farm and kissed her again under their favorite night sky. When they parted, her eyes pooled with the moonlight and in an instant, Garrett found he had a fantasy of his own.

Chapter Sixteen

"Look who's here!" Paige exclaimed as Garrett, hands full of boxes, approached their spot at the Sunday farmers market the following week.

The sight of Sage hit him like sunlight on an early winter morning before the truck had warmed up and the heat turned the frost to shining droplets. The thought surprised him in both its detail and power. He hadn't seen her for a few days because of his schedule and hers. He'd called her a couple of times and had caught her at The Yard for a few minutes. She'd texted him about getting dinner soon, but they never did. It seemed they were both comfortable being alone, but the pull to be together was getting stronger.

She looked rested, her hair was natural, the front down over her forehead, no makeup that he could see, and those lips were covered in something that made them look moist but not sticky. Wearing a light brown scarf and a white T-shirt with jeans, Sage looked beautiful in that way she alone was able to manage. He'd missed her.

He had been up to his ass in work, but he'd still missed her. What the hell was he supposed to do with that? Their eyes met as she listened to Paige talk about what they were featuring at the market. She smiled, shook his father's hand, and Garrett had that feeling again. The frequency was starting to scare the shit out of him.

"Hi there," he finally said, helping Paige pile bundles of Swiss chard onto the table separating them.

"Hi," Sage said with a smile that felt like it was made for him. A smile that said it would be all right if he leaned over and kissed her. Not that that was going to happen because they weren't, well, it's not like they were. . . *Shit!*

Garrett handed over setup duties to Kenna, who was now helping Paige. He dried his hands, walked around the table, and felt a pull toward her he couldn't stop. It made no sense; they'd barely spent time together since egg rolls. She was. . . a woman, Kenna's friend, and she worked with his brother—that was the extent of it, he told himself, but the closer he got to her, the more he felt like he was walking into fog.

The sounds of the market became muffled noise as his hand clinched instinctively at his side, wanting to find its way to the curve of her neck and to bring her into him. His whole body was on board with that, but need was not something he was familiar with nor something he entertained—definitely not in front of his entire family. Her eyes softened as he reached her. She must have seen the emotions in his eyes because she was returning them and in that moment, all he wanted to do was kiss her and stand in the sunlight.

"Be careful they don't put you to work," he said and patted her shoulder. Her T-shirt was soft and her shoulder felt small under his hand. *Holy fucking shit, I'm losing my mind.*

This was worse than the wooden roller coaster at Belmont Park. He suddenly wasn't sure what to do with his hands, whether to scream or laugh. He had no idea what to do with her. Well, actually he did, lots of ideas it turned out, but this was a farmers market.

He must have been standing like a complete idiot for a beat too long because Sage's eyes dropped and he could no longer hear

Paige or Kenna. There was no way he was looking back, and the truck was behind him, so he couldn't keep working.

"I'm. . . I'll be back," he called over his shoulder.

As he walked away, he heard his sister, always subtle, say, "What the hell was that?"

It was a great question. One he didn't have the answer to.

Paige ran after him. "Uncle, Uncle." He swooped her up in his arms, thankful for something familiar.

"Why don't I have a nickname?" The question suddenly came to him as he searched for answers.

Paige looked at him, puzzled. "What do you mean? You're Uncle."

"I know, but I'm not Uncle Rogan or Donk or My Travis. I'm only Uncle."

Paige nodded, as if she was following along but still didn't see the problem. "You don't need a name because you're. . . you're the first, like the original. It's like if I look up 'horse' on my 'puter, there's the main title and then all the different kinds of horses go down from there. You're a horse, Uncle. You're the top guy so"—she scrunched her face and Garrett could feel the lump in his throat—"you don't got time for silly nicknames. You're Uncle. Get it?"

His chest squeezed and for a second, it was as if a dam somewhere was about to break. Putting his face into her strawberry hair, he hugged her tight. "I do. I get it. Thank you."

"You're welcome. Now, where are you going? We still have a lot to do and Donk never gets the radishes right."

He laughed, setting her down. "I'll be right back. I'm going to. . ."

"The potty?" she asked with a grin that looked like she was feeding him an answer. Was it possible he wasn't as smart as a six-year-old?

"Yeah, that's where I'm going. I'll be right back."

"Okay." She slapped her hands to her jeans. "I'll tell Auntie you went to the potty because I'm sure she wants to see you." His niece wiggled her tiny blonde eyebrows and ran back to their tables.

Garrett sighed and hoped "the potty," as she put it, was far enough away for him to get his shit together.

❧☙

"So, Chris the lawyer sent flowers, huh? Look at you go juggling two men now. Soon you'll be writing your own book," Kenna teased as they walked around the market so Kenna could introduce Sage to "the frosted lemonade that will change your life."

After seeing Garrett, she'd forgotten all about Chris and the flowers that had been delivered yesterday. She'd texted Kenna as soon as she closed the door. Getting flowers was exciting, and Sage didn't care if texting her friend was foolish. She hoped she never grew too old for foolish.

"He left a voice mail last night."

"Really? Have you called him back?"

"No." She was still thinking about Garrett. Was he flustered? He seemed different; less sure of himself if that was possible. She looked over at Kenna, who was shaking her head. "What?"

"You were excited about the flowers when you texted me, remember?"

Sage nodded as they approached the frozen lemonade stand and ordered two from the young girl with the crayon-red hair wearing a threadbare The Decemberists T-shirt. She had clearly been recruited by her parents to work the market and wanted to be anywhere else.

"And now, one look from the nonlawyer, brooding farmer, and all bets are off."

"I care about him. That's not going to change because some guy sent me flowers. Although they are beautiful and he left a very nice message."

"He's so lucky," Kenna said as they passed the crystal booth.

"Chris?"

"No, my brother. I'm not sure what line he stood in. Maybe he has good karma because he spent so much time taking care of us, but he's a very lucky man."

Almost tearing up, Sage put her arm around Kenna.

"Yeah, well, you never know. Maybe Chris will take me up against a wall and I'll forget all about Mr. Dear-Lord-Kiss-Me-Again."

"What's with you and being taken against a wall?"

"It's in all the romance novels."

"You read romance?"

"Yeah, so do you."

"I know I do, but I didn't think women with engineering degrees read romance."

"Oh please, of course we do. We all do, and the women who turn their noses up are missing out."

"On being taken against the wall, it seems."

"Yeah, but I feel like it won't work out the way it does in the books. You know, when she jumps into his arms. There are so many things that could go wrong with that in my world."

Laughing, they both returned to the Ryeland Farms tables. There was a line, and Paige was charming all the customers by handing out baby carrots with tiny cups of buttermilk dressing that Her Travis had made for the market.

"Sage, Kenna tells me you're going to teach bridge down at the community center this month," Mr. Rye said, sitting in a chair off to the side where he could watch the action.

"I am. Mondays and Wednesdays in their small conference room. Do you play bridge?" She leaned on the table next to him.

"No, but I've always wanted to learn. You're a little young for bridge, aren't you?"

"It's often misconstrued as an old ladies' game, but it's great fun. My grandmother taught me bridge when I was little. All my sisters play. My dad does too, so there's room for men."

He looked at her, as if he were weighing his options.

"I'm going to sign up when I get home."

"Great."

"Do you like Oprah?" he asked.

"I do. Does she play bridge?"

"You know, I'm not sure, but she seems cool enough to, doesn't she?"

Sage laughed and nodded.

On the surface, Mr. Rye looked like the last person who would even entertain a daytime talk show host, let alone a black, female, self-improvement guru daytime talk show host. Watching him help Kenna bag up radishes for a waiting customer who sported a yellow hat, Sage saw what had made her friends so very special. She loved Oprah; it made perfect sense that a farmer in his sixties would find value in her, too.

Chapter Seventeen

Garrett rang the doorbell, still feeling out of sorts. He made a concerted effort to avoid disorder most of his life, but he couldn't stay away. She'd been at the market for a couple of hours but he still wanted more. Did she? He probably should have called. After the doorbell, he heard rustling and her voice as the noise of the television went silent. Hopefully she'd felt it too because it was too late to back out now.

"Hang on." Followed by a loud thud and then, "Oh, shit, damn."

It sounded like a war zone and then she swung the door open. Sweatpants, correction: tight sweatpants that read Berkeley up the leg, and a white tank top with pieces of popcorn and what looked like a glob of chocolate stuck to it. She wore no makeup and the front of her hair was pulled to the side with a clip. She had on a sports bra under the tank top, which was unfortunate, Garrett thought. Those things were like a lead curtain for men's eyes. After he was done taking her in, he pointed to the piece of chocolate.

Sage looked down, pulled it free from her shirt, and popped it in her mouth. "Eh, sorry. Milk Dud," she said, still chewing and holding her door open. "Did you want to come in?" She made room and brushed the popcorn off her shirt.

Garrett smiled and stepped into the entryway of her small house. The first thing he noticed was the floor. It was made up of rectangular slate tiles with a narrow grout line. The second thing he noticed were the roses sitting in a vase on a small, whitewashed, spindly type of table with a glass top. Beautiful roses, he had to admit, most of which he recognized. He found himself wanting to identify them so he could revert to something more familiar than standing in her doorway completely unannounced.

Sage cleared her throat and he went with the roses.

"Great flowers." He stepped closer, noticing the card and trying to ignore it. There must have been two dozen, and not one of them was the type you'd get from a typical grocery store or even a chain florist. These were every different color and size imaginable, as if someone had handpicked them from a garden. "Those are Claire Austin, and I'm pretty sure the ones in the back are Golden Celebration." He turned to her and caught the name on the card.

"Thank you. They smell great."

"Right," he said, trying not to think about the name. Maybe it was a brother, although she said she was one of four girls, didn't she? "I thought I'd stop by because. . . are you watching a movie?"

"Oh, um, no. It's *The Golden Globes*. I watch them every year." She ran her hand across her hair and must have realized she had a clip in it because she rolled her eyes, but not at him. Did people roll their eyes at themselves? Clearly, Sage did.

"Huh, well, I wanted to stop by—"

"Do you want to watch? I have taco shells in the oven and the stuff is all ready and on the table."

"I thought you were eating popcorn and Milk Duds?"

"Appetizer."

In an instant, the discomfort slipped away, replaced with something that made his throat tighten. He didn't know what to say.

"I like tacos." *Wow, way to melt the panties, man*, his brother's voice jabbed in his head.

"Great, me too." She took his coat and hung it on an old iron stand by the door.

Walking into her living room, Garrett noticed lots of old and realized he'd always thought of her as modern, new. He was wrong, and another piece of her puzzle fell into place. In the center of the living room was a big oval rug with blue and yellow along the edge and a large couch on wooden feet that was the same blue as the rug. He hadn't seen a couch like that since his grandmother was alive. A white knit blanket was thrown over the back and her coffee table looked like an old suitcase or trunk.

The Construction of the Cocktail sat on a side table on the other side of the room. She had two small bookcases filled with textbooks and fiction; a huge dictionary lay open on top. Garrett remembered her crossword puzzles. A kidney-shaped desk stood behind the couch, in between the bookcases. As his eyes traveled up, he noticed an art deco print over her desk and a smaller framed painting of what looked like two fairies eating raspberries. After only one turn around her living room, Garrett had almost forgotten about the card. Almost. Sage returned with the taco shells, plates, and two beers.

"I like your house," he said, taking the plate out of her hand and sitting on the couch. Sage sat next to him, legs folded underneath her.

"Thanks." She looked around as if living in her space gave her a confidence she struggled with outside her four walls. "It's coming together."

They sat and made tacos while the television was still on mute and scrolling through commercials.

After his second taco and the acceptance speech for best short animated film, Garrett asked, "So, who's Chris? Those are impressive roses."

Her cheeks went pink and she didn't meet his eyes. *Shit. Chris was someone.*

"He's a guy I met on the plane when I flew back after the holiday."

"Huh." He made another taco as Sage hit the remote and the sound of applause filled the room again. Garrett let out a breath, sat back on the couch, and tried to convince himself he didn't give two shits about Chris from the plane as some tall blonde took to the stage crying.

❧❧❧

Once Sage's heart had settled down after finding Garrett at her door unannounced and she accepted that she was in her laundry-day clothes and that was that, she allowed herself to be happy. Happy to see him and have him in her home. It occurred to her that every moment she spent in reality with him was far better than anything made up in her mind. After carefully sidestepping the flowers, they fell into conversation about everything from the farmers market to her first pet, all while managing to watch the awards.

Sage clapped for the best picture winner and Garrett wanted to know why blockbusters were never nominated. She laughed until her eyes watered as he made the pitch for Arnold Schwarzenegger winning a Golden Globe.

"His movies aren't about acting," she told him. "Blockbusters are a spectacle. I like some, don't get me wrong, but they only stand a chance for special effects or lighting or editing awards, not acting."

"No way. There's serious acting going on. Invisible evil alien? That takes all kinds of imagining, right? And, these guys don't even have that many lines, so when they say something, it needs to be good. Hello, 'I'll be back,'" he said in a pretty good Arnold voice. "That's iconic right there."

She cleared the plates, still laughing and feeling like she could do this every night with him. Movies, parties, dinner, sitting together reading, breakfast, her mind flooded with the ways in which real Garrett could fit into her life and she into his. That was love, wasn't it? Seeing a person in her world, wanting to be in his. They hadn't touched each other since her tiny panic attack and the big reveal that she was not, in fact, ever going to be naughty.

Not like that anyway. She needed more than surface flirty and dirty talk. This, she thought as he grabbed the remaining bowls off the table and followed her into the kitchen, was her kind of sexy.

"Do you want another beer or coffee?" she asked as he came up behind her to put the bowls in the sink.

"Coffee's good." He stood at her back, breath at her ear, and as much as Sage loved a clean kitchen, it could wait. Turning to find them face-to-face, her heart jumped and she didn't care that she hadn't showered after her yoga class. She reached up and touched the rough line of his unshaven jaw. He was looking at her different- ly, she thought, as her hands moved down his neck and found his chest. He was no longer entertaining her crush: something had changed in his eyes. Maybe for both of them because standing in her kitchen, pressed against his warm solid body, things felt even. Equally charged.

"I'm not sure what's happening here," he said softly as his arms encircled her waist and he touched his forehead to hers.

She said nothing because she couldn't. She only wanted to stand there with him while he figured out feelings she'd known for such a long time.

"I don't think I'm going to be good at any of this. The flirting and teasing, yeah, I can do that. But this"—he eased her back and looked into her eyes—"I've started missing you." He lowered his arms and turned from her. "I'm not sure I've missed anyone since Santa stopped showing up at our house. But when I saw you today, I thought I was going crazy." He leaned up against the counter as if holding on for balance.

"I'm used to not having you, missing you," Sage said, not sure how to help him navigate the fall. "This doesn't have to be any- thing more than it is right now, Garrett." She walked back to the living room, hoping she sounded convincing.

He followed her.

"I started all of this. I'm the one who was attracted to you." Sage moved some magazines back onto the coffee table.

"Loved me." He took her arm, the playful back in his eyes.

She laughed.

"What? You said you loved me."

"I did. I do," she added quietly, which was so stupid because he clearly thought she was nuts.

"I'm not sure how that's possible."

She shook her head. "Well, you're not me. You don't have my heart."

Sitting back down on the couch, Sage felt strangely comfortable in her truth. She supposed that came from spilling your uninhibited guts all over a guy's truck and then admitting to the naughty book.

Garrett sat next to her.

"Who's Chris?"

"I already told you. He's the guy who sat next to me on the plane."

"I've sat next to a few women on the plane. Never thought about sending them flowers." He teased.

"He wants to take me to dinner."

Garrett said nothing. Standing, he suddenly seemed too big for her tiny living room.

"Are you going to dinner with him?"

"Probably not." She stood as Garrett grabbed his coat by the door and eyed the flowers again.

"I need to get going."

She went to the door and put her arms around him.

"I was reading this book last year and it said there was 'power in the present' and that in order to be in the power position, people needed to not look back or too far ahead. Do you agree with that?"

"I. . . sure. Present is good."

"So that's what we're doing. Now that you know I don't want you to spank me—"

Garrett's grin was big and wide as he held up his hand. "Now, I don't think we should completely rule that out."

She laughed. "Let's try to be present. What do you think?"

"I think you sound like my dad. Do you watch Oprah?"

"Her show's not on anymore."

"Must be reruns because he watches her all the time."

"Oprah has amazing insights."

"Yeah, I guess. I do think it's good to live in the present and I guess if you're focused on what you're doing, then there is some power with that."

"I do too. I'm working on that."

"On what?"

"Being present and being powerful."

"You're not powerful?"

"I'm. . . well, no. I'm awkward and I'd like to be more in the moment. I want things."

"You seem pretty powerful behind the bar."

"That's my stage and I don't have to be myself. I can put on badass bartender, and it's fun."

"But you are badass bartender, aren't you?"

"I guess. Kiss me, Garrett." She put her arms around his neck, and as his warm lips touched hers, she closed her eyes and soaked in the present.

"Sage," he said after they'd slipped apart.

"Yes." She opened the front door for him.

"Don't go to dinner with Chris." He kissed her again lightly and walked to his truck.

Sage closed the door and leaned against it, trying desperately to not think about the future.

Chapter Eighteen

Garrett could now check "best man" off his life list or put it in his bottom drawer. Christ, he was starting to sound like Sage and his father rolled into one. But it was true, he'd never been in a wedding, let alone had the best seat in the house as a beautiful woman—dressed in what Kenna informed him was silk—walked toward them. It was cool, more change, a whole lot emotional, but great.

What was supposed to be another farm-to-table event for Senator Malendar and some of his close friends had secretly been turned into a wedding. Garrett, Kenna, and Travis were told late Thursday night, and Kenna, "no longer able to hold it in," told Sage Friday morning. It hadn't made much of a difference because all of the pieces were in place and Logan handled the menu. Things were all set when fifty people crowded into the barn to watch Logan Rye marry Kara Malendar on a crisp February evening under the stars and an arch of magnolias.

After a few months of going back and forth, Kara and Logan had decided they wanted a small, surprise wedding. To their credit, there was not one reporter, which appeared to make Kara very happy. "She wanted a day that was ours," Logan told them, and as Garrett looked around the barn, it was clear that's what she got.

Garrett and Grady, Kara's brother, stood ready as Logan walked over with their father to take his place right before the wedding started. Garrett felt a lump in his throat and a sense of imbalance at watching his family. They'd shared so many firsts, the four of them, and this was their first wedding at home. Kenna had married Adam in Vegas, which was the first quickie wedding, and now this one had all the bells and whistles. The beginning of many new and exciting changes, he tried to convince himself, because there was a weight in his chest. Letting out a slow breath and fixing the back of Logan's jacket, Garrett remembered what Sage had said about staying in the present. As the music started, he was pretty sure that's what kept him from crying like a baby.

Across the aisle, Kara had a man of honor, Jake, her best friend and a maid of honor, Makenna. Paige was the cutest flower girl in the world, of course, along with Eloise, Jake and Cotton's daughter. The entire place overflowed with what he could only describe as pure love and joy as his brother told the woman he'd waited so long for that "he'd loved her all his life," and "couldn't wait to cherish her forever."

"Married man," Garrett said, making his way to Logan as people milled around once the toasts were done and the food was eaten. Putting his arm around his brother, it was not lost to him how much time had passed since he'd taught Logan how to drive a stick shift.

"I think we pulled it off, right?" Logan asked, practically glowing under the evening sky and the string of lights surrounding the barn.

Garrett nodded.

"Did you see her face? My God, do you see how beautiful she is?"

Garrett swallowed back the emotions that crawled into his chest and began to wonder when he'd become so damn soft. Maybe he'd always been a little soft but never had a use for it before. "I did. It was a great wedding. I even got a little choked up. She's gorgeous, man, and for some reason, she loves you. Go figure."

"I know, right?" Logan's eyes spilled the contents of his heart. He almost looked like a little kid. "Thank you."

"For what? You made all the food."

"For being my big brother."

It was so damn basic that it almost knocked him down. Garrett couldn't speak.

"For teaching me and showing me how to be a man."

"Pretty sure Dad did that," he said, barely getting the words out.

Logan grew serious. "Garre, it's my wedding night and I'm trying to tell you that you're a big part of the reason I'm standing here. I've looked to you my whole life for how to be and it's never let me down, so I want you to know that —"

"Oh, for fuck's sake," Garrett said on a whisper, pulling his brother into a hug and holding him tight, which shut Logan up and filled Garrett with the love only family brought. His eyes welled up and it washed right over him. All of them, the house, the day in and day out of making their family work. "I'd do it all again. Love you, man."

"I love you too," Logan said as Garrett loosened his grip.

Patting him on the back, Garrett shook his head and muttered, "This shit is all Oprah's fault. We should take the damn television out of the house." He smiled at his brother and turned. "Go find your new wife. I need a drink." Logan laughed as Garrett walked toward the bar. He had to walk away. There was nothing he could say that would express the feelings watching his little brother get married stirred in him. The love between them was so pure that it almost didn't feel like it belonged in him. That was probably why he pushed it down, kept it in its place most of the time.

"Are you all right?" Sage asked as he approached the bar.

He nodded.

"Beer?"

"Please."

"Great wedding." He could tell she was keeping it simple. It wasn't in her nature, but she knew him.

He took a pull of the beer she handed him and tilted his head in thanks.

"Anything you want to talk about?"

"No."

"Okay. Do you want to dance?"

Garrett arched his brow to check her sincerity.

"You don't dance?" she asked.

"Not if I can help it."

Laughing, she stepped out from behind the bar. She was wearing a short gold dress that he hadn't noticed before, although looking at her now, he wasn't sure how that was possible.

"Nice boots," he said, looking down at the muckers she wore in stark contrast to the sparkle of her dress.

"Thanks. Kenna let me borrow them. It's muddy behind the bar, so there was no point wearing heels."

One of Grady's friends, the one with the bowtie, approached them and Sage slipped back behind the bar.

"What can I get you?" she said.

"Actually, I was wondering if you'd like to dance."

"Oh, that's so sweet. I'd—"

Back the hell up, man.

"Sorry, I beat you to it," Garrett said, taking her hand and pulling her to his side.

The guy looked confused as they walked to the dance floor. Garrett offered up thanks that it was a slow song and took her in his arms. She was laughing.

"What?"

"Nothing." She rested her head on his chest and Garrett felt a rush of breath leave his body. It was replaced with the sweet smell of her.

Another first, he thought. He did dance, as long as it was with her.

❧❧❧

The cake was delicious; it was the one dessert Logan knew how to make and it was Kara's favorite—chocolate cake topped with tart cherries. Paige was holding a group dance lesson for Travis, Garrett, Kate and Grady on the dance floor, so Kenna and Sage sat in two comfy chairs by one of the fire pits.

"Things are good. He stopped by and we had dinner at my house last week."

"Okay," Kenna said less than enthusiastically over the rim of her wine glass.

"I'm telling you, we're in a good place. I like him."

"That's not new, Sage."

"No, it sort of is. I like the real him, not the please-brush-by-me lusty kind of thing I had going on before. I'm getting to know him and he gets to see the real me. I told Travis yesterday while we were closing that things are. . . friendly."

"With benefits?"

Sage shook her head. "No. No benefits. He's been different, but. . . maybe we're good as friends."

"I don't pretend to understand my brother all the time, but I'm going to guess he doesn't want to be your friend."

She shrugged. "Well, he doesn't seem to know how to move forward and honestly, I'm happy to be with him without my awkward sexy talk."

"So you're back to being nice, no more naughty?"

"Yeah, I deleted it," she said, shaking her head.

"What book are you on to now?"

"*Acceptance: A Lifelong Journey*."

Kenna almost spit her drink onto the grass as Sage adopted her Zen voice.

"Okay, and how's that going? You've. . . accepted things and you no longer want to jump my brother's bones?"

Sage looked around as she always did because Kenna could be so damn loud.

"I. . . no. I mean"—she leaned in and whispered—"of course I do, but I put on the brakes because I can't do that casually, not with him. I'm trying to accept my life and enjoy whatever abundance comes to me."

"Uh huh, well, don't look now, but Mr. Abundance is walking over here with fierce purpose if you ask me." Kenna swung her legs to standing, kissed Sage quickly on the cheek, and held her beer up in a toast to her approaching brother before walking away.

"I need to talk to you," Garrett said, seeming almost winded.

"Okay."

He gently took her arm, and while she was still admiring the way he filled out a dress shirt, now rumpled and rolled at the sleeves, he led her farther away from the barn.

"So, here's the thing," he said now that they were alone. He was flustered or nervous maybe? "I'd like to, um, revisit the 'never ever.'"

She knew what he was talking about and as he crowded closer, she couldn't find her wit.

"I feel like we are heading off in a direction, and I'm. . . shit. . . did you tell Travis we were friends?"

Sage nodded.

"Why?"

"I didn't exactly say we were friends, I said that we were friendly. You know, now that I'm not simply lusting after you, we have gotten to know each other. Right?"

"Yeah, we are, but not as friends. I realize at your house last week I was weird and it may have felt like I was backing up, but then I said I didn't want you to go to dinner with Chris and"—he took her arms—"Sage, I don't want to be your friend."

"Okay. I thought since we'd sort of stopped being flirty and things cooled off that we should. . . if you don't want to be friends, what—"

"Things haven't cooled off. I want you," he said as if he had to get it out or he'd burst. "All of you. I'm losing my mind here. I can't sleep and that 'never ever' sex keeps rolling around in my head. I have absolutely no idea what I'm doing or how to fit things together, but tell me what you want"—his hands went to her face—"tell me how we move past 'never ever.'"

Sage's heart drummed steady and deep in her chest. It was heady to be on the other side of want for a change. Garrett was babbling, pouring out words she never imagined hearing, so she was honest. "I need something after sex. As fun as I'm sure your headboard is, when it comes to you, I need a relationship after I catch my breath."

He nodded. "I. . . can do that," he said, looking like his mind was racing, trying to order exactly what he was promising. "I want that."

Seeing him so vulnerable, straining to erase the 'never ever," Sage let go and allowed herself to love him all the way. The release made her playful.

"Is that so? Huh." She backed him up to the side of the house. The moon was only a sliver and the night sky was black. She took his hands and, up on her tiptoes, it was an effort even with both of her hands, to hold his above his head. Awkward but sexy awkward, which wasn't exactly naughty, but close. "What do I do now?" she said into the side of his neck, her lips grazing the softness.

Garrett grinned and looked up at his hands. "Kiss me." His voice low, sounding like he'd done this before.

She kissed along his jaw and made her way to his mouth, touching her lips to his, and barely allowing her tongue to taste. Garrett closed his eyes, releasing his hands easily as he grabbed her around the waist.

"What now?" she asked, not nearly as confident because her heart was racing something awful.

Garrett leaned in, his mouth close to her ear. "Now, we're going to say goodnight to the happy couple, we're going back to my place, and I'm going to. . ."

Sage inhaled slowly, letting the exhale slip past her lips as he continued whispering into her ear. The man should definitely be in charge of all fantasies going forward. She was grateful his arms were still wrapped around her as he kissed her collarbone, and she lost all sense of balance. *Nice to Naughty* didn't have a chapter that came close to the buzz of him telling her exactly what he was going to do. It wasn't naughty, it was being desired in a way she had never understood before that moment. He wanted to touch her body, show her what she did to him, his heart. It wasn't taking her up against a wall, although his words were certainly as bone melting. It was the slow whisper of a man who had waited, learned about her, and now knew exactly what she needed. When he was finished seducing her, she leaned against his chest, her head in the curve of his shoulder. Gently, he set her back, allowing her to find her footing.

"Oh my," fell from her lips as she pulled him back toward the wedding to say their good-byes.

Garrett smiled, the same way he had the day he'd been on his knees, and Sage wondered how long it would take to get to his house. "Never ever" had turned to "right now" and she was prepared to run there if necessary.

Chapter Nineteen

His house was tucked away near the orchard, and unlike the main house, this one was not painted white—it wasn't exactly painted at all. The wood, weathered gray and a golden color, blended together. It almost looked like a quilt. Opening the door, he gestured for her to walk ahead of him while he turned on the lights. The short drive from the barn had been quiet and filled with expectation. Standing in the entry to his home, her breath was unsteady.

"Can I get you a drink?"

Sage shook her head and walked into his living room. Two leather sofas the color of strong coffee sat near a table that appeared metal in the dim light. On one wall, a large flat-screen television was surrounded by floor-to-ceiling shelves. What looked like a river rock fireplace sat opposite. She stepped closer to the shelves and noticed pictures: some faces she recognized and others she didn't. Black and white, color, drawings that she knew were from Paige and some others with Spanish words written in crayon. Books on soil and plants. Several on plant pathology, but also more fiction than she had thought he would read. The shelves were full; pillows and blankets were arranged on the couch. She could feel

Garrett behind her, but he was quiet, so she walked to the fire-place.

"This is beautiful," she said, breaking the silence and noticing her voice carried in the high-ceilinged room. "Did you build it?"

"Sort of." He moved next to her. "These"—he ran a hand along the wall—"are all of the rocks we collected from the topsoil when we prepped the off-site acres. That land was a bitch and took us twice as long as it should have, so I knew I wanted to see these rocks every day."

"A reminder that things could be worse?" She smiled.

"I guess." His eyes softened and he reached out to take her coat.

"This is a real home," she said, not even sure what that meant.

"Were you expecting something different?"

She shrugged. "Maybe. I don't have a very good idea of what a man living alone looks like, I suppose. Four sisters. And our society sort of leads you to believe men live with the minimum until they find a woman to warm up the place, but this is full and rich."

"Thanks."

He showed her the rest of the house, which quickly led to the upstairs bedroom. Sage stopped at the door, trying to process exactly what she was looking at. Garrett's bedroom had a large attic feel to it, or maybe, she thought, a hayloft. She noticed a dresser off on one wall and a chair near another door she assumed led to the bathroom, but her eyes kept returning to the bed. King size and sitting front and center, it was made of the same wood as the rest of the house and positioned under a huge hole in the ceiling. Moving closer to get a better look, Sage glanced up and saw the night sky.

"My God," she said on an exhale.

Garrett laughed. "If I had known I'd get this reaction, I would have brought you here sooner."

"This is the most unbelievable bed, room for that matter, that I have ever seen. What made you, I mean, did you have a designer put this together?"

166

"No. I told the builder I wanted a big bed. That I need to watch the weather, and I like to watch the stars. The room came out of that discussion and a couple of beers."

Sage nodded, taking in the ink dark sky flooded with endless stars. She felt as though she were outside of her body in a different place or country instead of an hour away from her own house. Once again, he made her think of those twelve-dollar magazines, but this time, she was standing in the middle of one with him. When he turned to her, her hands went to his chest and Garrett kissed her, slow and deep. She'd always imagined he would be sexy anywhere, but surrounded by his home and the life he'd created for himself was overwhelming. Right when Sage thought it impossible, she loved him more.

Whispering into her neck, he unzipped her dress and as the sparkly fabric pooled at her feet, they both looked down and realized she was standing in nothing but lace and black rubber boots.

In the middle of all the heat, all the need, they laughed and he pulled her into bed as she kicked off the muckers.

❧❀❧

Garrett had never been a romantic when it came to sex. Sex was sex and as long as the woman he chose to get naked with had a smile on her face when he made excuses and negotiated a quick exit back to his life, he never questioned his motive or his abilities. Sex was fun. Sometimes, it was slow and easy and other times, it was a quick fuck, but it was always a good time. While he was occasionally sappy and did admit to crying at the end of the movie *Rudy*, he had no delusions that sex meant love. It was bodies moving and satisfying one another. He knew that to be true until his hands touched her skin, until his chest was pressed against hers, until she was under him and he was wrapped in her. As she reached up to kiss him, her eyes barely open and her lips panting his name, Garrett had no idea what was happening, but it was the furthest thing from sex he'd ever experienced.

He moved over her naked body, past the places that were still chilled by the night air and the parts that were warm and silky. She was stunning in his bed, under the stars and uninhibited. There were no more games for them to play or fantasies to joke about because this was it. Her hands claimed the ridges of his back, around his shoulders, and as his entire body grew taut with need, he hoped like hell he could give her what she wanted because never before had he wanted something so completely.

"Please," she whispered, and whatever plan he had for teasing her all night would have to wait as he slid into her and lost himself once again in the liquid silver of her eyes.

❧❧❧

Sage woke to the expanse of Garrett's back. It was early and the blue light of morning misted over them. She touched his shoulder. The man was a mountain of worn muscle that had nothing to do with a gym and so much to do with who he was, what he did. A faded scar ran across his left shoulder blade and a thicker, newer one on his elbow. No tattoos, only sun-kissed skin that was surprisingly soft in comparison to his hands.

Carefully turning under the weight of his arm, Sage thought it appropriate that all of Garrett's soft parts would be covered up. She'd seen him hundreds of times elsewhere, in motion, but there was something so intimate about watching a man sleep. She knew that sounded silly considering everything they'd done to one another last night, but watching him sleep seemed as sensual. Well. . . almost. Rolling onto her back, she pulled the covers up to her nose as if she could somehow contain the eruption of happiness as it spread across her face. Garrett shifted and pulled her closer into the warmth of him.

Sage had never thought about sex as giving herself to someone before. The two other partners she'd had were both more. . . experimental. One had been fumbling and figuring things out the whole way through, which was a fine experience for a first time. She wasn't complaining. She'd been a freshman in college and although the relationship hadn't lasted long, that time stood out as an education and milestone since most of her friends had reached it in high school. Missionary, simple, and perfectly un-bottom-drawer-worthy. After college, she met, and after the customary time, got naked with Brad Pierce, VP of development. Their relationship had been one-sided and what her very first self-improvement book called toxic. Sex with him was a series of internal monologues that went something like—*Am I doing this right? You want me to put what, where?* Brad, while starched and pressed in their staff meetings, had leaned toward kinky in his bedroom. For Sage, it had never been enjoyable. Things with Brad were always too much work for her and never exciting enough for him, which was fine because if sex with him was adult sex, she wasn't interested.

What she'd wanted, what she'd imagined it could be, was what had happened with Garrett. He had undressed her and touched her as if she were a present he never expected to receive. There was passion and need mixed with the hesitation of getting to know someone for the first time. It wasn't only about discovering what he could do to her or moaning and talking dirty to get him off. What had happened under the stars of his bed was a series of questions they asked one another with their bodies. He was gentle and then he wasn't as they melted together, teased, and let go. Sage finally knew what all the fuss was about as she burst into hundreds of tiny pieces and he held them all together.

She'd given a part of herself to him, knew she loved him, and that had made all the difference. There was a time she'd hung onto his every word, but this wasn't something as frivolous as all that; this was breathless sex with someone she knew she'd still enjoy once they put their clothes back on.

✿❦✿

"I'm not going to lie, the whole fantasy thing is messing with me right now," Garrett said softly because he knew she was awake.

He rolled over onto his back to find her naked in his bed, laughing. Letting out a breath, he kissed her shoulder, and in the muted light of early morning, tried desperately to silence the voice in his head.

What the hell did you do? You don't know the first thing about having a relationship or giving her more. But that sure didn't stop you last night, now did it?

It was true he'd been prepared to promise her anything to get rid of "never," but he'd expected they'd get to his place, have rushed, back-scraping sex, a couple of times maybe. She'd scream his name, throw her head back and forth, and he'd tell her how fucking hot she was. That's how he'd pictured it in his mind. His male mind would have gladly sacrificed a limb for that, but that's not what had happened.

The word hot felt stupid now like something left behind at a bar. She had stolen his breath and been achingly responsive. Every time she touched him, it felt like she was handing him a part of herself. Her eyes were open, looking into him as she arched off his bed and ran her hands over his body. Her lips were urgent and, when he thought he might go back to calling her hot, she'd soften and show him something he didn't feel good enough to take. They'd gone down to the kitchen sometime in the middle of the night and had eaten cold spaghetti. He would forever have the image of her, legs pulled up on the chair, tucked under his sweatshirt, smiling and teasing him until she'd climbed into his lap and made it impossible for him to ever look at his dining room again without seeing her in it.

"You're safe. You have nothing to worry about," she said, thankfully taking him out of his thoughts.

"Yeah?" He rolled on his side to face her.

She nodded slowly, turned toward him, and there went his breath again.

"How do you figure?"

"Are you looking for feedback?"

He laughed. "Not exactly, I *was* wondering how I measured up"—he pushed up on his elbows—"so to speak, to the fantasy."

Sage made a show of thinking. She was teasing. No way all of those moans were fake. *She'd had fun, hadn't she?*

Right when he was starting to get a little nervous, she said, barely louder than a whisper, "I don't even remember the fantasy."

He kissed her lightly. "Bottom-drawer material?" he asked, barely touching her warm skin.

Her eyes lit up and as she nodded, she slid on top of him and kissed him, surrounding him again with everything that came with being loved by Sage Jeffries. Just when he thought he'd seen all of her, she opened another space and invited him in.

Chapter Twenty

*A*s soon as the first sip of coffee hit his bloodstream a couple of weeks later, Garrett wondered about the weather. Last night, the forecast called for partly cloudy, but the sky looked thick like his shaving soap and almost as white. He moved to the cabinet and Jack sat up at attention, hoping for food.

He was tired, which was normal, and restless, which was not. He had no idea how he'd let this happen. How she'd gotten in, and how instead of working his way toward excuses and the inevitable let down when the relationship ended, he couldn't stop thinking about her—and not only at night. She was on his mind at work, he made extra stops by The Yard to see what music was playing before they opened and what kind of mood she was in. What had started as a bargain made in a lustful haze of fantasy had now turned to a look of knowing in her eyes. It was as if she could see into him now and that, he decided on the ride into the Rye family meeting, was the sole reason for the restlessness. He'd meant what he said when he told her he wasn't afraid of commitment. He wasn't afraid, he simply didn't think about it. Anything other than what he'd done his whole life, which was to keep the farm running, was uncomfortable.

For a moment last night, after he'd left her drowsy and curled up on her couch after a movie, he tried to convince himself it had been a mistake to cross the line, a mistake to make love to her. God that phrase "made love" could be added to the list of touchy-feely words Garrett tried to avoid. But, there was no denying that's what had happened after Logan's wedding and a few times since. They were making love, although when she'd pulled his hair in the shower a few nights ago, that was a whole lot more about pure and simple need. Whatever the label, while his restless brain now worried about the weather and the million things he needed done by noon, his heart sat warm and satisfied in his chest. If loving her created chaos within the rest of him, his heart didn't care. Where his heart was concerned, she was everything even if his mind scrambled for how "family" included room for anyone else. Tossing Jack a treat, Garrett grabbed his keys and his phone and set out for Libby's to meet, discuss, and most likely argue by the time he finished his pancakes.

❧❁❧

"I signed Libby and me up for bridge class at the community center. It starts next week, do you want to join us?"

"I do not," Garrett said, walking with his father out of the diner following their hour-long meeting.

"Sage is teaching."

"Is she? Well, I'm sure it'll be a great class. Why are you going with Libby? None of your male friends get excited about bridge?"

"She's my friend."

"Yeah, I know you see her at the diner, but I didn't think. . ."

His dad was suddenly uncomfortable. Garrett hadn't meant to make fun of bridge. Maybe his dad wanted the company. Maybe that's why he'd resorted to asking the woman who owned the diner. He barely knew her. Shit, he really didn't want to have to learn to play bridge.

"Do you want me to go with you so you don't have to take Libby?"

His father shook his head, and Garrett wondered by the way he'd stopped meeting his eyes if he'd hurt his feelings. "I'll go with you. It'll be. . . fun. You can tell Libby she's off the hook."

"Off the hook? She's totally into me." He climbed into his truck.

Garrett smiled. "Oh, is that so? I didn't realize you were in the market."

"I'm not," his father said, tipping his hat and driving away.

The man got a little loopier every day. Sage was teaching bridge. Was there anything the woman didn't do?

❧❧❧

Sage was in her first warrior pose on her deck by 5 a.m. the next morning. The sun was barely beginning to warm the sky so she could only see her body from the glow of the house lights. It didn't matter; she knew her set, could feel her way through it. On the exhale, she rolled her arms back at the shoulders and held the position, her eyes to the waning night sky. She loved early morning, the quiet and the newness of the day. This early in the morning, decisions for the day hadn't been made yet, and she imagined everyone on her block waking with their own set of worries, goals. There was something comforting about traveling the planet with other people. She didn't need to know them all, but it was good they were there.

He'd be awake, she thought, rolling her shoulders back the other way. He'd probably been for almost an hour before her. She couldn't begin to wonder what filled his mind first thing in the morning, but as hard as she tried to be sensible, she longed to be near him in the early sunrise hours. Sage had thought a lot about being in the "now" over the last few days, but now was filled with him touching her and loving her whether he knew it or not yet. Her now was the feel of his body, the rumble of his laughter, and that look he gave her as if he were learning something new about her every day. Her now was warm and delicious, but despite the comfort of it, she wasn't sure how it all fit into her tomorrow.

Placing both hands on the spongy black mat, Sage lowered her head into downward dog. The tension and questions hiding in her spine spilled off her back and she told herself to be conscious, to live her life because that was all she was given. There was no way to deny things were changing, but she still had her anchors in case she was heading into a storm.

After a set that left her drinking water in her kitchen on wobbly legs, Sage showered and dressed in jeans and an olive-green sweater. She had the day off today and once she picked up her dry cleaning and ran by the grocery store, she would be at Bao on Beverly Boulevard by eleven o'clock for her very first dim sum. It had been on her calendar for a couple of weeks, and she was expecting to love it. The pictures looked incredible, and the bartender there touted a cucumber martini that was "the best in LA." She highly doubted that, but she was intrigued. Her college roommate had gone out for dim sum every Sunday. Sage had never gone with her or with her sisters when they went into the city, because she was busy studying and then too busy trying to excel at a job she hated.

Since Brad, Sage enjoyed doing things on her own that were all hers. She didn't invite others along because she needed time "to be," as the book had said. She didn't want anyone's opinion on certain things before she had a chance to form her own. Her mother said this self-exploration was "lonely" and "kind of selfish," but Sage didn't see a problem with being a little selfish every now and then. If there was anything good to come of her time dating Brad, it was that she now understood the importance of keeping some things to one's self.

Walking out to her car, Sage wondered if Garrett liked dim sum. She felt certain he'd tried it, which was strange. Why did she project things onto other people and assume they'd done more exciting things than she had? Sage sighed and threw her dry cleaning into her trunk. She wondered if self-discovery ever ended. Was there a point when she would truly know herself? Sometimes after reading or watching something an expert suggested she integrate to be a "complete person," Sage wished she was like a grocery store turkey with one of those plastic things that popped up when she was cooked, finished.

As if he'd known she'd been thinking about him and was considering having dim sum with him instead of by herself, her phone vibrated with a text.

Crazy day today, but how about dinner?

Sage remembered her mother telling her that a boy should give at least two days' notice when he asked a girl out. Then and now, Sage thought that "rule" was ancient and weird, but as she glanced at her phone, she wondered if she was slipping. She hadn't seen Garrett for two days and had already started wanting him in her life—in all aspects, even the times that were meant for herself. This was no longer a fantasy. It wasn't something she could turn on or off in her mind. This was real, and Sage wasn't sure she'd done enough work on herself to be this close, this in love. She texted him back:

Sorry, can't. See you soon.

Chapter Twenty-One

"So here's what I was thinking after I showered and wondered if I should call you or spend another night alone," Garrett said, letting himself into her entryway after Sage opened the door a little after six the following evening. "Maybe now that I've given it up, that you've used my body several times, you're done with me."

She smiled, closed the door, and inhaled the smell of soap and clean cotton.

"We haven't seen each other and I know part of that is me, but I feel like part of it's you too. How was dim sum?"

Sage froze, not that she had anything to hide, but now that they were together, it did seem strange she had not invited him. "Kenna?"

"She didn't mean to, but we were talking about Chinese food and she mentioned you were trying your first dim sum."

"I—"

He held up his hand. "So, before those independent parts of us screw this up, I thought I'd drop by with Jack and food."

She looked around, not seeing Jack or food.

Garrett opened the front door to Jack sitting politely with a large paper bag in his mouth. "I left him outside in case you were busy again or had a hot date or—"

She took the food from Jack, set it on the table that no longer had the infamous flowers, and locked her front door. Pulling his jacket off and throwing it toward the rack, she kissed him fast and urgent as if all her fears, all her crap, could somehow be fixed if she kept touching him.

"I'm trying to keep a handle on things, but I'm slipping and you don't want. . . I honestly have no idea what you want. Sometimes I think we're even, but then I'm not sure we ever can be because of the way we started. Oh Christ, I sound nuts and I know you only came over for dinner, but I won't survive if I fall and you're not with me. Some other guy, sure, maybe, but not with you. And I'm not even positive you know how to love. I mean it's not like you've had relationships, right? Shoot, I'm sorry. Let's eat."

"Hold on, you already said you loved me, so now you're backing out?" He smiled and kissed her gently. "I know how to love," he said, and she almost believed him.

"Oh really? Have you ever been in love?"

"I'm not sure. I care about people, but I don't normally get involved."

"Why not?"

"Because I'm busy doing. . . things. You know how some people never buy a house or own a car?"

Sage nodded, hoping this was going somewhere productive, but probably not.

"It's like that. I spend my time doing other stuff."

"Don't you think love is a little different than a car?"

He shrugged and kissed her again. They separated, and she brought the bag into the kitchen.

"Sure, yes. That was what came off the top of my head. When you asked me if I've ever been in love, I'm trying to say that I've never gotten around to it."

Sage wasn't sure how to respond as she opened the cartons of Chinese and pulled out some napkins. This wasn't a typical "I don't do relationships" response. He'd never gotten around to it?

"You're thirty-four," she said, taking a seat on the couch and giving Jack one of those fried noodles they always sent in bulk.

Garrett nodded and sipped the beer she handed him, as if they were discussing a current event.

"Do you want to be with someone? Clearly you're into sex."

He smiled and Sage instantly replayed every touch, the way he closed his eyes right before they fell together as if he was collapsing into a warm pool of water.

"Sage, what we are doing is more than sex. I. . . care about you."

The brief hesitation spoke volumes, and Sage was sorry she'd asked.

"But that's not what we're talking about. You asked me if I've been in love, and that's different. I have some recent experiences with love considering both my brother and sister are stupid from it. Love, you know, after the honeymoon, seems to be all about living a life together. It's work. I can't say I've done that or that I've even thought about it. I plant, harvest, sell, and repeat. My life is about that farm."

"Like your dad."

"Yeah, I guess. But he was in love once. Didn't work out for him, but he went there."

"And you don't want that, you only want . . ." Suddenly feeling playful and desperately wanting to lighten the mood, she pursed her lips and squished her cleavage together.

Garrett laughed.

"What, are you laughing at my expert naughty? Here I thought I had mastered sexy."

"Sorry. I can't help it." He wrapped his arm around her waist. "Your sexiness has nothing to do with being naughty. It spills out of you. The sweet, the awkward, those eyes, and your hands, the way you dress, your neck, it's all part of something so much better than naughty. That's what makes it funny when you try."

"Are you sure you've never been in love?"

He laughed and kissed her neck. "Pretty sure."

She let out a slow breath as he unbuttoned her shirt. "That's a real shame, because I think you'd be excellent at it."

"Maybe I'll look into it." He picked her up, leaving the food. "Stay, Jack."

"You do that, put it on the calendar. You know, in between peas and spinach."

"We don't grow peas." He carried her into her bedroom.

"Huh, why not?"

"Joe Everett's farm does peas and celery. They cover that local market, so we don't step on their toes."

He put her on the bed. "I like that, how you work together. It's friendly and not competitive."

"We're up against the big guys. There's no time to compete. Besides, organic peas are a bitch to grow. Joe's good at it." He opened her last button, kissed his way around her neck, and found her breasts.

"Oh, well." Sage closed her eyes. "You grow spinach though."

Garrett nodded, his tongue gliding, making it almost impossible for her to speak, which was saying something.

"Kale?"

Garrett stopped playing with her body. She opened her eyes and he was looking at her, smiling.

"What?"

"Are you trying to turn me on with vegetables?"

She laughed and shrugged. "Does that work?"

He kissed her. "Everything seems to work with you."

❧❧❧

Sage woke the next morning before the sun and Garrett was gone. The note next to her on the pillow read:

Duty Calls
Garrett

Pulling the covers up over her head, she couldn't fall back to sleep. The card still lay on her pillow, she could smell him on her covers and for an instant, that wasn't terrifying. She felt surrounded by him. After a few more minutes of staring up at the ceiling, she got up, showered, and tried to talk herself into yoga over a piece of toast and tea. She'd resolved to be good when her phone vibrated with a text:

> *Sorry I had to leave.*
>
> *If you're not doing anything, I'd like to plant flowers with you.*
>
> *I'll be here most of the day. Come on up if you can.*

She smiled and texted back:

> *I'm not sure what I'm getting myself into, but I'd love to. See you soon.*

Chapter Twenty-Two

Sage arrived at Garrett's house two hours later, feeling as if they were more of a couple than she ever had before. The expectation scared her, but the sight of him standing among hundreds of cartons of flowers was worth the drive.

"Hey there," she said, walking over to him and taking in that he was even more beautiful among the dirt. He wasn't wearing the tool belt, but he was wearing the sexy gloves. When she'd told Kenna about the sexy, worn leather gloves, Kenna exclaimed that was the last straw and "only an insane person" thought gloves were sexy. Insane she must be then, because those things were deadly.

"Hey." He kissed her.

"I need to replace this section of the flower bed and I've always done this bed myself, but I thought I might invite you since…" He let out a breath instead of finishing his thought and then something shifted in his eyes. "So this"—he spread his arms wide—"is one of the projects on the calendar for today."

"Huh." She grabbed a pair of gloves that sat on a big tub of potting soil and put them on. It wasn't lost on her that he was letting her into something he did on his own or that she should return the gesture, but at that moment, she needed to keep things light. "So you're kind of like Martha Stewart. Is cleaning the gutters on the calendar too? Chicken coops?"

"You're very funny."

"I think so."

He laughed and even though he looked tired, he seemed happy. She knew she must be part of that because he was certainly part of her happiness these days.

"I'm not sure I've ever had my hands in the dirt, not like this."

"Well, you are in for a treat," he said, squinting and then putting his sunglasses on, which only enhanced the sexy gloves.

They scooped, squeezed, and shook root beds in silence for a few minutes. The smell of the morning dew and heat of the sun on her neck reminded Sage why she loved being out there. Jack sat obediently in the sun chewing on a bone.

"So, have you ever been in love?" he asked her.

Sage laughed, picked up a carton of tall purple flowers, and pulled her hat farther down on her head.

"So, have you?" he asked again, stopping to drink some water.

"Have I what?" The question with a question rarely worked, but she was having a great day and didn't feel like answering.

"Ever been in love."

She stood and shot him a look she hoped conveyed the answer.

"I mean other than me, and since we're on that subject, 'I love you' said while intoxicated does not count. So don't think you're going to get credit for loving me longer."

"Love credit, is that a thing?"

He laughed. "Answer the question."

"Yes, well, I thought I was in love. See, I've learned it all depends on where a person is at in their life. How they feel about themselves sort of shapes what kind of love they feel."

Garrett shook his head.

"I know, but it's not only Oprah. It's true. So, to answer your question, yes. I loved someone and. . . he didn't love me back."

Garrett kept working, so she did too.

"When were you in love with this asshole?"

Sage smiled.

"His name was Brad."

"Well, there's your problem right there."

"We worked together and things didn't work out. The end."

Garrett stood from his crouched position over square buckets of flowers and took off one glove. "Was he mean?"

Sage nodded. Garrett moved to planting flowers next to her, as if being closer would somehow help. For the next hour, they planted and Sage told the sob story she'd never told to another soul except for Kenna. Brad had been a few years older. She was infatuated. But some time into the relationship, she realized she was no longer a whole person; he'd made her feel small, like she wasn't enough. It was a tale told by women time and time again. Sage hated being part of it, hated that she'd allowed someone to make her feel less than. She explained to Garrett some of the things she'd learned about herself over the years and that she vowed never again to hand over her happiness to another person.

"So that's why you do so many things alone."

She nodded.

"I get that. I do things alone too. Especially since everyone's been moving on with their lives lately."

"Does that bother you?"

"That they've left? I. . . I don't think about it," he said, and she knew from the look on his face, that was a lie.

As promised, Garrett made sandwiches and they sat out on his deck.

"I have to check in with George, but do you want to go out later? Maybe somewhere that doesn't involve dirt or booze?" he said jokingly.

"I have the symphony tonight."

"I can't believe I'm going to say this, but I'll go with you."

"I only have one ticket and I. . . I'd rather go by myself."

"Okay, afraid to take a farmer?"

She laughed. "I've seen you cleaned up. No, it has nothing do with you. It's my thing."

"Do you want to explain?"

"Not particularly."

They sat in silence.

"When I remade my life, I decided there are certain things I do for myself and they stay that way, sort of like my anchors in case I need to find my footing again. Yoga, the symphony, and crossword puzzles are my anchors. I do them alone. They're mine."

He waited so she explained further.

"When the relationship ended, we had mutual friends and places we ate. I was a little lost for a while. Then I read in this book that every woman needs anchors. There was some metaphor about storms, not specific to men but life storms. I loved that idea, so I created some of my own. I guard them. You should understand. Isn't this place one huge anchor for you?"

"Yeah, but I invited you over to play in my dirt."

She laughed.

"I'm kidding. I get it. Anchors, I like that," he said.

"Yeah?"

"I like you." He pulled her close.

"That's good, because I like you too."

"I know."

"Oh, well, I'm not sure how you feel about me, so maybe you could show me?"

"But you're all dirty."

"And here I thought you liked it dirty," slipped right off her lips in a husky voice Sage barely recognized.

Garrett raised his eyebrows in surprise. "That"—he took her hand and led her into the house—"was very naughty. Damn, have you been practicing?"

She hit his shoulder. "You wish."

He kissed her and gently rolled her onto the couch until she was on top of him, looking down with those sparkling eyes. He wasn't sure if it was that she'd been hurt or if he was simply happy to spend a day off planting flowers with her. Whatever it was, he was so damn grateful and his chest filled with the need to tell her, to give back everything she gave him.

"I love you," he said, softly wiping a smudge of dirt off her cheek. "To answer the question you asked me before. No, I've never felt like this, but I know I love you. I can feel it everywhere."

Her tear landed on his neck. She wiped her eyes with a smile. "I love you too," she said, and then she showed him.

Chapter Twenty-Three

S age had managed to break two glasses less than an hour into the lunch rush. She was off her game. Too much time relaxing, she thought with a smile. Once everyone was refilled and happy, she stepped outside to catch her breath. Taking out her phone, she returned a text from Chris asking if she was free to grab coffee. When she'd told him she couldn't have dinner, he'd downshifted to coffee. The man was persistent, but it was time to let him know she was involved, unavailable, in love, all of the above. She went with the simple excuse that she'd reconnected with someone from her past and she wished him well. He replied with one of those crying faces and a request to keep him in mind if things changed. Feeling better that it was done, Sage took one more deep breath of the afternoon sunshine and returned to work.

Garrett's father was sitting at the end of the bar, talking with Kenna. Herbert Rye was a combination of all his children, as if he'd given pieces of himself to each one. Sage never wondered about their mother because so much of Herb was reflected in his kids. He sat with his reading glasses propped on his nose, and Sage couldn't tell whether he held an iPad or an e-reader from where she stood making a screwdriver at the opposite end of the bar. She handed the drink to the waiting server, poured a woman with a silver bob and bright red fingernails another glass of fume blanc, then moved down the bar, checking as she went.

"Hi, you two. I sort of feel like one of those geniuses at the Apple Store. Whatcha doing there, Mr. Rye?"

Kenna rolled her eyes, clearly frustrated.

"Hi, dear, and please call me Herb. Kenna made me donate all of my paper books and return my library books because she bought me this"—he held up what she could now see was an iPad—"for Christmas. Wave of the future and all."

"It's going to be great if you take a minute to get used to it. Change has never been his strength," Kenna said, shaking her head at Sage.

"That's not true. I'm progressive. I'm all for being kinder to the environment, but can you make this font bigger?"

Kenna took the device from her father and after a few touches handed it back.

He smiled and leaned over to kiss her. "Thank you, sweetheart."

"You're welcome. Now, promise you're going to use it?"

"I am. I downloaded *Grapes of Wrath*. Libby and I are going to reread some of the classics."

"That's great. Are you two part of a book club?"

"Yeah, our own." He winked at Sage, and she wasn't sure if he was joking or trying to tell her something.

Refilling his soda water with lime, Sage told them both about her evening at the symphony and made them laugh with her story of getting completely turned around and lost. No matter how long Sage lived in Los Angeles, she still managed to find opportunities to go the wrong way.

"Will I see you up at the farm this weekend?" Herb asked.

"No, I'm afraid not. I'm going back up north to stay with my parents. I have a hot air balloon ride scheduled for Saturday."

"That's exciting. Is your whole family going?"

"Nope, only me."

"Dad, you'll learn Sage does all these incredibly interesting things all on her own," Kenna said, smiling and then excusing herself when she heard a customer tell a server there were no more paper towels in the ladies' room.

"Why?" Herb asked.

"Why a hot air balloon?"

"No, why do you do things on your own? Isn't it more fun with a friend?"

"Sometimes, but I've been working on myself for a few years, and part of that is doing things on my own, being my own friend. Do you know what I mean?"

He nodded. "I sure do. You're loving yourself."

"Yes, I suppose I am." She smiled.

"And you don't want anyone getting in the way of that."

Sage nodded and excused herself to cash out two guys who looked like they needed to get back to the office.

When she returned, Herb said, "I noticed Garrett's flowers. You two did a nice job."

Sage knew her face was beaming at the mention of his son's name. She was learning to accept her reaction.

"Love is a wonderful thing, don't you think?" Herb asked, taking another sip of his water.

"I do."

"I've spent so many years with that boy, and I can tell you he never tries to steal your thunder. He's spent his life letting other people shine."

Sage felt her heart pulse. She wasn't sure if he'd meant it the way it came out, but the statement was sad. *He'd spent his life letting other people shine.* The words trickled through her mind again as Garrett's father gathered up his iPad and left a few bills on the bar.

"Thanks for stopping by," she said.

"Always a pleasure talking with you, Sage. You might want to ask Garrett to go with you in that balloon. George and I can hold down the fort for a weekend." He winked again and was gone.

Maybe she should.

He never tries to steal your thunder. She heard the words long after Herb had left. *What did that mean? What about his thunder, Garrett's light?*

For the first time in what felt like a very long time, Sage wasn't worried about herself or her anchors. She loved him and fearlessly wanted him on her adventures. It was time, she thought, clearing plates and wiping down her bar.

Sage took the remote and switched the music to Norah Jones.

※ぐ※

The USDA inspector presented his badge and then grilled Garrett in his office for over two hours on policies and procedures. He'd review the information and get back to them with his decision about a formal investigation, that's how he ended it. "Formal investigation" buzzed across Garrett's splitting headache as he watched the black sedan drive away. Sinking down at his desk, he put his face in his hands, but then at the bite of anxiety, he stood and began pacing. Apparently, the USDA had received a complaint from a former employee. This was what happened when things got so fucking big, he told himself as he grabbed the paperwork the inspector had left and walked out of the building. Makenna had asked him to meet her at The Yard when he was done. It was nearly five o'clock, but she mentioned their dad was taking Paige to a movie, so she'd hang around until he showed up.

There weren't many people at the bar when Garrett arrived and Sage called him over while he waited for Kenna, but his mind was on hearing from George. They were both racking their brains trying to figure out if they'd fired anyone recently who would hold a grudge. Garrett guessed a person fired from any job held a grudge, but there hadn't been any recent drama, not that he could recall. Distracted, he took a seat and tried to listen to Sage, but his thoughts kept wandering. They'd grown too big, and that was part of the problem. He no longer knew everyone who worked for them. The days of meeting workers in the early morning hours and confirming duties on a dry-erase board were over. He didn't look his team in the eye, know their stories, share coffee with them anymore. Things had changed. There was that damn word again—change, he thought, checking his phone for what felt like the hundredth time and wondering where the hell Kenna was.

"Yeah, so what do you think?"

"About what?" he asked, trying to tune back into Sage and not scream, "This is it, folks. Ryeland Farms is going to be brought to its knees by some disgruntled jackass!"

"Taking the weekend, hot air balloon, up north?"

"I thought you did this stuff on your own?"

"I do normally," she said, her tone less enthusiastic as she put three open beers on a server's tray.

"I'm. . . I don't think I can get away."

"Okay."

"Yeah, there's stuff going on and I. . . so no."

"No," she confirmed.

Garrett was instantly annoyed at the tone of her voice. Granted, he hadn't told her the whole sordid shit storm heading toward him, toward his family, but he wasn't in the mood for Sage and her get-out-and-experience-life campaign. That wasn't his world, and anytime he did step away, things went wrong. He couldn't afford for things to go wrong. The hum of the bar started to grate on him. He didn't need this shit. *Where the fuck is Kenna?*

"I need to go, but I'll talk to you when you get back." He stood and left as Kenna gestured to him and opened her laptop at the corner bar table.

Sage said nothing, and while he was grateful for her silence, he would later realize what Sage was offering and how badly he'd screwed it up. His family, their farm came first, and he'd face the consequences of that if necessary.

As Kenna began telling him things he already knew about the complaint that was filed two days ago, Garrett remembered his senior prom. He'd asked Michelle Miller. She'd been in his Spanish class, and her friend was going with a buddy of his. She had a crush on Garrett, or so he was told, so he agreed to go. It was May, which was harvest season for broccoli, cabbage, carrots, and citrus trees. They'd been busy and he'd forgotten to pick up his tux before the shop closed. He was sorry. That's what he'd told her at four o'clock the day of prom. She went with her friends and Garrett remembered being annoyed that she hadn't understood, that she never talked to him again. "It was a dance," he told Kenna later that night while they ate dinner. After trying to explain to him the importance of that particular dance, Kenna shook her head and he left the table.

Later that night, lying in his bed, he might have known something was not right, that he wasn't living the normal life of a kid his age, but he shook it off for two reasons—he didn't care because he was doing what he loved, and he was so tired that he hadn't had the energy to think about it for one more minute.

"So, George thinks it's one of the older guys we hired in shipping. He kept taking smoke breaks and was always late. According to the final warning, he loaded three orders on the wrong truck and the driver had to go all the way across town. He didn't get home until after seven and two of our restaurants were pissed. Richard fired him. It was clean."

"But he didn't file a claim for wrongful discharge, he filed with the AD?" Garrett asked.

Kenna nodded. "Yeah, I guess he figured that would hurt more. He's clearly pissed off. You answered all of his questions; maybe they'll schedule an inspection, maybe not. Either way they'll see there's no need for an investigation. George has been through inspections before. This isn't a big—"

"Please don't tell me this isn't a big deal. It is a big deal. Who hired this guy?"

"I don't think that matters. I looked at his application. He came from Highland Farms, no complaints. We followed procedure."

He let out a deep breath. Garrett had never been a fan of "that's how it is." He liked things he could fix and because he was distracted playing relationship and not around to personally do what needed to get done, they'd now have an inspector up their ass. *Shit!*

He stood and walked out.

Chapter Twenty-Four

*S*age would look back on the argument and realize she should have let him go, but she'd felt foolish for asking and her pride was hurt. He was distracted and clearly upset, but pride was a powerful thing and she wanted to clarify she didn't *need* him to go with her. I was silly, but at the same time, there was no reason she should feel uncomfortable asking him to go away with her, to do something other than watch movies and eat. They were in a relationship. That's what people in love did—they shared parts of themselves, went to the airport occasionally.

Catching up with him in the parking lot after he stormed out on Kenna, she sensed as she approached his truck that he was ready for a fight. She wasn't sure what happened back in the bar, but whatever it was, he didn't need to be a complete ass. Maybe she was looking for a fight too, which was good because that's exactly what she got.

"Garrett?"

"Jesus," she heard him say under his breath as if she were some nagging woman. "Can we please talk about this later?" he asked, holding the door handle.

"Is something wrong? You're pissed, I can see that, but I was simply trying to—"

"Okay, here's the thing. I'm giving this relationship thing my best effort, but I have shit that I'm dealing with that has nothing to do with you."

"Okay. Why don't you talk to me about it then?"

He laughed over seething anger. "This isn't going to be something you'll find in one of your books, Sage. This is real life, my life, and all the pressure that goes along with that. I told you I couldn't go with you on a hot air balloon ride. Work is my priority. What we do on the side—"

"Excuse me?"

"What?"

"What we do on the side?"

"Come on, Sage. I'm not getting into this. That's not what I meant."

"No, that's exactly what you meant. And you know, I should be grateful for what I'm getting, right? Seeing as you're Mr. Fantasy, I should be honored you're even keeping me on the side." Now she was seething too.

"You're being ridiculous. And you're the one who came up with the whole fantasy thing, spilling your heart all over my truck."

"That's right, I did and you've been going along and why not, you're getting laid." Garrett walked toward her and she jumped back. "This was good. I'm glad I talked to your father today. I'm glad I asked you to do something that would require you to step into my life for even a weekend. This is good information. Whatever this is"—she gestured between the two of them—"you're free to go."

Garrett shook his head in frustration tinged with what looked like exhaustion.

Sage laughed. "This was never going to work because we are not on equal footing."

"Did you read that in one of your books?" he scoffed.

"And the minute things get interesting"—she ignored him and continued—"that you have to give of yourself, you default back to 'Hey, I never wanted this,' and you're right. You didn't. So, I'm done."

Garrett looked at her for a few beats. She could see him start to sort through his feelings and then she saw it in his eyes the minute he shut down. Without another word, he got in his truck and left.

❧❧❧

Garrett would have given anything to simply go back to the way he felt the night he picked her up from the restroom. Things were simple, the boundaries were clearly drawn, and he didn't have this goddamn ache in his chest every time he remembered the look on her face. He could brush this off as their first fight, right? If he did read the same books Sage did, wouldn't that be in there somewhere? Dropping to the couch, what happened earlier felt like more than a fight, heavier than a disagreement. She had asked for more that night they had done away with "never ever" and he'd given her more than he ever had with any other woman. They'd been out to eat. Maybe it was more like takeout, but there was a lot of cuddling on the couch, which was something. They'd planted flowers, but now she wanted even more. Well, didn't that just figure. Every day couldn't be a damn fantasy. He had work, things on his mind, and she didn't seem to care. That wasn't fair either.

"Shit," he said out loud to Jack. "This is why, exactly why we don't. . . oh, forget it." Jack licked his leg and fell back to sleep. Garrett grabbed two pillows off his bed and settled on the couch for the night. There was no way he was sleeping in his bed. His sheets still smelled like her. Hell, if this was the ending it felt like, he'd have to burn the damn house down because she was every-where.

Putting a pillow over his head, he tried to sleep and when that was no use, he opened his laptop and did what he did best—he worked.

Chapter Twenty-Five

Driving the rental car from the airport to her parents' house, Sage replayed the argument for what felt like the tenth time. The painful truth came out in arguments and since this had been their first one, there were probably lessons to learn. She had his attention when she was in his bed and out of his bed as long as something didn't come up. She was on the side, that's what he'd said, and although most of what they had said was clearly in anger, the "on the side" part stuck. She didn't do the sidelines anymore and she didn't wait or beg. "You see," she told herself, pulling into her parents' driveway, "this is why we have anchors, for this very reason." And then she started to cry. *Damn it. The upside, find the silver lining, Sage.* She wiped her tears and grabbed her bag out of the trunk. Taking in a breath of crisp air before she walked through the door of her parents' home, Sage told herself she was away and she would be in beautiful Napa on Saturday. A hot air balloon ride, her solitary adventure; that's how she liked it anyway.

He'd screwed up. By the time he had finished breakfast the next morning, things had already settled down. Kenna and George had provided additional documentation. They were doing everything they could and Garrett spoke to the inspector again, who hinted that there would "most likely" not even be an inspection, let alone an investigation. They weren't out of the woods yet, but Garrett felt better. Until the anger and frustration subsided and he realized what he had done.

He'd known from the minute he told her he loved her that he would screw up. He couldn't have guessed it would be this soon. The responsibility of running things, the sometimes burden of supporting what had been done for generations, had messed with his head and gotten in the way of loving her. *This is why we don't get involved*, some stupid voice he barely recognized whispered.

Standing alone on his deck, he looked over at the flowerbed. They'd only finished half, but it looked beautiful and fresh, like her. Garrett fed Jack, dropped him off at the main house, and did one of the things he'd always committed to in life—he set out to fix his mistake.

Driving up Highway 10, he tried not to question what he was doing, where he was going. This wasn't him. He didn't do "gestures" as his annoying sister had put it. He'd led his entire life being practical, right and wrong, simple. He liked it that way, or at least, he thought he did until her. Until she looked at him, touched him, and filled him with things he had no idea he even needed. He'd been perfectly comfortable with his world, his work, until she came along. How was it possible that now he was more himself with Sage than he ever was without her?

Keith Urban was singing something sad and desperate from the speakers, so Garrett hit the volume and rode in silence. When he was younger, maybe ten, his dad took him for new boots. He had argued all the way to the store that the boots he had were fine. They were comfortable, he'd said, but his dad insisted it was time for a new pair. They tried on a few different styles at Millie's Western Wear, and nothing was working until the guy with a handlebar mustache brought out a pair of handcrafted leather work boots from Rick Leighton. Rick was a local and Garrett could still remember the smell of leather when the guy crouched in front of the chair and opened the box. He slid his foot into the boots. Garrett laced them up himself, and was never the same. He may have been a kid at the time, but he grew to learn that the boots fit him like a glove because they were made by a man who knew how boots were supposed to fit. Corners weren't cut, and right there he learned about craftsmanship. Rick still made boots, and Garrett bought three pairs a year without fail.

Sage was like his first pair of those boots. The sweet pull of her mouth, the way her eyes woke up every time he walked into a room as if he meant something to her. He never imagined meaning something to any woman, let alone a woman like her. She had five or six holes in her ears and her nail polish was nuts. She dressed in a way that made him dizzy most of the time and her legs and ass had the same effect. All of it ruined him and as he pulled off the freeway to grab another coffee, he had a sinking feeling he was never going to make it back. Back to his life before she told him she loved him, before she became more than something glittering behind the bar.

She felt so right that he hardly remembered what it was like before he was allowed to touch her, kind of like the boots. The road stretched out in front of his headlights and Garrett flipped to podcasts Kenna had loaded on his phone. Talk, at least someone else talking, seemed safe.

❧❀❧

Sage heard the doorbell ring, both dogs bark, and continued trying to figure out seventeen down. Dylan. . . Aquinas. . . She knew it, it was right there on the tip of her brain, but instead, she kept humming Bob Dylan's *Blowin' in the Wind*, which was distracting. She set the newspaper down when she heard Hollis say, "Oh well, let me get her," and then call up the stairs. Damn it, who was at the door for her? She hoped to God it wasn't Christian, her barely-a-friend from high school, back for another round of look how gorgeous my fiancée is, because she was not in the mood. Swinging her legs around, Sage decided whoever it was could handle her red-and-pink-striped socks and the few specks of mascara below her eyes because she was still sulking. Hollis called her name again as she opened the door and went to the stairs.

"I'm coming." She tried to find a smile, but she about fell down the stairs when she saw her sister standing next to Garrett Rye with her wide eyes and dangling wine glass.

"Sage, your friend stopped by or drove, how long did you drive, Garrett?"

His eyes were on her. "It doesn't matter."

"It doesn't matter, did you hear that, little sister? This. . . man drove all day and you've decided to greet him in. . . Dr. Seuss socks."

"He's seen me in worse. What are you doing here?"

Hollis pursed her lips and slowly backed out of the entryway. Garrett said nothing, so she walked down a few more stairs, leaned against the railing, and folded her arms. He looked ruffled, tired, and as hard as she tried, she couldn't stop from visualizing him in her bed. *Damn it.*

"I'm sorry, I probably should have called."

Sage remained silent.

Garrett dropped a small leather bag off his shoulder and she watched it fall.

"Are you planning on staying?"

He walked to her.

"I'm sorry."

The heart she thought was properly broken began drumming in her chest. "For what?"

"You. . ." He looked over his shoulder as Hollis and Annabelle ducked their heads back into the living room. "Is there somewhere we can talk?"

Sage tilted her head and realized she was still pissed. Sure, he was standing in front of her and he'd worn the leather jacket she knew smelled like all kinds of wonderful male, but he'd hurt her, so she wasn't in a rush to make him comfortable.

"Here's good."

She saw a hint of a smirk, the acknowledgment he knew she was going to make him work for it. Clearly up to the challenge, he stepped up to her.

"You invited me," he said, and she swallowed a lump in her throat. "I should have been paying attention because that was a big deal. I was pissed about work and. . . there's no explanation. I was an asshole and I'm sorry. You had every right to assume I'd want to go on a hot air balloon ride with you, that I'd want to meet the people important to you."

"My family."

"Right, your family. We are. . . together."

"Were."

"Sure. We *were* together. It was special, different that you wanted me to come with you. I blew it and I'm sorry. It's gorgeous up here, by the way."

Sage said nothing. She'd learned silence from the master.

Garrett slowly stepped up two more steps and touched her shoulder.

"I like the socks."

"Thank you."

He waited her out, his chest moving in and out. She could smell the coffee on his breath.

"So why the change of heart? Things aren't as bad as you thought, so now you're feeling all warm and fuzzy?"

"Did I ever tell you about when my dad took me to buy new boots?"

Sage shook her head, still trying for stoic and uninterested, even though his cheeks were flushed and she couldn't reconcile his beautiful mass standing in the entryway of her parents' home. *Who was watching the farm?*

"Well, it's a good story. I'll tell you and"—he looked over his shoulder again—"your sisters sometime, but right now, I drove up here because I love you and I want in on your adventures."

"And that you're sorry."

"Yeah, that too. I *am* sorry." His smile reached his eyes and he played with her dangling starfish earrings.

"They're not all adventures, and I love you too."

Their eyes met. "It's all an adventure with you, Sage."

She had tried to keep it together, put him in his place, act cold even, but she simply wasn't that woman so she jumped into his arms, wrapped her legs around his waist, and kissed him. She would have let him take her up against the wall if only to finally have a story to tell Kenna, but her father came around the corner and asked Garrett if he wanted a beer.

Chapter Twenty-Six

*I*t was still dark when they left for Napa the next morning, armed with a Thermos full of hot coffee and a blanket. It was her hot air balloon ride and not only had she invited him, her excitement was contagious. He found himself wanting everything she wanted for this bottom drawer that seemed so important. He checked his phone once and then shut it off.

Garrett had never considered himself an artsy guy, but standing in that grass field in the early hours with her, he was sure he could have written a song or a poem, maybe even painted a canvas. Sage wore a multicolored sweater, which she informed him was a poncho. The morning was cold enough for him to put his hands in his coat pockets and stood in contrast to the surge of open flame warming the air inside the huge rainbow balloon lying on its side. Garrett had been to Napa a few times, even did a wine tour once, but he'd never been in a hot air balloon. It was strange, he thought, that he had never even considered if he wanted to go for a balloon ride. Now, holding her hand, her smile was brighter than the flame, he'd never wanted anything more. Love was dizzying that way.

As the basket tipped upright with the now-inflated balloon above it, Garrett wondered if he should be nervous. He wasn't sure how these things worked or what to expect, but the guy helped Sage into the basket first and when she held out her hand for him, he knew he was a goner. He couldn't think of a place he wouldn't follow her to.

It turned out hot air balloon rides were a little touch and go. Garrett understood the hot air part, but the steering felt a bit unreliable. As he peeked over the edge, Sage laughed.

"What?"

"Nothing." She stepped in front of him and wrapped herself in his arms. "I'm not sure I've ever seen you this uncomfortable."

"I'm not uncomfortable."

She leaned forward, taking his arms along with her, and Garrett jerked back. Smiling over her shoulder, she said, "You were saying?"

"Fine. Maybe it's a height thing."

"I'm pretty sure it's a control thing."

"That too." He laughed and was rewarded when she kissed him, her cold nose touching his cheek.

"Look at all the boxes," she said.

"Vineyards."

"Kind of like farms."

Garrett shrugged and held her tighter. "Eh, not exactly. We like to call vineyards 'pampered farms.'"

"Why is that?"

"Because they're temperamental, not as forgiving. The families down there working those vineyards know what they're doing. It's a crazy amount of TLC."

The basket shifted and the flame, which seemed like it should set the whole damn thing on fire, blazed on a whoosh, and they climbed higher. Garrett kissed the top of her head, finding comfort in the way their bodies fit together.

"So why a hot air balloon ride?"

Sage pondered for a minute and then said, "I think it's important to feel small."

"Okay."

"No, I do. I like going up and looking down. It reminds me that I am tiny by comparison."

Garrett didn't know how to respond to that. He'd never thought of it that way, but being with Sage had led him to see many things differently.

"What made you decide to take a hot air balloon ride?" she asked.

"You."

"Me? That's your answer?" She glanced back at him. "Okay, well, what do you think?"

"I... think I prefer feeling big. I like being on the ground. I guess you're right—I can't control things up here and honestly, it all looks a little overwhelming from this angle. I'm happy on my own square."

"Okay," she said, turning in his arms to face him instead of the view. "So what's on your list?"

"I don't have a list."

"You don't have things you want to do?"

"I didn't say that. I have things to do, but I don't have a list like yours. I'm not sure what's in my bottom drawer, but I haven't thought about filling it... I guess ever..."

"As Paige would say, 'If you had to pick,' what would you put in your drawer, on your list?"

Garrett thought for a moment and was happy as the basket began lowering closer to the ground.

"Maybe... the running of the bulls in Spain. I'd like to see that."

"Run in it, or watch?"

"Running. It seems very Hemingway."

"It is. I noticed Hemingway on your shelves at home. You're a fan?"

"I am. He drives Kenna nuts, but I get him. I understand the..."

"Pain?" Sage asked.

Garrett looked out at the rising sun. He'd never thought about it, but maybe he did connect to a certain sadness. "Yeah, I guess."

The basket began to skim the ground and as they prepared for the "bumpy landing" they were told to expect, Garrett had one more question.

"Do you like Hemingway?"

Sage shook her head. "He wallows too much in the past."

Before he could respond, they hit with a thud and Garrett held tight to her as they tumbled back to being big.

Well into the afternoon, they took pictures and drank wine. Garrett was amazed how normal it all felt—as if having a life with her would be the easiest thing. They talked about their childhoods and on the drive home, Sage showed him her high school and shared a couple of stories about her family. Garrett learned more about her every day and he never tired of the layers. He still hadn't turned on his phone, which must have been some kind of record.

That night, they sat down to dinner at the Jeffries' house.

"So, hot mystery guy, what do you do?" Hollis asked.

"I'm a farmer."

"Seriously?" Hollis took another sizable sip of her wine.

"Seriously. I manage Ryeland Farms down in Ventura."

"Shit, that's like saying you're a writer or a dancer or like you're Bob the Builder. A farmer, huh."

"Hollis," her mother said, bringing in the coffee.

"What?"

"You're rude."

"No, Mother, I'm miserable, so anyone remotely happy or alive is fucking fascinating."

"Hollis! That's enough. I know you're. . . going through something, but I will not have that language in my house. You were raised better."

She nodded. "You're right, I was, Mom. I apologize," she said in earnest as she set her empty wineglass down and put two sugar cubes into a small white coffee cup.

"What do you do?" Garrett asked.

The room went silent and as his father loved to say, Garrett felt like he'd "stepped in it." He thought he even heard Sage's mother gasp as she went back into the kitchen for the cake.

Hollis contemplated her wineglass for a moment but then sipped her coffee. "I'm in the circus." She smiled.

"Seriously? Which one? I remember seeing this awesome Russian circus on tour when I was a kid. They had a bear, which I remember pissed me off because bears shouldn't wear clothes. They also had this woman who could fold herself into a tiny box. Was that you?"

Silence again. This time, their mother was standing holding an enormous chocolate cake and forks. Hollis burst out laughing.

"Oh, Sage, if you're not in love with this one yet, I am. Yes, I was definitely the fold-me-up woman."

Garrett had a feeling Hollis had a pretty substantial story and recognized raw pain when he saw it. He would forever remember it in his sister's eyes when she'd lost her husband, but this registered like a different kind of ache. Whatever Sage's big sister was going through was something else altogether different than an unfair twist of fate. Hers almost seemed self-inflicted.

❧❦❧

The questions continued as they were cleaning up before heading out to a late movie. It wasn't lost on Sage that Garrett would be the first man to take her on a date while she was under her parents' roof.

"Our weather is pretty mild, so we grow all year long, but we slow it down in winter. December and January are all about fixing equipment and getting ready, so I've had some time. I can't believe it's March already. Things will get crazy before long," Garrett told her father while they cleared up the cake plates.

"Oh, well, I'm sure Sage can help you with most of that equipment."

"Dad."

"Really?" Garrett said in a mocking tone that quickly grew inquisitive as her father appeared serious.

"Dad, why not tell Garrett about your latest remodel? He loves retro stuff. I think he'd get a kick out of what you're doing."

"Sure. Yeah, we're turning an old gas station into one of those drive-through coffee shops. I'll break out the plans later if you want to see, but our Sage is a wonder."

"She is." Garrett put the coffee cups on the counter.

"I always liked to say that Sage had a degree in fixing things. Mechanical engineering, UC Berkeley. Graduated in three years. Brilliant, as I'm sure you already know."

"I. . . I'm not sure I knew that." He looked at Sage and she registered the change in his eyes right away.

No one ever tells a girl when she's staying up all night cramming for impossible exams that once she graduates people will treat her differently. That if a man knows she can build a robot he might find that intimidating. Garrett's gaze was more one of discovery and admiration, but it still held the weight of a past where Sage no longer dwelled.

"Oh well, she has always been modest. I guess being a. . ."

"Mixologist," Garrett added, smiling at her in a way that said he could read her mind.

Her father laughed. "Yes, that. She's making things work together."

"Dad, let's not get into this, okay?"

"I'm always proud, you know that."

"I do."

Garrett still had questions. She could almost see his thoughts as he ran through the time they'd known each other. When she'd had knowledge most bartenders didn't possess, times she'd fixed things. The ice machine, she was certain the ice machine now made more sense in his logical mind. Sage put some effort into hiding her nerd, but she knew that little overachiever surfaced more often than she realized.

Later, sitting in the movie theater, they were still discussing the past and Sage desperately wanted to enjoy her present.

"I don't get it. All of your accomplishments are things that people brag about. Mechanical engineering? Come on, why would naughty or a bottom drawer matter? Look at you."

"It's hard to explain."

"I've got all night. Let's give it a try because from where I'm sitting, you're more than the fantasy, Sage."

"I never went to my prom," she said, taking a handful of popcorn from the bucket in his lap.

"So."

"Did you?"

"Yeah, well, the first one, no, but my senior year, I went. A damn nightmare."

"You see, everyone who has a bottom drawer always says that. Ever cut class?"

Garrett nodded.

"Go to Mardi Gras or a bar for St. Patrick's Day and pass out drunk?"

Garrett nodded slowly this time.

"Been on a bull?"

"Sage, everyone's life is different. I've never graduated from UC Berkeley, or had an article published in an international journal. Do you want to ride a bull?"

"I don't know, maybe. I want more than being nice and neat. I want to break something, mess things up. I want stories to tell my children. I'm thirty-two. My twenties are over and I have straight As and framed certificates."

"Ever made out in a movie theater?" He looked over his shoulder as the lights dimmed. "A pretty packed movie theater?"

She shook her head. Garrett put his hand on her leg and leaned in.

"Stop. I grew up around here. Plus the movie is starting and I always hate when people suck face during the movie."

He laughed. "Suck face. I like that one." He took her hand, kissed it, and then kissed her.

"You know why no one ever made out with you in a movie theater?" he whispered.

"Shhh."

"Because the poor bastard wouldn't have been able to stop at only kissing you. You're an all-or-nothing sort of woman," he whispered, grabbing his own handful of popcorn.

And just like that, she loved him more.

Chapter Twenty-Seven

*W*hen they returned from the movie, Garrett thought about having a beer but decided it was time to check his phone, sift through any e-mails. Grabbing it off the nightstand of the bedroom Sage grew up in, he stopped cold when he noticed there were at least half a dozen text messages and two voice mails. Some from Logan, most from Kenna. Their dad had fallen off a ladder while he was changing a light bulb in the barn. There was more about the emergency room and a cast.

"He's resting at home. He's fine, but I wanted you to know," Kenna said when he finally got a hold of her. "Are you having a good time? How was the balloon ride?"

Garrett barely heard the rest of what she said as he stood in the Jeffries' kitchen. His heart was thundering in his chest and in the back of his mind, he knew this had happened because he'd left. Like the balloon, what went up always came down. He was part of a unit, an integral spoke in the wheel. While it had been surreal spending time with Sage, this was not his world, never would be. What had happened to his father made that crystal clear. He wouldn't have been on that ladder if Garrett had been there. *What if something worse had happened?*

The rational part of his brain knew his father would be fine, as Kenna had said, but the other part that pictured him alone and hurt was more than Garrett could bear. He knew it made no sense to a normal person from a normal childhood if there was such a thing, but it was the way he had always felt about his family. They needed him, and as much as everyone joked that he should "lighten up" or "go have fun," Garrett knew he had no business having a life away from his responsibilities. Logan and Kenna were the ones with separate lives, but he was the rock, the piece left behind so everything stayed together. He didn't mind being that guy until Sage changed everything. She kept rolling down the window, pointing out the scenery in a world where he needed to focus on straight ahead. His family's history, the jobs of hundreds of people. . . All counted on him to stay focused. Floating around in the clouds with a beautiful woman, there simply wasn't time for it.

He told Sage what happened, thanked her family, and then went back to where he belonged.

❧

Garrett drove through the night, his mind racing even more under the silent hum of his truck. This happened because he left. He knew it was stupid; he wasn't usually superstitious but that was the only explanation. His father fell, alone in the barn, because Garrett wasn't there. Christ, the thought of him lying there on the barn floor made his stomach turn. The man had given his life to them, put their happiness above his own. He didn't deserve to be alone.

Whatever the hell he thought he was doing with Sage was secondary. It had to be because people were counting on him. Garrett had been there when Kenna needed a boost to the water fountain at recess or when Brody Pierce needed the shit kicked out of him for bullying Logan into doing his homework in junior high. Garrett was always over their shoulder, right around the corner, and he liked it that way. He was at his father's side when their mother abandoned them, and he'd never left. Sure, he'd been places, seen things, but emotionally, he was always at the farm with his family. As he drove up to the dimly lit porch of the main house, his father's house, he was exhausted and right where he belonged. Everything else, everyone else, would have to stay on the sidelines.

Garrett walked through the front door to find Jack asleep at the foot of the stairs. He lifted his head, tail wagging and once he realized it was Garrett, he sleepily walked over for a greeting.

"Hey, Jack, where's the patient?"

"We're in here," said a female voice over the sound of the television.

Walking through the archway of the living room, Garrett saw Libby putting on her coat while his father sat on the couch.

"I'm fine," his father said. "There was no need for you to drive all the way home."

"Sure there was." Garrett threw his coat over the chair on his way to finally setting eyes on his father. "I was worried about Jack. He can't have a cripple looking after him."

His father's laughter was exactly what he needed.

"Well, fortunately, it's only the forearm and you still have your elbow."

"True. Doctor says eight weeks in the cast and then some kind of brace until it heals all the way."

Garrett nodded and looked to Libby, who was smiling at both of them.

"Thank you," he said, a little surprised to see Libby out of the diner. "Did you feed him?"

"You know I did. There's some chicken in the fridge from last night and some cinnamon rolls I brought over this morning if you're hungry. I have to get back to the diner," she said. She hung back momentarily in some sort of weird limbo before squeezing his dad's hand, patting Garrett on the shoulder, and leaving.

"That was nice of her to stop by." Garrett sat on the other side of the sectional couch.

His father nodded, looking at the television but not watching it.

"Dad?"

Their eyes met.

"You all right?"

He nodded. "You didn't need to leave your girl."

"She's not my. . . don't worry about that. I'm sorry I wasn't here to help with the light. Why didn't you ask George?"

"Because I was changing a damn bulb. If I can't change a lightbulb on my own, then it's time to hang it up. It was a fluke. I stepped on the ladder the wrong way and went down. No one's fault."

Garrett let out a breath.

"No one's fault, do you hear me? If you'd been here, I'd have still been on that ladder."

Garrett started to disagree, but his father held him off.

"You're not the only man in this house, Garre. I was changing lightbulbs long before you could reach them. I'll continue to change the damn things until the day you put me in the ground. I'm not some invalid."

"I never said you were."

"Then why the hell are you back here when you should be up there winning that woman?"

Garrett felt the tension creep into his back and shoulders. He ran his hand over his face. He was tired and suddenly the urge to rush home felt foolish.

Something shifted, almost as if things would be fine without him.

He didn't like it. "I have work to do."

"Aren't you going to sleep?"

"No. I'm hopped up on coffee and George has finished redirecting those drip lines. I want to make sure it's the coverage we were expecting. You all right here?"

"Yeah, I'm going to watch some Oprah. I think it's a master class today on body acceptance."

Garrett laughed. "Is that something you're working on?"

His father shrugged. "Not exactly, but she always has little lessons in there. Most of it applies to me."

"Is that so?"

"Yeah," he said a bit defensively, "she's — "

"A bright woman, yeah, yeah, I know."

"You sure you don't want one of Libby's cinnamon rolls?"

Garrett put his coat back on and went to the kitchen, returning with one roll in his hand and another in his mouth. His father laughed.

"Careful out there. Will you ask George to take a picture of Bird and send it to Paige? I promised."

Garrett grunted, filling his mouth with Libby's incredible baking, and let the screen door slam behind him.

After a few hours of reworking a couple of the drip lines and doing an inventory of the seeds that still hadn't arrived, Garrett took a picture of Bird, one of their goat's newest babies, and sent it to Paige. She promptly replied that she was "looking good, but maybe needed more sunshine." Garrett laughed and slipped his phone back in his jacket. He slumped down in the office chair, propped his feet up on the desk, and fell asleep.

Chapter Twenty-Eight

Sage flew home the next morning. It was raining as the taxi pulled up in front of her house. She hadn't heard from Garrett and didn't want to call Kenna to pick her up. She'd texted Garrett a couple of times, without response, so she tried to leave it alone. They were with their father and when the Rye family circled up, they didn't appear to need anyone else's help.

Sage worked at bringing her focus back to her own life. She'd started a new book, fiction this time. She was a few chapters in; it took place in England and it was lilting and literary. That's what she wanted. She was tired of working on herself, analyzing. She needed escape—her mind and her heart wanted to pretend. After losing her place more than a few times, Sage closed her Kindle. Her energy felt off and she was restless. It was as if she could feel him, feel for him. His fear and anger mixed with whatever else he kept bottled up in his big brother routine. Another side effect of love, she thought, getting out of bed and glancing out the window on her way to the kitchen for ice cream. It was still pouring. She stood in her dark kitchen with nothing but the dim light over her stove and the occasional flash of lightning. Sage opened the freezer and closed it. She couldn't eat; she couldn't sleep. This was ridiculous.

Pulling a sweatshirt over her tank top, Sage zipped her jeans. She still had Kenna's boots and there had to be a raincoat somewhere in the back of her closet. Within minutes, she was ready for the weather and grabbing her keys. *He doesn't need you*, something reminded her as she stood with her hand on the doorknob. As if in defiance, she lifted her hood and walked out into the rain. She was done waiting, done dancing around. She loved him and they needed each other. If she had to fight for that, then challenge accepted. She knew exactly where to find him.

Sage drove through for burgers on her way to the farm and ate some of the fries as she drove. Nothing but the haunting voice of James Morrison and the slap of her wipers filled the car. She cursed the long drive to get to him. The lights were on as she pulled into the gravel parking lot. She tucked the bag of food into her coat and ran to the awning that hung over the front door of the Ryeland Farms offices. The door was unlocked. Shaking off the rain, she walked toward the sole light cutting through the darkness of desks and cubicles. She found him going through paperwork and tried to steady her breath, to rein in the need to hold him.

"I brought you some dinner."

"Thanks, but I already ate." He didn't look up and with the exception of a slight dent in his clenched jaw, there was no sign of surprise that she was dripping wet in his doorway in the middle of the night.

"How's your father?" She unzipped her coat, setting the bag on the edge of his desk.

"Fine." He was a robot, moving from one piece of paper to another. She would have bet he wasn't reading any of it—he simply needed something to do, someplace to hide his pain. After a couple of minutes of silence, except for the rain thumping on the roof, Garrett looked up at her, eyes vacant. "Thanks for coming by, Sage, but he's fine."

"Don't do that. Don't you dare make me feel stupid."

Garrett almost laughed. "How the hell would I begin to make you feel stupid? You've got a degree in mechanical engineering.

Turns out you know everything. If you're feeling stupid, maybe that's your issue."

She swallowed. She wanted to run away, but instead she stood her ground, her lips tight. Garrett did the same.

"So, are we done here?" he finally asked with a raised brow and a cruelty she'd never noticed before. She recognized the fear.

"Do you want to talk about this?" She already felt foolish, but if there was a chance of breaking through, she had to try.

Garrett stopped shuffling through papers, stood, and walked past her. Pushing through the front door, he walked out into the rain without a word or a jacket. Sage hesitated for a minute and watched him move to the barn. He was drenched by the time she could see him under the outside light. She went after him.

"Garrett, please let me—"

He held up his hand and walked farther into the darkened barn. She wondered if the smells, the warmth of the wood helped him, gave him any peace. She caught up to him and put her hand on his shoulder. He turned on her so fast that for a heartbeat, she was scared. He held her by the shoulders, his chest heaving in and out, and wiped away tears barely visible below the glistening green of his pained eyes.

"What is it with you? I don't need help. I need to work, keep things running."

"You're scared and you should be, your father—"

"I am not scared. Stop. That shit doesn't work on me. I don't need some book to tell me how to live my life, Sage. I have to get back to work. I'm fine. Please leave." He was still holding her, so she gave it one more shot.

"I can't. I love you, and you're hurting."

"Oh for fuck's sake, please stop. You like being alone and I have to be alone. The fantasy is over, Sage. My father needs me. I need to be here."

She let him squeeze her arms. He wasn't letting go, so she took a page from his playbook and waited him out.

"I mean, enough. This was incredible, but seriously, look at our lives. I can't leave and you're... you deserve something real. I can't give you that. This was fun, but it turns out I can't give you the 'more' you're looking for." He was shaking, and Sage called on strength she didn't know she had until that very moment.

"Yes you can, you already have. You're scared. You've had a lot of changes and things going on. Your dad falling was probably the last straw, but that doesn't mean there's not room for us. I want all of you and that means this too, your pain. I want to help you. Let me be there for you."

"You want to help me? You want to be there for me. Fine." He grabbed the back of her neck, hard, and before his lips smashed into hers, he looked at her, a storm of anger and pain swirling through his eyes. When he pulled her in again, she remembered the first time her father had taken her white-water rafting. "It might look scary like it can overpower you, but it's only doing its thing. If you want to ride, you have to hold on and be willing to get wet." Sage held on, let him share some of his need, his pain. His hand moved to her face, held her chin in a kiss that was frantic, meant to intimidate, but she was made of tougher stuff. She hoisted herself up and Garrett caught her as her legs wrapped around his waist. He backed into the barn, still kissing her, and once they were covered, Sage lifted her wet shirt over her head and the night air made her skin dance. Every breath felt like a wave, a splash of water to her face. Garrett's mouth took her neck, between her breasts, as he leaned her against the wall.

"Sage." His fist was tight in her hair.

On a rush of breath, she started unbuttoning his shirt, but felt the next wave approaching, so she ripped the rest of the shirt open and ran her hands over his damp chest. If she could have climbed inside of him, held his heart, steadied him at that moment, she would have. There was nothing she could say that would help him deal with his father's mortality or the responsibilities he'd carried since he was a little boy. There were no words at that moment, so she simply set about showing him that she loved him, that he was full of the life and vitality she'd seen the moment she met him.

Sage dropped one hand to the waist of his jeans while the other was still wrapped around his neck. Garrett closed his eyes and she felt the pressure of his hands dig into her thighs. With air seemingly racing in and out of her lungs, Sage opened his zipper, found him and lifted. Garrett's eyes were fierce, on the edge of a place she'd never been with him, but she wasn't looking away. When he slid her down onto him in one fast thrust, Sage could see the puffs of breath between them, feel the drops of rain still on their skin. Her back against the barn wall, Sage held on as Garrett frantically searched for everything he said he didn't need with every thrust. How many people gave into that cold stare of his and left Garrett alone, she wondered as she felt her nails dig into his back until they both fell apart.

❧❧

The rain had stopped as they lay on the blankets thrown over bales of hay in the darkness of the early morning hours, moments before the moon handed the sky over to day. Sage threaded her fingers through his as if he might slide away with the moon. His chest slowly pulsed up and then down as her eyes fell to the scar on his shoulder.

She swallowed. "How'd you get this?" She gently traced the smooth faded line.

Garrett closed his eyes and said nothing. He had declined to share before, but somehow this was different. The intimacy of allowing him to take her was more than she'd ever offered to another person. It left her empty, needing something in return. She hated that feeling and was getting tired of asking for more. They were somehow able to speak with their bodies, but once the passion passed, he was often so hard to find.

Sage sat up and grabbed her clothes in the dim light. The scratch of the blanket beneath them was now uncomfortable on her bare skin. She climbed off the hay and suddenly wanted to be anywhere other than where she was. As if someone had slammed a door, she saw things as they were. She loved him to complete distraction, probably always would, but there was no way she was going to give away all of her light if he couldn't—wouldn't—keep her warm. She'd been left in darkness of doubt before, in the cold with nothing. No way in hell would she go back there, not even for him.

Garrett shifted and pulled on his jeans, still without a word. Bare chested, he sat with his hands on his knees. The curve of his beautiful body was lit by the first glimpse of morning. He broke her heart. Every time. She grabbed her jacket and walked toward the light.

"Where are you going?"

"Home." She turned back as he jumped off the hay. "Did you have something you wanted to say?"

He ran his hand over the stubble of his far-too-tired face and shook his head. "What time is it?"

Sage pulled out her phone, wondering why she was still standing there as if one moment or one word would wake him up and change things. "It's five."

He blinked and appeared as if he'd been called to attention. "Shit, I've got. . . we've got harvest and I need to check on Dad. Where's Jack?"

Tears slid down her face. Sage walked into the early dawn toward her car, ignoring him as he halfheartedly called her name.

❧❧❧

Garrett spent the morning getting back on schedule. Jack was asleep in the corner of the bedroom. He'd driven them both home and stepped into the shower. Eyes burning as the warm water hit his face, and with an exhausted will, he tried not to think about her. The look on her face, her beautiful naked body rushing to redress while he lay there unable to tell her that he knew. He knew he was fucked up. Everything he'd ever understood was growing apart, falling apart, and it frightened him. He should have held her, held onto her, but he couldn't move. He didn't know how to make something new. He should have told her that, let her help him, but even with his mind screaming, "Don't let her leave feeling like this, you asshole," there was nothing he could do. He was trapped in a past that simply wouldn't allow him to have her.

After drying off, he dressed and went to work. Harvest of anything was usually a great time. Fields so teeming with life, he couldn't help but leave the office and join his men in the sunshine. As he jumped in his truck, all he wanted to do was work himself to within an inch of his sad, selfish life.

Chapter Twenty-Nine

Garrett walked into the kitchen at The Yard almost a week later. He'd put Logan's order on the delivery schedule, telling himself it was for the best, but somehow there he was, the blaring sounds of some hair band bringing back the faint memory of the garage his father used to take the truck to when it needed repairs or new tires. Every now and then, when Garrett heard bad eighties rock or smelled used oil, he was transported back to a time when getting a Dr. Pepper with his dad on a summer afternoon or scoring a lollipop at the register was all it took to make his day. Things were different now. Nothing was simple about the music or the woman he knew had turned it on.

"What the hell did you do?" Travis asked, his hands tossing something in a large silver bowl.

"Specifics please, and try not to sound like a damn chick."

"This is Motley Crew. Do you have any idea what that means?"

"No, but I'm guessing it's not flowers and running through a field?"

Travis shook his head and washed his hands. "Hair bands are 'I don't give a shit' music. It's a personal favorite of mine, but Sage never plays this. She's been listening to it nonstop for the past week. It feels like the whole damn world is off its tilt."

Although he always thought of hair band music as mindless, "I don't give a shit" worked too. He put the delivery down on the counter. "That's the last of the brussels sprouts, and tell Logan we had a run on the chard, so he needs to pull from his own garden to supplement this week."

"You could tell him yourself," Logan said, stepping out of his office.

Garrett nodded his head in greeting and was quiet.

"I'm guessing this is you?" He gestured toward the speakers playing overhead.

"Probably."

"You know, both of you are a real pain in the ass. First Travis, and now you. Quit messing with my damn restaurant."

Travis laughed. It figured he would laugh, he was probably sleeping soundly, his story had worked out.

Garrett wasn't feeling as good about his chances.

"Are you going in there?" Logan glanced at him.

"I was going to, but according to your man here, Sage and hair bands are never a good idea."

"Things that bad, huh? You're relying on Travis's musical horoscopes?"

Garrett turned on him and wasn't sure if his brother actually looked good or if Garrett felt like such shit that any kind of happy was accentuated. "You putting on some weight?"

Logan's eyes sparkled with sarcasm. "Too much bread."

Garrett laughed at the inside joke, remembering the early morning he had walked in on his brother and Kara. A moment into their joking, Sage came into the kitchen.

"Oh," she said, stopping short, "I didn't mean to break up the party."

Logan and Travis looked at each other and before Garrett could say a word, they were gone. Was there some sort of escape hatch when thoroughly pissed-off women entered the kitchen? Sage, ignoring him, plucked at the herbs laid out on the counter and walked back to the bar.

Garrett closed his eyes. He hadn't slept well since somehow managing to screw up the hottest rain fantasy he didn't even know he had. Grabbing a tomato off the counter and popping it into his mouth, he contemplated walking out the back door. But never one to walk away from a fight, he headed into the bar instead.

The music was still loud and still eighties. Smashing something in a marble bowl, Sage didn't look up, so he took a seat at the empty bar.

"Can you talk for a minute?"

She looked up, feigned being unable to hear him, and continued smashing at the bowl.

Garrett stepped behind the bar and turned off the music.

She stopped smashing, blew her bangs out of her face, and didn't say a word. Extending his hand, Garrett stepped closer, hoping she would take it.

After a moment of hesitation that gave him a chance to see she was tired and masking hurt behind being pissed off, she put her hand in his. He gently pulled her to the wine cellar and thought he caught a glimpse of a smile break through, but it was gone by the time he closed the door behind them.

She spoke first. "I told you the first day you touched me that I wouldn't be able to go back. I meant it. All of that seems so ridiculous now because you were right. I didn't love you then, not like this. This is going to kill me if I don't walk away. So I'm leaving."

Garrett felt the tiny room turn.

"Hollis is with my uncle. I'm going to see her for a few days and hopefully get myself together. When I get back, you can start doing deliveries again so you can see Logan. I'll work nights so you don't have to avoid me."

"You don't need to do that."

Sage picked up one of the bottles surrounding them and for a minute he thought she might throw it at him, but she only stared into the glass, and Garrett had never felt more helpless in his life. Her playfulness was gone; she was serious and hollow. Was it possible he'd made her this way? He had spent his life in the background, working and protecting when necessary. That was his role, but if he had been meant to protect her, he'd failed.

"I slipped off the roof of the barn when I was sixteen. I was drinking with some friends and lost my footing. Broke my shoulder, but it didn't heal right so they had to go in."

"What?"

"My shoulder, you asked about my scar."

Sage gave him that dumbass look he recognized from his sister. Then she laughed before her eyes returned to the same vacant gaze.

"What are you looking for, Sage?"

She turned the bottle in her hand. "You can't give me what I'm looking for, you said it yourself. It's not your fault."

"What the hell does that mean? I've told you I love you and I do, but maybe I'm not who you thought I was, maybe the reality isn't what you want."

"This whole thing was messed up from the beginning. I didn't represent myself, who I am or what I'm about from the beginning. It's my fault." She slid the bottle back into its place.

"Stop."

"No, it is. I pretended to be something I thought would free me and then it let me have you. But you're right, I'm more than that woman. I can't change me, and you can't handle all of me."

"I wouldn't say that."

"Right, sorry you *won't* handle me. You want sex, banter, and the occasional conversation. I want you, all of you."

"I can't be something I'm not. I know I'm messed up, but I work."

"I get that. We all work, Garrett, but then we go home, we have time off. People love, have a family, lie on the couch, it happens."

He didn't respond.

"I don't want to want anymore. I need to *be* wanted. I'm not the same woman who sat back picturing fantasies. I know the rush of it now, what it is to hold a man while he sees himself in my eyes. I know his laugh, his touch. I can feel him in a room before I've even seen him. I've experienced all of that now and I can't go back to the sidelines. I want the whole thing."

"All the time? Life doesn't work that way."

"Mine does, or it will. Remember when we were in Napa in the hot air balloon? You drove all the way up there to be with me."

Garrett nodded, and his chest tightened at the memory of her flushed and beautiful against a blue sky.

"I felt so. . . desired and alive. I don't need you all the time, but for that hour, we were suspended. It was like we were kids. I want that in my life. And you've helped me figure out what that looks like."

"Stop."

"It's true. I read this book once on visualization. A person needs to see what they want if they are ever going to make it real. I won't be afraid the next time I want something. I won't need tequila next time. I'll grab it, grab him. So, thank you for that."

The thought of her with another man hit him square in the chest because there was no question it would happen, that someone would find her and love her. She knew what she wanted now, and it wasn't him.

Sage sighed, probably because he was once again silent. He wasn't sure what to say, had no idea how to keep her.

"I need you to leave so I can get to work," she said, giving up and stepping back from him.

"When will you be back? I don't want you to go."

"Sure you do, it's easier this way."

"I love you."

"I know you do, it's simply that I've loved you longer. I'll always be ahead of you. Things should have stayed the way they were before we ever walked into this room." She tried to smile and backed up toward the door.

He touched her face. She started to resist and then closed her eyes. "Please, go."

Garrett had been at some crossroads in his life, moments when he could turn right or left, and he liked to think that he'd made good choices. That he'd acted in ways that honored his family and who he was as a man. All that was about to change because he was going to let her go, and that felt wrong in every way possible. She would go back to her family and someday find a man who could return everything she'd given to him. He'd make her feel loved, which was something he'd apparently been unable to do, and Garrett would go back to his work. A life he understood.

Sage crossed her arms over her chest. He noticed the tiny pineapples on her shirt; details that would normally make him smile now made him sick with longing. He missed her already. Brushing past her, Garrett left his heart behind in the tiny wine cellar. Fine by him—he wouldn't be using the damn thing anymore.

✿❧✿

Sage had a full bar and three orders from the floor forty-five minutes after they opened. She thought maybe Garrett had the right idea because she was thankful for the work, grateful for the familiar hum of conversation, laughter, and clinking of glass. She fell into a numb routine, her hands moving as if they didn't even need the rest of her. Which was good because the rest of her wasn't there. Turning toward the register to cash out three guys at the end of the bar, she realized she was out of register paper. She gestured to the bar that she'd be back in a minute and pushed through the door to the back office. She managed to make it around the corner before she collapsed. The pain came out of nowhere, as if someone was lying in wait for her and the moment she stepped into the silence, they'd punched her. She bent over, hands on her knees, and cried. *Oh God, please God take this away. Please.* Sage closed her eyes and tried to stop. Breathe in and breathe out, she told herself right as Logan soared around the corner.

"Sage! What the hell is going. . ." His words fell when he saw her, and she quickly wiped her eyes.

"Oh. . . okay, hold on." He walked up to the front kitchen and whispered something to Travis, who went to her bar.

She knew they were covering, that she should suck it up and get the hell back out there, but she simply stood and watched them as if she were watching a play.

"Okay, we're good. Come here." He pulled her into his arms and Sage was suddenly filled with the memory of her first mock trial in high school. She'd lost because she'd become too emotional and that skewed her focus. The coach had hugged her almost exactly the same way Logan was now, helped her accept defeat. In high school, she'd graciously pushed away, embarrassed by her failure and dreading facing her family in the audience. Now, wrapped in the arms of another man trying to help her through defeat, she held on tighter. Clearly adult failure packed more of a punch.

"I'm fine," she said, stepping back as Logan let her go.

"I need to get back to work and so do you, so I'll make this quick. He is. . ." Logan's eyes teared up and Sage thought she might die right there. "Shit, sorry." He blinked back his emotion. "When he says he doesn't know how, he means it. We are a million shades of screwed up. Our mom left and we became a tribe to survive. The tribe is scattering now, changing, and he's in a free-fall whether he knows it or not."

"Logan, you don't need to tell me this."

"I do. He's given me so much in my life. It's the least I can do for the idiot."

She laughed and wiped the rest of her own tears. "You need to get back."

"I do." He took her hands. "Don't give up on him. I know, be-lieve me, I know exactly what this is, but he loves you. He'll figure it out. Don't give up. He's like. . . what's the hardest crossword?"

"*New York Times*, Sunday."

Logan nodded and let her hands go. Larry, the pizza guy, called for him. "Yup, that's him. He's Sunday. A pain in the ass, but once you get him"—he turned back right before he disappeared into the kitchen—"well, I don't need to tell you."

Sage caught a few more tears, wiped them away, and returned to her bar.

She did know, but there was no solving Garrett. She had tried, and going completely against her nature, she had failed.

Chapter Thirty

By the grace of some higher power, Garrett heard his father before he saw him. He'd planned on spending the day in his office catching up on all the paperwork he'd put off until Kenna threatened his life, but then George called saying they still hadn't received the new seat for tractor four. Garrett followed up and learned it had been delivered to the main house instead of the office.

That was why he was there unannounced. It was the middle of the damn day, so he hadn't thought twice about walking right into the house he'd grown up in. He'd been in a shit mood and wanted to check off the damn tractor. As he stood in the entryway, he heard them. At first he thought he was delirious and then he distinctly heard a female moan, followed by his father's voice.

"You like that, baby?"

Garrett looked around and turned to check the front door, making sure he was in the right house.

"Oh, Herb, right there. Don't stop."

Garrett froze, closed his eyes, and wished he had the set of earplugs he normally carried in his pocket during harvest. The front door was still open about halfway. Hopes that he could back up slowly and get out of the house unannounced right when he began to hear Libby's voice chanting, were shattered when a gust of wind hit the porch and slammed the front door closed.

Garrett felt like one of those deer on the hunting shows his grandfather used to watch. Frozen, unsure what his next move was, only his eyes moving.

Following a few thuds and some muffled laughter from upstairs, his father emerged at the top of the stairs buttoning his shirt. *Jesus Christ!*

"Garre, I wasn't expecting you."

"Obviously," he said under his breath and cleared his throat. "Yeah, did Newmark deliver a tractor seat to the house? They said it was dropped here."

"Yes, yesterday," his father said at the foot of the stairs, now with a mixture of happy and busted on his face. "I put it on the side table in the kitchen. I was going to bring it down after—"

Garrett raised his eyebrows and glanced at the stairs. "After?" He wasn't in the mood to let even his father off the hook.

"Right. After. Let me get that for you," his father said with that look that said Garrett was near the line, close to being disrespectful. His dad handed him the box and he tucked it under his arm.

"How's the arm?" Garrett asked.

"Better every day." He held up his arm and Garrett noticed his shirt wasn't buttoned correctly.

They both looked down and before the look on his father's face grew any guiltier, Garrett left.

He couldn't have been more shocked if he'd walked in and found his father having tea with Oprah. *Holy shit!* How had he not seen this, not known his father was in a relationship? It seemed like everyone now knew how to move on, to have someone in their lives—except him.

※❧※

Entering The Yard through the back kitchen, Garrett found Logan at the prep table.

"Did you know Dad and. . ." He could barely get it out. "Libby. Did you know Dad was. . ."

"Come on Garre, use your big boy words." Logan rounded him, went into the walk-in, and returned with butter. "Did I know Dad and Libby were in a relationship? I found out last night."

"And you didn't think that was worthy of a text or a phone call? You texted me a picture of tennis shoes last week to ask me what I thought. But our dad, oh I don't know, sleeping with the woman who runs our favorite diner, the woman we've known since we were kids, didn't warrant a call?"

"It was late. Kenna called me and we agreed you were in a crap place already since you screwed up with Sage, so we decided to wait. Oh, and I bought those shoes by the way. Love 'em."

Garrett stood there for a minute, willing his pulse to slow down before he lunged at his smug brother.

He took a deep breath, let it out slowly, and even that simple act reminded him of Sage. Being there reminded him of her.

"Well, thank you for letting me know because I walked in this morning to find my tractor seat and Dad and Libby were. . ."

Logan stopped chopping.

"They were having sex."

Both of them yelled like they'd been kissed by a girl in kindergarten and held their hands up to their faces.

"Huh, monkey dumb and monkey dumber. Did I get it right?" Kenna asked as she walked in.

"You tell her," Logan said, hands still to his eyes.

"I walked in on Dad and Libby going at it."

"Holy shit, did you see anything? Oh wow, was she on top?"

Garrett dropped his head. "What the hell is wrong with you? What are you even asking me?"

"Oh, I would have loved to have seen the look on your face."

Taking his hands away from his eyes, Garrett saw Kenna chewing on licorice, genuinely interested in the position their father and his girlfriend were in. He looked at Logan, who started to laugh and before he knew it, the three of them were close to tears.

It was funny, like something out of a comedy sketch. Garrett felt the bond of his siblings and thought maybe that would hold up anywhere.

Maybe it had nothing to do with him, a house or some job. Being with them in the kitchen, the ability to forget his troubles and laugh with them until his sides hurt, maybe that was their whole foundation. What if something as abstract as their feelings for one another was what made up the rock? Garrett looked at his brother and sister and suddenly felt some room open up in their ever-growing family. For the first time since Logan left for culinary school, the shift didn't scare the hell out of him.

Chapter Thirty-One

Mitchell's Cove was on the northern end of Tomales Bay and just under a two-hour drive north of San Francisco. Sage flew into San Francisco, had lunch with her parents, then rented a car and drove up Highway One. She could have taken the 101 as her family did every summer since she was a little girl, but she loved going through Stinson Beach. Hollis came out to meet her car when she pulled up to the cabins a little after five. She had a bottle of wine and two glasses.

"I thought we'd watch the sunset," Hollis said, kissing her on the cheek.

"That sounds like a very good idea. How are you?"

"Oh, I'm sorry, that question is off-limits here on the beautiful bay. Throw your bag in my cabin and get your ass on the dock or I'll start without you."

Sage laughed and watched her sister walk away wearing fuzzy slippers. Hollis wore her hair in a ponytail and sported big dark sunglasses. She should look like crap, but somehow Hollis managed to pull off breakdown as if it was some new trend everyone should try.

The Cove was a place from their childhood, owned and operated by their Uncle Mitch, who was the junior to her grandfather

Mitchell Edward Jeffries. He bought the restaurant and eight bayside cabins in the 1930s at auction. Mitchell's Cove had been in the family ever since. It was a place of celebration and healing. Her family had gathered there for years and Uncle Mitch was like this icon in her life, in all of her sisters' lives. He was both a wise sage and a kick in the pants when they needed it. Sage had been filled with memories on the drive up, longing for a time when all she or her sisters cared about was getting their parents to play Monopoly and buying ice cream at the only store in town before it closed. It was fitting that Hollis had come back here to try and figure out her way forward. Sage still wasn't sure what had happened to her. She wasn't exactly speaking unless she had wine, and then the truth was muddled somewhere behind her biting sarcasm. Sage's oldest sister was only two years older, but she had played up those twenty-four months for as long as Sage could remember.

Hollis was a force, and similar to watching a racehorse fall during the derby, seeing her sister down was almost unfathomable. But here they were, propped on their forearms, leaning on the dock, and looking out as the last bits of sun tickled the smooth surface of the dark water.

"This is a bump," Sage said, shifting to her other foot and squinting at the sunset.

"Yeah, well, it's one of those big ones. Remember the speed bumps in the parking lot at Christ Lutheran? The ones that always scraped the bottom of Dad's Wagoneer, no matter how slow he went?"

"Yeah, I remember."

"If this is a bump, it's one of those damn things."

They both laughed at the memory.

"Come on, you are crazy successful. You have so much under your belt and—"

"And, I've worked my entire life. Since I was like fifteen when I lied to the Dairy Queen so they'd hire me."

"Oh God, Mom was so pissed."

Hollis nodded and poured them more wine.

"That's been my whole life. I'm thirty-four. Not that I care much, but maybe I want to get married or hell, have a man in my life for more than a couple of weeks when he gets tired of sleeping with my laptop between us."

They watched as the horizon faded from orange to purple while the dock creaked and moaned and swayed beneath them.

"So how long are you going to stay here?" Sage asked.

"No idea. I'm not sure why the hell I'm even here. Mom wanted me to get away and Uncle Mitch said he'd make me chowder and I could help him out come spring and summer. I have an MBA from Stanford, but shit, I'm sure I can still make a bed and put that paper strip on the toilets."

Sage laughed and sipped her wine. "I'm sure he's not intending for you to clean. Like we ever cleaned here when we were growing up." She bumped shoulders with her sister and noticed she was too thin.

"I was perfectly happy drinking myself blind and staying in bed all day back at Mom and Dad's, but this just in, that's not healthy." They both laughed and clinked glasses. "I didn't think they were going to summon you. I'm sure you have better things to do."

"Not really."

Hollis looked at her. "Oh no, is your life all fucked up too?"

Sage shook her head. "I'm fine. I'm finding my way."

"Work good? Do you still enjoy making drinks for people?" Hollis asked in that way she had that made every job other than hers seem trivial. Sage thought her sister might even be able to reduce the president of the United States to, "Do you still enjoy making little speeches?" She didn't mean harm, it was the way she was, always had been. Hollis worked harder than everyone, and that brought with it a sense of entitlement and probably a splash of bitterness.

Sage was beginning to wonder if all the competition, all the pushing to be the best, had had the opposite effect and screwed them all up.

"I do. I love where I'm at and what I'm doing."

"Good for you. How's the naughty going? Are you still with Farmer Garrett?"

"No."

"Oh boy, that was chilly. Let's talk about it. I could use some time in someone else's problems."

"There's nothing to say. He's emotionally unavailable."

"Yeah, I thought all men had that ailment."

Sage sighed. "I guess they do, but he makes me feel stupid and I don't do that anymore."

"Feel stupid?"

"Yes."

"You know what Mom would say if, God forbid, she were here?"

Sage nodded, prepared for what was coming.

"No one can make you feel foolish without your permission," Hollis said, imitating their mother perfectly and touching Sage on the nose.

"Yeah, well, I'm no longer giving him permission. I'm fine. It didn't work out. I'm over it. It's so nice to be here. Are you hungry yet? Should we eat, or stand here and get drunk?" Sage pulled her sweater closed as the night air turned chilly.

"I bet the sex was amazing, huh? I mean I was clearly in a state of despair, but when that man walked in, all my mind said was, 'look at that body,' you know?"

Sage finished off her glass of wine and enjoyed the warmth it brought to her cheeks.

"So, was it?"

"Was what? I need to eat something." She turned to walk back.

Hollis pushed off and caught up with her. "It was. I didn't even need to ask. You can tell everything you need to know by the way a man walks."

"Is that so?" Sage kept moving.

"Oh, yeah. You know how you'll see those hot guys and their bodies look perfect?"

Sage didn't answer, knowing it was hypothetical and her sister would keep right on talking.

"Well, watch them walk. Some of them look like they have a

spring shoved up their ass. I don't know if it's that their muscles are so tight they can't move, but hot bod is not necessarily a guaranteed orgasm, you know?"

Sage wondered if Hollis had started drinking earlier than she had as they rounded the corner to the cabin. Sage breezed by a man walking in the opposite direction along the small path, but Hollis swung too wide around the corner and smacked right into him.

"Whoa, sorry," he said, steadying Hollis, who was looking at his feet and then whipped her head up in preparation for her usual, "take two steps back asshole" look, but when her eyes met his, *she* was the one stepping back in shock and then after a beat, she laughed.

"Oh now, isn't this perfect?" She looked at Sage with her arms spread wide, empty glass in one, empty bottle in the other.

The guy, who was tall with brown hair and big eyes, grinned, and Sage wondered if Hollis was sober enough to see the heat or that dimple.

"So weird running into you, Hollis," he said in a low, smooth voice that hinted at his own brand of sarcasm.

"Literally," Hollis said, moving past him.

"I see you finally made it back."

Hollis shook her head and turned toward the cabin.

"Better late than never, isn't that what they say?" he asked.

Hollis held up her empty glass and kept walking toward Sage. Mr. Big Blue Eyes stood there, arms crossed, looking completely unfazed.

"Like, twelve years late, right?" he kept poking.

Hollis swung around, looking like she'd almost tip right over, but recovering. "Why are you here, Matt? Did the devil call and tell you I was circling the seventh circle of hell and you wanted to gloat?"

He laughed, and Sage saw her sister's entire face go soft in a way she'd never witnessed in all their years together. She couldn't blame her—it was the rolling laugh of a man with the upper hand.

"No, my world stopped revolving around you a long time ago, Holls."

Ignoring him, she walked away.

"I live here," he said. "Well, sort of."

Shy of the cabin door, Hollis spun around again. "What?"

Their eyes held and Sage could feel the air swell between them. Blue Eyes took a few steps closer but appeared to lose his confidence, dropping his gaze and rubbing the back of his neck as he turned to leave.

Sage finally closed her mouth, which had fallen open during the scene, and turned to her sister. "Do you want to tell me what that was about?"

"No," she said and pushed through the gate in front of their cabin.

"Who was that?" Sage closed the distance between them.

"Matt Locke. Junior year. We've known him since the first summer we came here. How the hell do you not remember him?"

"Oh God. That was him? Huh, he's. . . grown up. And correction, you've known him."

Hollis snickered. Taking Sage's wineglass too, she put everything in the small kitchen sink.

"You ready to eat?" Hollis asked, pulling on a sweatshirt.

"We're not going to talk about this?" Sage put on socks and shoes in lieu of her flip-flops as her sister stood by the door.

"Do you want to tell me what happened with definitely hot-in-bed farmer?"

"No."

"Then no, I have nothing to say about Matt."

"He has great eyes," Sage said.

Hollis was looking at her nails as if they needed a manicure.

"Fine. Can we talk about why you left San Francisco?"

"No." She looked up.

Sage shrugged. "Well, at any rate, there'll be bread and more wine."

"Yes there will, my dear sister, yes there will."

Hollis shut off the cabin lights and they walked through the crisp coastal air holding hands, two women united in a lifetime of memories and pain they were so sick of trying to figure out.

Chapter Thirty-Two

Garrett managed to stay on task and on schedule through Friday, but by Saturday night, he was shit-faced. Sitting at her bar because he needed to be near her, he thought about how many times he'd walked past her and never knew that she loved him. What he wouldn't give to go back to each and every one of those times he'd barely noticed her so he could pull her into him and hold her beautiful face. This was going to kill him, he thought, throwing back another shot of whiskey. His family was one thing; the general fucking disorder of his life was enough to warrant drinking, but the pain of living without her never went away. He'd tried everything to get back to where he was before she touched him, loved him. Nothing worked, so he thought he'd try drinking. The fact that he rarely had more than a couple of beers would explain why he was now glaring at Sebastian, the so-not-Sage bartender for the night.

"I need you to make a drink for me," Garrett said, barely realizing his lips were moving.

"I'll do my best, but don't you think you've had enough, man?"

Garrett shook his head. "One more. This one should finish me off. Make me a drink called The Rye."

Sebastian looked confused. "You mean a shot of rye, straight up?"

"No, it's a drink. Named after our family. I want that drink."

"I'm. . . not familiar. Do you know what's in it?"

Garrett pressed his hands to his head, remembering why he didn't drink like this. "I have no idea what goes into it. It's rye whiskey and some other stuff, but it's the best damn drink I've ever had. Can you make that?"

Garrett didn't wait for him to answer because he knew, even in his drunken haze, the answer would be no. He walked into the bathroom and rested his hands on the cool concrete of the counter. No one knew how to make it; no one knew what went into something so perfect except her. She held the key to everything, including that damn drink, and he'd lost her. He had a key box in his office. It hung on the wall, and everything was labeled. He knew every damn key in the place and what it unlocked. It figured she'd be outside that box. Make him want for something he didn't already have. Shit, his head was spinning.

❦

Sage had only been home long enough to shower and make some soup when her phone rang with a call from The Yard. It was Sebastian.

"Yeah, Logan's brother is down here and he's asking me to make some drink called The Rye. He said you would know and he's pretty gone, so I thought I'd call you and make the guy happy."

After Sage found her breath, she told him how to make her drink, clarifying he needed to serve it chilled, but not over ice. She hung up and a few minutes later her phone vibrated with a text.

If yoor home why arent you here?

She stared at her phone, at the letters of his name. It had been a while since they had popped up on her screen. She had not heard from Garrett since he walked out of the wine cellar. It had been a little over a week, not that she was counting. Prepared to leave the text unanswered, Sage plugged her phone in right as another text came through.

This is garrett in case you forgot. Thanks for tellin this guy my dink.

Sage found herself smiling. She'd never seen Garrett drunk, and it was as if everything had come full circle. Hopefully, he wasn't in the ladies' room, but he was drunk and texting her. She texted back.

You're welcome.

Less than a minute later, he replied.

I know youre home. But I've had too much to drnk. Could you come get me.

She felt her heart leap. It was stupid, but her heart had never been all that smart. Apparently, she wasn't either because she texted back.

Sure. Be there in 15.

Telling herself not to think, she grabbed her wallet and keys.

By the time she made it to The Yard, things had started to wind down. She waved to Summer and went to the pizza counter first. Travis was working.

"Thank God you're here. Put the bastard out of his misery, will you?" he asked, flipping mushrooms in a small frying pan.

She learned that Garrett had been at the bar since a little after five. Sebastian was trying to be helpful, but if Garrett told him one more time he was nothing like Sage, he might lose his mind. Sage laughed at Travis's animated story, took in a cleansing breath, and rounded the hostess station into the bar.

Her pulse still jumped. That was probably never going away. He was the only one at the bar, his head resting on his hands. She caught Sebastian's eye and mouthed that she was sorry as she put her hand on Garrett's shoulder. The charge of touching him was another thing that wasn't going away anytime soon. He closed his eyes and leaned his head over to her hand.

"Let's go."

Garrett put his hand on hers and when he looked at her, she almost lost her breath. His eyes were bloodshot and he had at a minimum two days of stubble. If she had been Kenna, she would have told him he looked like crap.

"I'm sorry."

"It's okay. I'm glad you called someone."

"I didn't call someone. I called you, and that's not what I'm sorry about."

"I know."

"You know I'm not sorry or you know I called you?"

"Both."

"Why are you answering in one or two words?"

"I'm not. Let's get going."

Garrett stood at her urging and put his arm across her shoulders. Sage felt the weight of his body and found herself drowning in the familiar warmth. Garrett took a deep breath after he waved to Summer, and they stepped out into the warm spring night. Sage clicked open her car and went around to the passenger door.

Garrett let out a laugh Sage had never heard. It vibrated from his chest, and she thanked the alcohol for allowing him such a carefree moment. "I can get into the car myself. Not sure I've ever had a woman open the door for me."

"Yeah, well, there's a first time for everything," she said, sliding into the driver's seat. She watched Garrett struggle with and finally manage to fasten his seatbelt.

Resting his head back, he closed his eyes.

Sage found herself staring. She should start the car, drive him home, but her heart wanted a moment.

"You're staring at me."

"I know."

"I'm sorry I messed everything up. That's what I meant when I said I was sorry." He turned to face her in the darkness of her car. "Tell me how to fix this."

Sage was starting to forget what had actually been wrong. Her heart had a way of screwing with her mind when it came to Garrett. She started the car.

"Sage."

"You've had too much to drink. We both know things are said when a person drinks too much. Before you say something we will both regret, please rest. I'll have you home soon."

He let out a sigh and fell quiet for a moment before saying softly, "I love you, Sage Jeffries."

Damn him.

❧❧❧

By the time Garrett started snoring, they were home. She left him on the couch because she didn't have the will to bring him to his bed. Too much had happened in that bed. The simple act of opening his front door, kissing Jack, and getting Garrett's boots off before he told her one more time how much he'd screwed up and how much he loved her had drained all her strength. Letting Jack out back to run around, she stood on Garrett's deck, suddenly flooded with memories.

The Saturday she came over when he was giving Jack a bath that ended with both of them soaked and laughing so hard they could barely breathe. The night she came over because she needed him. They'd made love and had sat outside, near the very spot she now stood, wrapped in blankets. That was the night she learned Garrett collected comic books when he was a kid before he sold his collection to buy his truck back in high school. That was the night she gave him a crash course on how to play bridge and he had carried her over his shoulder back to bed. Firsts. Sage closed her

253

eyes on the night sky, as if she could block out the stars and the memories of what was and what she could no longer have—unless she was willing to accept she would never have all of him.

Whistling for Jack, she wondered if she was doing the same, if some great guy would tell her she was holding back. Maybe she and Garrett were always drawn together in their reluctance to connect. She was the fun bartender with a crush. He could play when he wanted, so long as she never wanted more. He was a vision; a character in her mind, and that suited her because she only had to deal with glimpses of his world, which left all kinds of time for her solitary bottom drawer. They'd worked until she wanted more than the banter and he wanted her on the side.

Sage crouched to pet Jack, collar jingling as he panted happily. She kissed him on his nose and felt the familiar burn in her eyes. It was time to leave. Strange how homes were like time lines, she thought. Even if there weren't snapshots of memories on the mantel, the feel, the smell of it managed to remind her. All the love and pain, the laughter and the arguments, were stored between the walls of a home, floating in the spaces. It was hard enough that every time she looked at her couch she still saw him there, or no matter how many times she washed her sheets, she swore he was there in the early hours of the morning. That was hard and yet somehow manageable. But it was late, and being surrounded by the extra moonlight and the stars that had watched them fall in love was too much.

Sage locked the back door and covered Garrett with the blanket folded on one end of the couch. He rolled into the cushions, pulling one under his head. She wondered if he would dream. Resisting the pull to kiss his cheek, she reminded herself that he might look harmless, but it had become about so much more than his looks. She gestured for Jack—now curled at the foot of the couch—to stay, and left Garrett and their memories safely locked away.

Chapter Thirty-Three

Garrett was late for work for the first time... ever. His head had been reenacting that Broadway show where the people banged on trashcans. Kenna had dragged him to it a few years back, but now, as he walked into the greenhouse a little after ten, he remembered why he rarely drank anymore. Squinting even behind his sunglasses, he slowly sipped his coffee as his father walked in.

"Morning," his father said, unzipping his jacket. "It's warm in here."

Garrett slowly looked up.

"Don't give me that smart-ass look, I know it's a greenhouse. I'm saying it seems warmer."

"It's probably all this new life. Did you see the tomatoes? Logan is going to shit his pants."

They both laughed and then Garrett winched in pain.

"A little too much to drink last night?"

He closed his eyes behind his sunglasses. "You already know."

"Yeah, it's not my fault you picked that bar. News travels fast."

Garrett carefully opened his eyes and decided there was nothing else he could say. His life was a fishbowl.

"Might be our best year yet." His dad said, walking up the aisle. "Everything going according to schedule? I noticed George is stepping up quite a lot lately."

"He is. I know we pay him, but I swear the man would do what he does for free."

"I'm not so sure Angela would be happy about that. I was thinking maybe we should give him more money and let him take on more of the operation."

"I'm sure he'd appreciate the money, but I think he has enough on his plate."

"I spoke with him last week, and he said he'd be up for more responsibility."

"Dad, what's going on?"

"You're screwing this up," his father said, and Garrett knew immediately they were no longer talking about crops.

"And you know that, how?"

"I've been in love. Twice. Both times different, but I know what it looks like, how it feels."

Garrett set his coffee down on the paint-stained worktable.

"She's so good for you, Garre. And you love her, but I think you've been lonely for so long that maybe you're not sure how to be any different."

"I'm not lonely."

"Sure you are, we all are. It's never more glaring than it is once we're loved."

He carefully glanced at his father. "Oprah?"

"No, those are my words actually, but I'm sure O would say they're worthy of an *ah-ha moment*."

"Christ."

"What? It's true. You're so busy being this place and standing silently by while your brother and sister go on living a life that you're almost invisible, son. All the while, pretty, happy Sage noticed you. She saw you standing there, and from what Kenna tells me, she can see everything you are."

"Dad, I appreciate the pep talk, but I'm not like Kenna or Logan."

256

"I know. You were older when your mom left. It affects you differently. That, and you love the farm. Which I respect so much, Garre. Don't get me wrong, what you've done over the years, the time and work put in, it's what we needed. I'm so proud of you, son."

"It's a group effort, always has been."

"I know, but there's a time for everything. The group is changing, your brother's married now and Kenna—"

Garrett could feel the tears well up in his eyes. He didn't want to talk about any of this because his father was right. His past was all he'd ever known, the routine of farming, the comfort of the same thing, give or take, year after year. He took off his glasses, cursed the sunlight, and wiped his eyes.

"It's change, Garre. Kenna has someone else to help protect her now and Lo got to go off and be the man we all knew he could be. But he's home now too. We have help now."

"I know, and I'm happy for them."

"I know you are, but it's time for you to get yours. Find some balance and love her all the way. We'll all still be here for you."

"Jesus, Dad," Garrett said, now with the balls of his hands pressing up against his eyes, "you sound like a therapist."

His father laughed. "Well, the other night when we were in bed, Libby said—"

"Okay, okay, that's enough."

He laughed again and Garrett caught his father's eyes, saw himself in them, and like he had when he was a kid, he found direction, a gentle guidance that allowed him to make his own shadow rather than getting trapped under his father's. He put his glasses back on and decided to take the rest of the day off.

❧

"Well if that isn't the tables turned, I'm not sure what is," Kenna said, sitting at the end of Sage's bar that afternoon. "Did you tell him you didn't think of him that way?"

Sage laughed as she shook a martini for a table out on the floor. "No, I put him to bed."

"Oh, is it wrong that I want to go over there eating a disgustingly greasy pork sandwich and slam all the doors?"

"Yes, that's awful."

Kenna shrugged. "Eh, he'd do worse if it were me."

Sage stepped away to cash out two couples.

"Are you okay?" Kenna asked when she returned.

She feigned reflection and for what felt like the hundredth time, she lied. "Yes, I think I am."

"Fantasy shattered?"

She nodded.

"Well, that's good. Maybe he can rebuild into something more substantial now."

Sage wanted to say something, to tell her friend it was over between her and Garrett, that she was working on accepting and she hoped it wasn't going to be awkward.

"How's Chris?"

Okay, so much for worrying.

"He's good. We're going to the theater on Friday."

"So you finally accepted a date. Nice. He seems very. . ."

"Nice?" Sage said, shaking her head and cashing out another couple.

Kenna laughed. "There's nothing wrong with nice."

"Oh, okay. Then why aren't you marrying the dog guy you dated? He was nice."

"First of all, that was an isolated incident of a crazy man, and we did not date. I went on one date, half a date. Chris is not crazy and he does the same things you like to do."

"He does."

"Do you think you'll have a sexy story for Sunday coffee?"

"No! It's the first date. I'm not jumping into bed with him. Come on."

Kenna quietly returned to her laptop.

"What?" Sage said after a few moments of silence.

"You're not okay."

"Why, because I don't want to have sex on the first date?" Sage was still whispering the word "sex" more like a librarian than a bartender. "I'm fine. It takes some time to. . . get over things."

"Maybe you're never going to get over it."

"Don't wish that on me — that's cruel."

"I'm only saying, if he gets his act together, maybe he's the person for you."

"You don't believe that."

"I do. I have to believe he's going to make this right."

"That's because he's your brother. You want him to be happy, but I need to be happy too."

"I know. It's the strangest thing watching the two of you in pain. I know you both have to go through this, but I want to make it better, and I can't." Kenna wiped a tear away from her face.

"Hey" — Sage leaned across the bar and took her hand — "it'll be fine. We need to give it time. People live through much worse and there are no mistakes. Life is a continuous journey, like a river."

Kenna furrowed her brow. "What book are we onto now?"

"*Liquid Living*."

"Sorry? Like fish?"

Sage laughed. "Like stream of consciousness. You are what you think, that sort of thing."

"Haven't we already covered that in like. . . the last fifty books?"

"Each one is a little different."

Kenna wiped another tear away.

"Please don't be upset. I'm fine."

"Look at you comforting me. You are nice, Sage. There's not a damn thing you can do about that."

Adding a few ice cubes to her mixing glass, Sage knew her friend was right. Nice, it appeared, was to be her curse, or her gift, depending on how she chose to look at it. Either way, Kenna had been right about a lot of things. Everyone had a basic core that couldn't be changed without messing up everything else. She'd wanted a change and in doing so, she'd fallen and broken her heart.

Garrett had failed to accept change, and Sage guessed that came with consequences he'd have to deal with if he ever chose to even notice them.

Sage wiped down her bar and kissed Kenna on the cheek as she left to pick up Paige.

You're fine, she told herself, and suddenly Sage knew that fine would have to be enough.

Chapter Thirty-Four

Garrett knocked on the door, takeout from Sesame Garden in hand, but this time he'd left Jack at home. It had been almost a month since she'd driven his drunk ass home and Garrett had racked his brain for an answer. Finally, he decided the only way to fix things was to talk. He had never said enough, shared his feelings when they were together before. This time would be different. They'd make it work; it *had* to work. Footsteps approached the door and his heart charged to his ribcage.

"Oh. . . hey," the guy standing in the doorway said. "I don't normally answer the door, but she's getting her. . . I'm assuming you're here for Sage?"

Kenna had Barbies when she was growing up. Garrett remembered them mostly because they were usually in his way or left in the bottom of the tub when he wanted to take a shower. Garrett remembered Barbie had a big pink Jeep, a couple of friends with brown hair, and a boyfriend. Barbie's boyfriend in real-life form had just come to the door, and Garrett felt like he'd slipped into some messed-up commercial.

He was about to turn around and leave when she walked

through the entryway carrying a small purse and wrapping something around her shoulders.

"We're going to be late if we don't leave now. Who's—" Her words fell away as shock registered on her face, and Garrett decided that was something at least. Sure, he'd been hoping to convince her to give them another chance, eat some takeout, and let him take her to bed, but shock was a decent consolation prize. Not exactly, but it was all he had standing there in her doorway looking like a complete fool.

"Garrett."

"Oh, this is Garrett. Hey man, I've heard a lot about you and your family." The Ken doll extended his hand. "I'm Chris."

"Chris, you're the roses." Garrett shook his hand, not exactly a "pansy" handshake as George would say, but he'd bet this guy didn't mow his own lawn. His hands were Ken doll hands too, tan and perfect. He had one of those big watches too, the ones that looked like they served no other purpose than being big.

"I'm sorry. I didn't know," Chris said, looking to Sage, who handed him his coat.

"Neither did I," Garrett said, hoping if he engaged, found his sarcasm, maybe they could stand there all night bantering until it was past Ken's bedtime.

"Babe, we need to get going or they'll make us wait until intermission to take our seats."

Babe? They were already to babe? Shit!

"Where are you going?" Garrett asked, obviously abandoning any remaining dignity or pride.

"The theater," Sage said, gesturing them out the door.

"I'm taking her to see *Chicago*. It's hard to believe she hasn't seen it."

"Yeah, that is a shame. Wait. . . do you like plays?" he asked Sage.

She whipped around and there they stood, the three of them, on the little walkway that led through the grass to Sage's house. He'd traveled it a few times; usually during happier moments and never once thinking that time might be his last. Had he taken her for granted? Was that a side effect of knowing she loved him first, or was he an asshole? Garrett had a feeling, trying to soften the death stare on Sage's face, that he was the asshole.

On a huff, she shook her head. "I'm not doing this. Goodnight, Garrett."

"Actually, *Chicago* is a musical. Although we did love that play *Art* we saw last week," Chris added.

Right, thanks for the clarification, Ken. I get it. You and Sage have been going on theater field trips for a little while now. Too bad you don't have a tractor, my man. The lady loves the tractor.

"Do you like the theater?" He followed as she and Chris walked toward his clean black Audi with glistening midmarket rims. *Of course he had rims.*

Sage didn't like flashy unless it was her skirts or her earrings. This guy wasn't for her. She wanted to breathe, she loved him, not this. . . *Um, good-looking, successful guy who wears a suit well and is taking her out, treating her the way she deserves to be treated?* He heard Kenna's voice in his head as clear as if she were one of those shoulder devils on Saturday morning cartoons.

"Yes. I love plays," Sage said, and the night air turned colder. "I like getting dressed up every now and then and going to the theater."

"You're not going by yourself?"

"No."

"Why not?"

"Because I'm here," Ken doll piped up, apparently oblivious to what was going on right in front of his perfect face.

See Kenna, he's not too bright. You want your friend dating a dumbass? he asked the little cartoon devil still in his head.

"So no more bottom drawer?" Garrett's voice sounded juvenile to his own ears.

"This is bottom drawer. These are my life experiences now."

He felt the punch and got the message. She was letting him, Barbie's boyfriend, into her world. This guy was willing and appeared to be kind. He would get to share her light now.

Chris, in an attempt to move things along, beeped his car and the interior light went on. There were some benefits of new cars Garrett liked; mood lighting was one of them. Chris then put his hand at the base of Sage's back and adjusted the purple wrap around her shoulders like she was some kind of child who needed that extra button done up on her coat.

Garrett wanted to punch him in his perfectly stable face. Instead, he took Sage's arm and gently pulled her aside.

"Hey, we should get going," Chris said, a little tense this time.

Garrett held up his hand and hoped the guy knew that meant back the fuck up because he didn't want to actually have to punch him. After a little eye contact with Sage, Chris left them and waited by the car.

"Why are you here, Garrett?"

He held up the take-out bag as an answer while trying to swallow the huge baseball suddenly lodged in his throat. She smelled so good and her hair had a little sparkly barrette, sort of like the ones Paige wore, but more adult. It held her bangs off her beautiful face, and Garrett couldn't help seeing that face in the early morning or laughing at him in the sunlight.

This was going to kill him.

She had a date with Chris—flowers Chris. He immediately remembered that night, replayed the two of them standing in the entryway of the house now behind them. He'd asked about the flowers and she'd told him they could stay in the moment, that there was no need to panic or worry about change. Back then, he was supposed to gather her in his arms and tell her he wanted her in that moment and every other moment. Kissing her, back when she softened into his arms, held his face, that's when he was supposed to make her feel loved. He'd screwed that up royally and now the woman who was once longing, laughter, and sexy fun stood in front of him with shifting eyes as she let out a laugh laced with pain.

"You. . . simply stopped by with Chinese for old times' sake?"

"I wanted to apologize."

"Yeah, you already did that last month when I drove you home. All done. Now, if you'll excuse me."

She turned toward the car and Garrett, having no idea what the hell to do anymore, took her arm again. Sage tensed at the touch and then leaned into him. "Stop. Let go of me and stop."

"I can't. We need to fix this."

She shook her head. "This is not fixable. Let me go."

"So you can go out with him? I can't let that happen."

"This has nothing to do with you. You don't get to control this. Now please." Her eyes turned glossy as if he was hurting her. Garrett let go.

Sage straightened, took in a deep breath, and left with Chris, the flower guy, Barbie's damn boyfriend.

Shit!

He saw the whole thing going differently in his mind on the drive over. He'd somehow thought she'd be sitting on her couch eating ice cream and watching romantic movies. That she would be missing him, wanting him to come and rescue her, to love her back. Garrett climbed into his truck. He should have known better. Sage didn't need rescuing. She was fine on her own and even though she'd invited him into her world, under her rainbow hot air balloon, he'd been too wrapped up in his own shit to realize what a gift that was.

Starting his truck and pulling away, he didn't care if things had changed, if she hated him or was hell-bent on spending time with some guy she didn't love. It didn't matter that he had two inspections at the assembly plant in the morning or that George pointed out there was some weird shit growing around the base of three apple trees in the orchard. It would all wait, or he'd give it to someone else because the urgency of this made his chest hurt. If he couldn't figure out how to get her back, nothing else for the rest of his life would work.

Garrett rolled down the window, suddenly needing relief from the stifling air, and scoffed at his thoughts. *Don't be stupid. Your life will go on and work will continue without her.* He supposed it would.

He'd go through the motions and return to the way life had been before she'd climbed into his truck with her glittery skirt, quirky mind, and that look that had made him want more for the first time in his life.

He would be fine, but he would never go back. That's not how it worked. Good or bad, life moved forward. He'd learned that. Pulling onto the freeway toward home, he noticed the music playing right above a hum from his radio. He didn't know the song, but it was slow and maybe a little sad. Was slow music always sad? He hoped not. Garrett's chest squeezed. He needed a plan forward.

❧❧❧

Sage was grateful for the darkness of Chris's car and wondered if it was possible to disappear into the soft leather seats rather than have the conversation that was surely coming.

"Are you all right?"

"Please don't ask me that. I'm so tired of people waiting for me to be all right."

"So, you and Garrett are more than—"

"I love him," Sage blurted out, as if keeping it in was somehow detrimental to her health.

"I see. Do you want me to take you home?"

"No."

They drove in silence.

"Sage, we can do this another time or not at all. I don't want to get in the middle of something."

She put her hand on his. "I'm sorry. I'd like to still go on our date. I want to see *Chicago* and spend the evening with you. I do."

"But, there's definitely a 'but' coming up."

She searched for words. "You're a lovely guy, Chris. You're funny and we have a great time together. How about I keep the 'but' to myself and we enjoy the evening? Can you do that? If not, I totally understand and you can take me home."

"Are you going to start crying or randomly talking about him during dinner?"

Sage laughed. "No."

"Okay, then I'm good. The last woman I dated with an ex sort went off the deep end when I ordered an artichoke at dinner. Apparently she and her ex did that."

"Ordered artichokes?"

He shrugged. "I guess. She had to leave."

"I think maybe she was crazy."

Chris laughed. He had a great laugh and a warm, wonderful smile. She wanted to love him as much as she liked him. She wanted to date him, go away for a weekend or two, make love, and settle into a life with him. He was a good man and she could be happy with him. She wanted to be happy. She also wanted longer legs and to be able to eat Indian food without having to take Tums before she even got home. None of that was ever going happen because she couldn't control where she belonged, where her blind heart wanted to be.

Life didn't work that way. She loved Garrett. Had probably loved him from the moment she'd met him and had only fallen deeper and messier in love as the years went by. So, as much as she wanted to fall in love with Chris, her heart was already gone.

"I'm sorry for what happened back there," she said as they pulled into the valet line at the restaurant.

Chris looked at her, his sharp jaw highlighted by the dashboard light. "Don't be sorry. Can't blame a guy for fighting for you."

She shook her head. "He wasn't fighting."

Turning his car over to the guy in the red shirt and joining Sage on the sidewalk, Chris put his hand to her back as they walked into the restaurant. "It's been a while since I've groveled, but I think I still recognize the gesture. Poor guy."

They were seated, enjoyed dinner, and Sage loved *Chicago*. When Chris walked her to the door, she said good-bye and had a feeling it was for good. He didn't strike her as any woman's second choice.

Chapter Thirty-Five

S age arrived home from work a couple of days later to her first rosebush. She received another one every three days until she had eight rosebushes. Each looked like a different type, and each arrived without a note. She didn't need one, she knew who they were from.

Having worked the lunch shift or evenings, she hadn't seen Garrett since she'd sent him away and gone with Chris. Of course, she knew the rosebushes were from him, but she didn't call or text him when they arrived. She loved them, loved him, but instead of telling him, she planted each one in her backyard and allowed the silence. Surrounded by their fragrance, she didn't want to change a thing, didn't want to ruin it. As if she could somehow simply continue receiving the gift and let him love her that way, she put a few clippings in water each day. When they dried to muted colors, she put them into the bottom drawer of her nightstand.

The delivery truck arrived at Sage's house three days after the last rosebush. It was early morning when she heard the hiss of the hydraulics and the beeping as they backed up her driveway. Sage looked out her bedroom window to find a delivery truck, far too large for another rosebush. Ready to tell them they had the wrong address, she put on her robe and ran to the door. By the time she opened it, the tall gentleman in brown coveralls was already there, clipboard in hand.

"Ms. Jeffries?" the man asked.

"Yes."

"We have a delivery for you if you could tell me where you want it and sign here."

"I didn't order anything," she replied and asked him to confirm her address, which he did.

"Says here on my paperwork that it's a gift, already paid for."

"Who sent it?"

"I did," Garrett said, now standing in her doorway as the delivery guy searched his clipboard.

"Well, there you have it," the guy said, pointing at Garrett.

"You can put it right in the living room. I'm sure we'll move it later."

We, Sage thought. *Since when was he having things delivered, and what the hell would "we" be moving later?* "Garrett?"

After talking with the guy, who disappeared back out to his truck, Garrett took her by the shoulder and guided her toward the couch.

"What are you doing? I have bridge class to teach in a couple of hours. I don't have time for this."

"Shhhh." He held his finger up to her mouth and then proceeded to hold up a scarf. "Trust me?"

Sage managed to laugh. *Was he kidding?* Apparently not, because he tied the scarf around her eyes and the room went black except for a few large shadows. She sat back, wondering what he was up to and why he couldn't leave her be. She heard men's voices, some thuds, and the sound of her front door closing.

"Can I take this thing off now?"

"Yes," she heard him say, taking a seat next to her.

She pulled the scarf off her eyes, and sitting smack dab in the middle of her little living room was a huge dresser. It was an antique, Sage could tell, and it was gorgeous. Way too big for her house. It would have to go back, she thought, but it was a stunning piece.

She stood and ran her hand along the wood of the center cabinet, which was in between two rows of drawers, one on each side. There were two larger drawers underneath and a piece of paper sticking out of one. Sage looked back at Garrett, who said nothing. She knelt and removed the piece of paper that said, *Open me first*. It was the very bottom drawer, and Sage felt her chest tighten. The drawer was huge and she wasn't sure what kind of game he was playing. Pulling on the metal wreath-shaped rings, she tugged the drawer open. It was stuck so she pulled harder and when it finally gave, it was overflowing.

Sage picked up a few pieces that had escaped. One was a drawing from Paige of the two of them dancing. Her pulse jumped and she held the drawing to her chest. Turning over the other piece that had escaped, it was a picture of her behind the bar and Travis making a face with two red stir sticks in his mouth like a walrus. Sage laughed and held the photo to her chest as she looked into the drawer and saw pictures of her sisters, ticket stubs, train tickets, a picture of her in Paris, and a picture of her on the beach with Kenna. There was a certificate from when she won the science fair in high school and one of the research papers she worked on her first year out of college. Keys with little notes attached to the rings explaining what they unlocked. And letters. Sage picked one up and through the glistening of her tears read a thank-you note from a customer going through a divorce, another from one who had a sick child and came in for lunch. She couldn't take it anymore.

Her arms filled with the contents of the drawer, she pivoted on her knees to Garrett who was now next to her, the width of him competing with the dresser. He dried her eyes, helped her stand, and pointed to the very top drawer. It was small compared to the bottom drawer, with a note that read—*Open me last*.

Sage set everything she was holding back in the bottom drawer and pulled open the smaller one. She strained to reach because it was so high she couldn't see inside, but felt a small box. By the time she pulled it out, Garrett was on his knees in front of her. Her tears were out of control now.

"This is your bottom drawer," he started with a shaky voice full of emotion. "You have one. A huge one, filled with people who have loved you, people you have touched, and incredible things you've experienced and achieved." He cleared his throat and Sage squeezed the box and tried to breathe. "There may not be any dried-up corsages or Mardi Gras beads in there, but your bottom drawer is overflowing." He took her hand. "I was going to bring you an actual box or a chest, but when I spoke with all of the people who love you I knew I was going to need more room."

Sage looked at the dresser. "This was a little overkill, don't you think?"

He smiled and shook his head. "I don't think so." He took the ring box from her hand and opened it. "Sage Jeffries, I love you. If you'll have me, invite me along. I'm ready to give you more. I'd like to spend the rest of my life helping you finish your bottom drawer and then we can fill up all the other ones too. You are the only woman who can rescue me from myself. I know you said you loved me first, but I'm sure I love you more, so that makes us even." Garrett stood and Sage looked at the ring in his hand. It was old with a thin band and a square-cut diamond that glittered as if it were bought yesterday. He touched her face and wiped her tears with his thumbs. "I love you, Sage. You've stirred things in my life I never even knew were there. And I don't ever want you to stop. Please marry me."

"Well it took you long enough."

He laughed and his eyes filled. "Is that a yes?"

Sage nodded a bit like a child that had been asked if she wanted more candy. "I love you too. I always have. Of course I'll marry you."

He slid the ring onto her finger.

She'd loved herself enough to let him in, and he had found a way to her. Real life was so much better than the fantasy.

Oprah would be proud.

Sage held Garrett's face, gazed into his watercolor eyes, and knew she would never ever get tired of the storms in them.

"Wait, was that a bartending reference? Stirred, I've stirred things in you. Are you trying to seduce me with drink lingo?" she asked, so grateful as playful swirled around her.

"Does that work?" He pulled her close.

"Everything, Garrett, everything and always." She kissed him and realized the book was wrong. Sometimes nice girls did finish first.

❦

Thank you for reading *Stirred – A Love Story*! Sage and Garrett were so much fun to write and finished off the three Love Stories centered around The Yard restaurant. If you enjoyed the book, please consider leaving a review at the book retailer of your choice, as well as Goodreads, to help other readers find this story.

Please make sure you're on my newsletter mailing list at: tracyewens.com to keep up with the latest news about my books.

Thank you, wonderful readers, for the tremendous support. I appreciate each and every one of you! Keep reading for a look at *Vacancy – A Love Story*, Hollis and Matt's story.

All the best,
Tracy

❦

Chapter One

*H*ollis Jeffries wasn't exactly a religious person. She had gone to church a few times as a child, mostly holidays, and attended a Lutheran grammar school, but that was it. She seldom prayed as an adult, yet now, as the curtains of the large window overlooking Tomales Bay were ripped open to let in the ruthless light of late morning, she found herself offering up the same feeble plea she was certain so many other "heathens," as her grandmother would say, cried in similar situations.

Dear Lord, please make this jackhammer going off in my head stop and I promise never ever ever to wash down an entire bag of cheese popcorn with two bottles of Prosecco again.

She wasn't sure why they bothered, she or the other heathens, because God had no time for poor little privileged pity parties. Hopefully, God was busy with bigger, more far-reaching issues, but as Hollis raised her forearm to cover her eyes, she wished this once he, or maybe she, would make an exception.

"Rise and shine, Tiny Tots. You didn't check into the Betty, and even if you had, your twenty-eight days are up," her uncle said in a voice that sounded a lot like the jackhammer, but more madras shorts and springtime flowers. Come to think of it, even without a hangover, her uncle often sounded like springtime flowers. The man was entirely too peppy, entirely too positive, and entirely too much. Hollis once again called on her recently rediscovered deity.

"Dear God!" She gingerly rolled onto her side.

"Shower's running, and once you're dressed, we're heading to the market."

Taking in a breath and letting it out slowly, Hollis precariously opened one eye to find her uncle holding out sunglasses—big, obnoxious sunglasses with rhinestones on the sides. *Where would a person even buy those?*

"Water," she croaked.

"Put these on first and then we'll get you sitting up for water. No sense drooling on yourself."

Hollis thought she nodded as she took the glasses, but she couldn't be sure. By the time Uncle Mitch hooked his arm through hers and began pulling her up like a child after a long nap, she was swatting at his hands until he stepped back.

"Yeouch, you've got claws."

"What time is it?" Hollis asked as her legs now dangled over the side of the bed. With her toes barely grazing the warm wood floor of her beach cabin, she tried to rationalize how at the age of thirty-four she was still stupid enough to drink too much.

"Eleven thirty," her uncle answered, now keeping his distance.

"In the morning? As in almost afternoon?" Easing the sunglass-es onto her nose, Hollis was certain her head weighed a hundred pounds all by itself. She once watched a documentary and learned that the brain was 2 percent of a human's body weight, and it was a testament to the neck and the spinal cord that it managed to hold the whole thing upright. This morning, her spinal cord was struggling through the haze of wine and white cheddar because she felt like one of those bobbleheads vendors peddled at sporting events.

When she could finally lift her head, Hollis found her uncle surveying what she already knew was a hot mess. She scratched her head and took a slow drink from the water glass he'd carefully placed in her hands. At some point, she was going to need to get her shit together, get back to her life. It had been over a month since the second biggest failure of her thirty-four years, but this time, no amount of wine or junk food could disguise that she had no one to blame but herself. She continued to check in with the office, but she didn't have a plan. She couldn't recall a single moment in her life when she had not had a plan.

Yesterday, she'd spent the better part of an hour-long conference call listening to Reese Winterford, one of their project managers who liked to think he was the boss, confirm that the lead programmer for the game Fat Pigs, Zeke Walderblast—she couldn't make this stuff up—had, in fact, not been arrested as previously reported. He was "hanging" in Mexico with some friends and detained for possession of Aunt Mary.

"I'm sorry. Did you say he was detained with his Aunt Mary in Mexico?" Hollis had asked, rubbing the bridge of her nose.

"No, he was in Mexico when he was busted for possession of Aunt Mary," Reese clarified over laughter.

Hollis searched her brain then quickly Googled Aunt Mary. A type of marijuana. Right.

"Hollis, do you know what Aunt Mary is?" Megan liked to lurk in the background during conference calls, sort of like a sulking, bitchy party guest. She was Reese's boss.

"Yes, thank you, Megan. I may not smoke it, but I'm well aware. While he was puffing on his Aunt Mary, did he find any answers? Did it help him figure out why a nine-year-old was able to discover a flaw in his game after one afternoon of playing?"

"No. He said he's doing a lot of meditation and has a massage scheduled for tomorrow. He's hoping that will clear out his chi." Reese had to be smirking. Hollis could actually feel the bastard through the phone.

"His what?"

"Chi. His life force."

"Fan-damn-tastic." She bit into her second oatmeal cream pie. "Any idea how blocked his life force is?"

"He said he'd call us in a few days."

Hollis licked her fingers, having finished the entire cookie, pie, whatever in less than three bites. "Anything else? How are the investors holding up? I spoke with Greg on Monday. He'll be on vacation for a couple of weeks. I bought us some time. How are the rest of them?"

"We're burning platform here," creepy, lurking Megan added. "Zeke needs to finish this and fast. If we can't do something to move the needle on this soon, they're pulling out. They want it all functioning and the disaster-recovery plans in place by the end of the third quarter or they're pulling funding."

"That gives us about four months to get our ducks in a row. I suppose the silver lining is that he's not in jail. I'm guessing jail is not good for the chi."

Strained laughter again.

"How long will you be out of pocket?" Reese asked.

Hollis, who had been pacing her cabin, finally caved under the stupidity spilling from her phone. She'd used the "out of pocket" in e-mails before but never understood the phrase. If she was "out of pocket" when she was away from the office, did that mean when she returned she was "in pocket?" Why did all of this corporate crap sound so ridiculous when her feet were bare? Dropping to the edge of the bed, she rubbed her face. "I'm not sure."

Silence.

"What? It's a few days," Hollis said, trying to deflect.

"Thirty," bitch-face Megan clarified.

"Whatever. I'm working remotely. That guy in accounting was out for three weeks while his damn dog had surgery. Back up."

"Should we be worried, Hollis?" Megan had become a ginormous pain in the ass ever since she'd lost the partnership position to Hollis about a year before. Hollis was entrenched in the corporate culture as much as the next pair of expensive shoes, but Megan Tiffany was on a whole other level. She was known to say things like "in the brown" and "let's not boil the ocean" instead of "let's not waste time." She was the true definition of kiss ass.

"Megan, you can worry if you'd like, but I would direct your angst toward making sure the Plimpton and Inc. merger goes through without a hitch. You don't need to worry about me." Hollis heard some mumblings and was certain she'd hit her target.

Megan cleared her throat. "I suppose you're right. With the hot water you've landed us in, we need all the leverage we can get."

Hollis opened the wrapper of another oatmeal cream pie and felt the "go screw yourself" perched right on her lips, but since her "leverage," as Megan put it, was in short supply these days, she decided to chomp into her junk food instead. Hollis had worked hard to make sure she always had the upper hand, but this last bump had shaken all she knew to be normal. Megan was right—it was not something Hollis would ever say out loud, even alone in her cabin—but it was true. Hollis had screwed up royally, taken her eye off the ball, failed to "see the granular," as Reese enjoyed saying.

After a few less-heated exchanges and an agreement to "circle back around" again on Friday, Hollis ended the call and walked to the restaurant to see if her wine order had come in yet. The box had been sitting on the bar, and that was precisely why she was now playing host to her uncle and his jackhammer backup singers dancing around her cabin.

"Someone likes oatmeal snack cakes." Mitch plucked the wrappers from Hollis's bedside and threw them in the wastebasket. "All right, let's get you up and at 'em." He handed Hollis two Tylenol, which she promptly swallowed. She hoped there was a way to fix this mess and fast because there was no way she was failing without a fight.

Matt Locke opened The Bean fifteen minutes early because Mr. Trumble had been standing outside for almost a half hour holding three jars of something. Even though he had been helping out with his parents' coffee shop for a little over two months now, Matt still couldn't predict what bounty from Mrs. Trumble's garden would end up in the jars, but it was guaranteed to be interesting. He'd asked Poppy, the manager who was currently out on maternity leave, the first time Mr. Trumble handed him jars and was told, "It's a weekly thing. You'll get used to it." He had gotten used to it and had even grown to like Mr. Trumble, so with the coffee brewed and pastries arranged in the three glass-covered displays, Matt pulled the dairy from the refrigerator and flipped the sign.

"Morning, Matt." Mr. Trumble handed over the three jars.

"Morning." Matt had no idea what Mr. Trumble's first name was, and it was never offered.

"The missus did something crazy cool there for you. Spicy cauliflower and carrots in one and the other two are smoking hot okra. Do you do okra?"

Matt smiled. He'd never quite thought of it as "doing" okra, but according to Poppy, since Mr. Trumble retired a couple of years ago he'd been watching way too much reality TV and enjoyed being "hip with his lingo."

"Yes, I like okra. Thank you."

He nodded. "Welcome. So, what's good in the pastry case, bro?"

Matt walked behind the counter and set the jars down. He would add them to the others he'd placed out of sight in the storage room later. A mother and daughter arrived, accepting the "after you" gesture of a cop in uniform as they filed in behind Mr. Trumble, who appeared like he might take well into the afternoon choosing his breakfast.

"Scones. There are a couple of orange cranberry ones that I think you and Mrs. Trumble might enjoy." Matt tried to move him along. When his mother called him to ask a "little favor," he had agreed to stop by and help out in Poppy's absence, but once his dad hurt his hip, stopping by had turned into nearly full-time. Most of what Matt was working on at his own company could be done remotely, so he didn't mind, but the pace of things, the slower, lazy-day way that floated freely throughout the cove, was an adjustment. He'd grown up around coffee but never worked a shop for any extended period of time. Matt was reluctant to return, especially to Tomales Bay, but now that he'd been at it for a while, he had to admit he was enjoying himself.

Mr. Trumble hesitated for a minute and then smiled. "Sweet, those are it. Two of 'em and your usual brews."

"Great. Be right with you, folks. Good morning, Officer Hernandez."

"Morning. Do you have any coffee cake today?"

"I do." Matt put the scones in two separate bags, knowing that was Mr. Trumble's preference, and poured two medium roast coffees—one with a Sweet'N Low and a splash of cream, the other black.

Paying with singles and change as he usually did, Mr. Trumble commented that he and his boys played poker and he was nearly "baked," but he managed to pull through. Matt knew "baked" meant something else entirely, but he wasn't going to say anything. Instead, he smiled as Mr. Trumble gathered up his bags, stuck brown plastic plug sticks in his coffee, and left.

Matt met Officer Greg Hernandez for the first time the summer he turned seventeen, the year he was allowed to drive his own car up to the cove for their summer stay. His parents wouldn't be up for another week, but Matt had worked the roaster with his dad the Saturday before and convinced him he could be trusted. Matt could still conjure up the restlessness of seventeen, a time when hours felt like days and one week was a lifetime.

He'd finished his last final early and used his lunch period so he would be done by Thursday. The old blue Nissan, with the dent on the rear bumper, a little reminder from backing into a cart pole in the Safeway parking lot when he was learning to drive, was packed to the windows. He drove the first hundred miles listening to a playlist she'd sent him and the last forty-five minutes with his windows down feeling the ocean breeze on his face as if she were sitting right next to him. It was one of his best memories made perfectly movie worthy when the lights and sirens appeared in his rearview mirror about fifteen minutes from Mitchell's Cove.

Officer Hernandez, then quite a bit younger, had requested license, registration, and proof of insurance. It was all painfully professional and Matt's heart was drumming in his chest with equal parts nerves and frustration at being so close to seeing her. As Matt impatiently waited for the inevitable ticket, Officer Hernandez informed him how fast he was going and asked why he was in such a hurry. It had felt pointless, glancing up into the officer's dark, almost machine-like, neutral face, his eyes invisible behind the standard-issue mirrored cop glasses, but back then Matt was more compulsive. He remembered rubbing his neck as he tried to decide how much to share, and also because one of the springs of his seat poked through the upholstery and into his back. Matt never missed that car, not one day.

"I'm sorry. I know it's wrong to speed, but I finished all of my finals and I'm excited to see my girl." He had tried to maintain eye contact even behind the mirrored shades. His father had drilled into him that eye contact was the key to winning a person over and when Officer Hernandez spoke again, Matt offered thanks to his dad.

"Understood. These turns can be tricky as I'm sure you know, Mr.... Locke"—the officer glanced at his license and then back at him—"so if you're planning a long life with this girl, you might want to take it easy." He handed back the paperwork with a stern nod followed by a smile.

Matt had been stunned. He sat waiting for something else: the reprimand, the call to his parents. No way it was this easy.

"You better get going. It's never good to leave a pretty girl waiting," he said and then patted the top of the Nissan.

"Yes, right, sir. Thank you." Since a cop was watching, Matt checked left and then right, exactly the way the driving manual had instructed, and pulled back out onto Highway 1. After kissing Hollis that night and then kissing her some more, he had told her all about being pulled over as they walked to the pier. Matt knew it was one of the few moments growing up when he'd looked at an adult and known they must have been a kid at one point too.

About a week into that summer, Matt had noticed Officer Hernandez's patrol car parked in one of the cutouts in the road near the 76 gas station one night. He brought him a cup of coffee and some of his mother's maple cake, and that was the beginning of their friendship. Nothing too heavy, it was simply a mutual understanding of the journey every guy took toward becoming a man. Matt learned over time that Officer Hernandez was married to "the love of my life" and they had a son and a daughter both in high school too.

Matt stood facing Officer Hernandez on the other side of the counter and was struck by how many years had passed. He still slowed down when he saw that patrol car, but lately it was to wave. Matt wondered if Greg, that was his first name although Matt never used it, saw the years too, if he noticed that Matt had grown into—what exactly had he grown into? Annoyed at the tension his moment of reflection stirred, Matt returned to the present because most of the past, anything that took place in this little corner of the world at least, reminded him of her. It was an ache that had dulled to manageable but never quite went away.

"How was Ruby's wedding?" Matt asked, warming up the coffee cake.

"Great, she looked beautiful and I managed to get her down the aisle without disgracing the father-of-the-bride title."

Matt smiled. "I'm sure you made her proud."

"It's a tough business. I read some article that this guy in Florida started having a heart attack while he was walking his daughter down the aisle."

Matt's eyes widened.

"The man finished the walk, handed his girl to her fiancé, then walked to the side of the church and quietly called 9-1-1."

"Wow."

"I know, wedding heroes, right? Who knew?"

Both men laughed, and Matt handed him his coffee and cake. As was routine, Greg tried to pay and Matt wouldn't take his money.

"Thanks, Lead Foot." He turned back right before the door. "Hey, I noticed your girl is back in town."

Matt tried to smile, unable to meet his eyes. "She's not my girl anymore and you know it."

"Eh, you never know where that road out there will take you." Their eyes met and Officer Hernandez lifted his coffee cup in a toast. "Tell her I said hello." He flipped his sunglasses down over his eyes, smiled, and was gone.

Matt shook his head and turned to wipe the counter.

His girl. Had Hollis ever truly been his girl? All these years and Matt still couldn't answer that question. It had seemed about as perfect as a love story could be, but great love should be effortless, shouldn't it? There was never anything effortless about Hollis and she eventually left him, or he stopped trying. Matt was never sure which it was and it certainly didn't matter anymore. Between Hollis arriving at the cove and his father coming home from surgery next week, things were bound to get complicated. Matt didn't do complicated. Even with his business back home, things were streamlined and he liked it that way. Poppy would be back part-time next week and he'd be closer to wrapping all of this up and getting back to a life he understood.

By the time the door tinkled again with arriving customers, Matt slipped the memory of a time so simple, so happy, back where it belonged.

OTHER LOVE STORIES BY TRACY EWENS

Acknowledgements

I would like to thank:

Katie McCoach and Nikki Busch because without them there would be no books.

People who get their hands dirty, literally and figuratively.

My family for putting up with my closed door, imaginary friends, and often absent mind.

Readers for inviting me into your lives. The honor is never lost on me.

Tracy Ewens is a recovered theatre major who writes smart contemporary romance from a beautiful piece of Arizona desert. When not working on her next book, she drinks copious amounts of tea, prefers an exit row seat, and reads well past her bedtime.

www.tracyewens.com

www.ingramcontent.com/pod-product-compliance
Lightning Source LLC
Chambersburg PA
CBHW020414260626
47156CB00007B/2376